Candles and Roses

Alex Walters

ISBN: 978-0-9955111-9-4

To Helen – for everything.

CHAPTER ONE

It was starting to rain and she was feeling well and truly pissed off.

Where the bloody hell was the cab?

She should have waited inside. She could always have locked up the bar herself if Josh was so keen to get off. But she knew Josh wasn't comfortable leaving her with the keys. It wasn't that he doubted her honesty, or so he said. It was just that the owners had given him the responsibility and—well, you know. Yeah, she knew. Josh was the manager and he wanted everyone to be clear about that. Well, fair enough. If anything went wrong, it would be Josh's arse on the line and not hers.

So she'd agreed to wait out here so Josh could bugger off home. And she hadn't realised that her phone was out of battery. Now she was locked out on the street with a dead phone and no sign of the sodding taxi she'd ordered. A perfect end to a perfect bloody day.

She didn't even know for sure what time it was. Long after midnight now, obviously. She'd called from the bar before leaving and been told the car was ten minutes away, max. How long ago had that been? A lot more than ten minutes, anyway.

The road was almost deserted at this time of the night and she peered hopefully at every passing car. There were several cabs, but no sign of the familiar logo of the company she always used when she was working the late shift. Christ, she ought to be a favoured customer by now, not just another punter to leave standing in the pouring rain.

She contemplated walking home, but it was nearly a mile and the rain was coming harder. In any case, the reason she always booked a taxi was because she hated walking home at this time of night. Unless she took a lengthy detour, the route took her through a largely unlit stretch of parkland. She'd heard from one of the other girls that, a year or two before, there'd been a spate of sexual assaults in the area. She didn't know how much truth there was in that but it was enough to make her cautious. She'd decided early on that, if she was working late, she could justify the expense of a taxi home, even though it would eat into her already small earnings.

That was, of course, as long as the bloody taxi turned up.

For the moment, at least, she was dry, sheltered under the bar's garish front awning. But it was bloody cold. This was supposed to be the start of summer but after a few misleadingly bright days in early May they'd had nothing but grey skies and rain for weeks. She'd caught the TV weather forecast that morning. Back up north, in the place that, even after everything that had happened, she still somehow thought of as home, they were having some of their best early summer weather in years. Wasn't that just bloody typical?

She was still deciding whether to cut her losses and risk the walk when a car pulled up at the kerbside. For a moment, she thought it was the taxi but there was no logo. In any case, she realised now, it was just some superficially tarted-up junk-heap. Kids.

The driver's window wound down and a pimply face peered out. 'How much, love?' She could hear raucous laughter from the rear of the car. Drunken kids.

'Oh, just fuck off,' she said.

'Whatever you're charging, love, it's not worth it.' The youth guffawed at his own wit and then slammed down the accelerator and pulled back out into the road, tyres spinning on the wet surface.

That was enough to decide her.

She had no umbrella but she turned up the collar of her thin coat and stepped outside into the rain. She'd be soaked by the time she got home. Even so, it felt better than being jeered at on the street by some spotty-faced idiot teenager.

She'd walked less than fifty metres when she saw another vehicle approaching. She squinted at it, the rain dripping from her hair, hoping it might finally be the cab. But it was only a small unmarked van. It passed and then, seconds later, she heard it pull into the kerb behind her. A voice called: 'Katy?'

She turned, baffled. The van's passenger door was half open and a figure was peering out, leaning over from the driver's seat. 'It is you, isn't it? Katy? Katy Scott?'

She was even more confused now. How had the driver known her name? She took a step or two nearer to the van, trying to recognise the figure looking back at her.

'Jesus, Katy, I thought I was seeing things. What are the odds? After all these years.'

She knew now, though it didn't make it any easier to believe. 'Bloody hell,' she said. 'What you doing in these parts?'

'Ach, you know. Work things. Usual story. What about you?'

She gestured back towards the bar. 'I work in there. Just heading home. Ordered a taxi but the bastard never turned up.'

'You can't walk home in the rain. Let me give you a lift.'

'You're going the other way,' she said. 'I couldn't—'

'It can't be far if you were going to walk it. I'd never forgive myself if I left you standing in the rain at this time of night. Anyway, we can have a blether for a few minutes. Catch up. We can maybe arrange to meet up properly sometime. I'm down here plenty.'

'Well, if you're sure—' She was already walking towards the van, cheered by this unexpected late-night miracle.

She pulled open the passenger door and climbed inside. Almost immediately, she felt she'd made a mistake, though she couldn't have said why. 'Look, I don't know—'

It was too late. Even as she clawed frantically at the car door, a hand was clamped firmly across her mouth, the full weight of the driver's body pressing her back into the seat. Something wet was being pressed between her lips, and the stench was unbearable, acrid and burning in her throat. Her skin felt as if it had been doused in acid.

Her first thought, even as the hand pressed tighter across her mouth, was that she was going to vomit. Her second was that she was going to die.

And then there was just darkness and nothing. And no time for any further thoughts.

CHAPTER TWO

No-one had ever called DI Alec McKay a sentimental man. But even now, a year on, he remained troubled by the case, and not only because it had never been formally closed.

Occasionally, in a rare quiet hour, he dug out the file and thumbed aimlessly through the thin sheaf of documents, as if hoping to spot some lead, some connection that had eluded them at the time. There was nothing, of course. He'd end up staring blankly at that scanned image, the gaunt face, the pale blue eyes staring smilingly into the camera, the corona of blonde hair caught by the sun, a carefree moment snatched out of time. Lizzie Hamilton.

On the face of it, just another missing person. They couldn't even be certain that a crime had necessarily been committed. It was possible, but it was equally possible she'd just chosen to escape, to re-boot her life in another place, with new friends, new surroundings. McKay found that almost the more disturbing possibility.

She'd vanished at the end of June, midsummer. And last year for once they'd actually had something of a summer, three or four weeks of half-decent weather. Unclouded skies translucent through the long light evenings, the temperatures high by local standards, the sea a deep blue along the Moray Firth.

Nobody had missed her for a couple of days, which told its own story. She'd worked three or four evenings a week in a bar up in the Black Isle, did some cleaning and housekeeping for the holiday lets around Fortrose and Rosemarkie. She was friendly with the regulars in the bar, but no-one knew much about her. It had been Denny Gorman, the pub landlord, who'd contacted the police. He'd been the only person who expressed any interest in her private life, and McKay had assumed that was just because Gorman had secretly had the hots for her.

It was another couple of weeks before they finally registered her as a misper. McKay had insisted on being there when they gained entry to her rented bungalow, having secured a spare key from the landlord's agent. He'd been tense beforehand, not knowing what to expect. He'd had more than one experience of walking into the stench of death in some lonely bedsit, a decomposing body in a bed or on the floor.

But the bungalow seemed in good order, as if Hamilton had tidied the place before leaving. It was sparsely furnished, with only a few signs of a personal touch, but there was no indication of any disturbance or anything missing. There was milk and food left in the fridge, clothes in the wardrobes, a half-read chick-lit novel splayed on the table in the sitting room. If Lizzie Hamilton had done a runner, she'd left most of her current life behind.

They tracked down her widowed father living in Inverness, but she had no siblings or other close relatives. McKay had driven over himself to visit the father. For no particular reason, he'd expected someone frail and elderly. But the father, one John Robbins, was a well-built man in his mid-fifties who looked as if he worked out. He was living in a decent Edwardian semi on the south side of the city and gave the impression that he'd made a bob or two, one way or another. He greeted McKay on the doorstep, showing no intention of inviting him inside. He was wearing tight black jeans and tee-shirt that no doubt had designer labels inside and which seemed intended to show off his toned physique. He was bearded, his greying hair caught back in a short ponytail. Some sort of wheeler-dealer, McKay thought dismissively, too keen to hang on to his receding youth.

'Police?' Robbins said, unimpressed, when McKay had brandished his warrant card. 'What do you want with me?'

'Your daughter, Mr Robbins. We're trying to track her down.' In other circumstances, McKay might have been tempted to insist on going inside, but he'd already formed the view that Robbins would have little or nothing to tell him. 'She seems to have gone missing.'

'That one went missing ten years back,' Robbins said. 'Not seen her since.'

'You've no knowledge of her whereabouts?'

'God knows. Dundee? Aberdeen? Back in Glasgow. You tell me.' Robbins took a breath. 'On second thoughts, don't bother.'

'You weren't on good terms with your daughter, Mr Robbins?'

'I can see why you're a detective.'

'Any particular reason for the bad blood?'

'Every reason. She was trouble. Took advantage every chance she had. Walked off with half my worldly goods. What more do you want?'

'She was your daughter, Mr Robbins.'

'So they say.'

He got nothing more from Robbins. But it seemed Lizzie Hamilton had made a habit of disappearing. She'd walked out on her father—taking his wallet and various items with her, as he'd said—and headed down to Glasgow with her then boyfriend, Kenny Hamilton. They'd married within weeks and split up acrimoniously a couple of months later. Again, she'd walked out without a word and Kenny Hamilton reckoned he hadn't seen her since. He'd no idea what had happened to her, and no-one seemed to know what she'd been doing or where she'd been living till she'd arrived back up in the Highlands three or four years later. If he'd put the effort in, McKay might have been able to trace her movements over that period, but resources were scarce and, whatever McKay's own feelings, the case had never been the highest priority.

When they were able to check Lizzie Hamilton's bank account, they discovered that she'd withdrawn all £200 of her painstakingly accrued savings a few days before her disappearance. There were only a few pounds left in the account, and no attempts had been made to access it since.

Over the previous weeks, at least as far as the regulars in the bar could judge, she'd been her usual self. Cheerful enough, friendly, chatting amiably with the regulars, but as private and reserved as ever. She'd rarely talked about her private life, and had given no indication that anything might be troubling her. But then, McKay thought, people don't always need a reason.

Maybe it was as simple as that. She'd come up here to start a new life, but life hadn't come running to greet her. Perhaps she'd simply grown tired of the endless round of work and sleep. Perhaps she'd wanted more. He could imagine her, walking along the sea shore, staring out at the clear sky and the blue waters of the Moray Firth and the North Sea beyond, thinking that there must be something else out there. Something she could aspire to.

The summer weeks had dragged by, and no further leads or clues had emerged. The last time she'd been seen was at a housekeeping visit to one of the holiday lets the weekend before her disappearance. One of the assistants at the local Co-op thought he might have served her on the Monday, but couldn't be sure. If he had, she'd paid cash, as no credit or debit card transactions were recorded to her name. They'd checked the CCTV in the store as well as elsewhere in the village, but could find no images of her in the relevant period. They'd been unable to trace her mobile phone and no calls had been made from its number since she'd left. None of her neighbours could recall when they'd last seen her but that wasn't unusual, they said. She'd never been what you'd call sociable.

McKay had made routine contact with the relevant missing persons agencies and with his colleagues in the larger cities and towns. They'd checked the local hospitals. That image—the picture that still sat in the front of the file—had been sent to all parties. Nothing had come back.

It still seemed extraordinary to McKay that, in the modern world, anyone could simply disappear. He felt tracked and trailed every minute of his waking life, always conscious of the countless surveillance tools that, for good or ill, were now simply part of the landscape. But people vanished every day. They stepped off the grid, sometimes by choice, sometimes by accident, occasionally for sinister reasons. And it was easiest for people like this, with no ties, no obligations, no reasons to stay.

Even so, aspects of the case made McKay uneasy. Lizzie Hamilton had made no effort to cancel the tenancy on her bungalow or to contact the utility companies. The fridge had contained perishable food bought in the days immediately before her disappearance. She had left behind a number of apparently personal items, though admittedly nothing of great value. She'd had no car, and there'd been no sightings of her on the local buses or records of her booking a taxi to leave the village.

But as the weeks went by the case, which had never been a high priority to begin with, inevitably slipped further down the list. McKay had half-expected that eventually she might reappear, one way or another, alive or dead. Her body would be discovered, lost in woodland or washed up by the tide, the victim of an accident or something worse. Or she'd simply return one day from wherever she'd been and resume her humdrum life in the village. Maybe she'd be tracked down, living back down in Glasgow or here in Inverness.

But it never happened. When her rent direct debit bounced for the second time, the property company foreclosed on the tenancy and repossessed the property. As far as McKay knew, it was still standing empty. The owners of the holiday lets found new housekeepers. Denny Gorman no doubt found himself a new barmaid to lust after. Life ground slowly onwards.

And every once in a while, McKay would pull out the file and sit staring at that scanned image. Not even a particularly good likeness, he'd been told, and clearly taken a few years before she'd arrived up here.

But it was a good likeness, he thought.

Of another young woman. Another lost soul.

Another Lizzie.

His own daughter.

CHAPTER THREE

'Just five minutes.'

'I know your five minutes, Greg. And I know what you can get up to in five minutes.'

'Aw, come on. We've got time.'

'I've told you, I don't like it. Place gives me the creeps.'

'Ach. Just a wee walk. Breath of fresh air. Blow the cobwebs away.'

'You sound like my mother. And it's not blowing cobwebs that you're interested in.'

Greg Johnson laughed, but said nothing more as he pulled off the road down the short track to the makeshift car park. It was a Monday morning in midsummer, but theirs was the only car there. Other people had more sense, she thought. They came here only if they were desperate. Even more desperate than Greg, she added to herself, as she noted his eagerness to leave the car.

She knew well enough what was on his mind, and in truth she wasn't exactly averse to the idea herself. Christ knew, they got little enough time together. It would be different come the autumn when they both went off to university.

She just didn't want to come *here*. The place really did freak her out. She should be used to it by now. It was just part of the landscape, and she'd been walking round there more times than she could remember. But every time she felt the same frisson, the same sense that the place wasn't quite right.

'Fancy a quick walk, then?' he said.

'A quick what?' She laughed. 'Yeah, go on then, loverboy. But straight into the woods. Not up there.' She glanced behind them to where the low hill rose gloomily above the car park, a dark tangle of trees endlessly festooned with strips of fabric and items of clothing, some new, some long-faded, fluttering in the summer breeze like the banners of a defeated army.

They both knew the story of the Clootie Well. A Celtic place of pilgrimage, a running stream with supposedly health-giving properties. People still came here when their friends or relatives were unwell, tying pieces of cloth—sometimes wiped on the skin of the invalid in question—to the trees around the stream. The theory was that as the fabric rotted away the illness would dissipate. No doubt some people believed it enough to make it work.

It was a harmless piece of superstition, and these days, for most people, the place was no more than a quaint tourist attraction. Somewhere the summer trippers visited on their way to their holiday lets on the Black Isle, traipsing along the paths, chattering patronisingly about the gullibility of the locals. While, in some cases, no doubt stopping to attach their own votive offerings, just in case.

Even so, the place disturbed Kelly. It was partly the disparate and often poignant nature of the offerings. Nearer the stream, it wasn't just shreds of cloth. It might be baby clothes, old stuffed toys, football scarves or shirts. Things that had belonged to real, identifiable human beings, left here in a last, desperate hope that the act might cure a terminal disease, remove a cancer, allow a child to live beyond her first birthday. Kelly assumed the magic would mostly have failed. That the former owner of the rotting teddy-bear or the faded Caley shirt would be long since dead. For Kelly, the place was infested by ghosts, the spirits of those who clung on, earthbound by their last dregs of hope, watching as the worthless waters poured endlessly down the wooded hillside.

Well, she thought, as she followed Greg into the woods, he might be in the mood but she certainly wasn't. Not now, not in this place. Still, maybe five minutes in the company of Greg's caressing hands might be enough to change her mind. Even before they'd become an item, she'd found him attractive—well, for a Scotsman, anyway, she added to herself. Most of the lads at the Academy had been all ginger hair and freckles. Greg was more the tall, dark and brooding type, or at least that was the image he tried to cultivate, with his swept-back black hair and incipient stubble. He was probably aiming for a cross between Heathcliff and William Wallace.

She glanced behind her and then, allowing herself a smile at her own thoughts, she ran ahead of him into the shade of the trees. He jogged behind her, laughing.

It was a fine sunny day, one of the best they'd had so far this year, and it was relatively warm even in the woodland. Greg led them off the footpath, tramping through the undergrowth until they were out of sight of any potential passers-by. 'Well, here we are.'

'We seem to be.' She threw herself against him with sufficient force to knock him off his feet. He stumbled, regained balance, and then allowed himself to fall sideways into the thick heather, pulling Kelly down with him. They lay for a moment, looking up at the dappled sky through the shifting leaves, listening to the rustle of the breeze. Greg rolled over and kissed her, gently at first, then more hungrily.

She responded enthusiastically, enjoying the feel of his firm body against hers, conscious of his arousal and finding that, whatever her earlier feelings, she was beginning to share it. They kissed for a while, losing themselves in each other. Finally coming up for air, she said: 'It's good to have some time together. Just the two of us.'

He rolled over, peering through the grass. 'It is. It'll be even better when we're at uni. As much time together as we want.'

'I think we're expected to do some work as well.'

'I suppose. We can fit it in between the bouts of rampant sex.'

'It'll need careful scheduling.'

'We'll be very organised.' He began to turn himself back towards her, and then he paused, staring along the rough ground. 'What's that?'

'What's what?'

'That. There.' He sat up and pointed. She hoisted herself up and sat beside him, trying to follow the direction of his gesturing.

At first, she could make out nothing but the rough undergrowth. Then, between two thorn bushes, she saw what he was indicating. Evenly distributed blurs of colour, something crimson.

'Flowers?'

'I don't know. It looks very neat, if it's just something growing wild.' He climbed to his feet and took a step or two forward. It was typical of Greg, she thought. Lost in the throes of passion, but it took only the mildest tug of curiosity to drag his mind, if not necessarily his body, elsewhere. It was one of the qualities she found endearing. 'Think you're right, though. It is flowers. Looks like roses. Weird.' He walked forward another few steps. 'Jesus. What is that? Come and have a look.'

Reluctantly, she stumbled after him. 'What is it?'

'Look. There.'

It was a line of alternating candlesticks and small black vases, positioned some fifty centimetres from each other. Each candlestick contained an unlit candle and each vase was filled with cut red roses. As she moved closer, Kelly realised there were two parallel lines, each comprising three identical vases and two candles, with a further vase positioned between the lines at the two ends to form a rectangle. It took her a moment to realise what the arrangement resembled.

A grave.

It was the right size, she thought. The size of a human body.

'Jesus,' Greg said. 'What is it?' She could see the same thought had struck him.

'Somebody's idea of a joke?'

'Strange joke. Some sort of installation piece, you reckon? On the short list for the Turner prize?' He was talking too quickly, more rattled than he was letting on. Kelly realised that both of them had been glancing involuntarily around, as if someone might be observing them. 'Maybe we're being filmed for some TV programme?'

'Greg.' Kelly had moved ahead of him, conscious of Greg's reluctance to approach the vases. She was a few metres away, staring down.

'What?'

'Look at this.' She pointed to the grassed area between the vases. The turf had been cut into several sections and then had been lifted and, slightly unevenly, replaced. As a result, the surface was raised above the surrounding grassland, although the difference was partly obscured by the positioning of the candles and vases.

'What does that mean?'

'I don't know,' she said. But she had a growing feeling she knew all too well. Greg had moved past her now, embarrassed at his own previous trepidation. He crouched down to pull at one of the sections of turf.

'Greg—'

It was too late. He'd already dragged back the heavy lump of earth and was staring at what lay beneath. Kelly turned her head away, unable to look.

'Jesus,' Greg said. 'Jesus fucking Christ.'

CHAPTER FOUR

'**R**ight,' McKay said. 'Let me explain how you should handle it.'

DC Josh Carlisle, a young fresh-faced figure who looked to McKay as if he might have bunked off school for the afternoon, nodded earnestly. 'That would be good, sir.'

'You don't need to call me sir. Boss will do.' McKay stretched back in his chair, chewing on his habitual gum with the air of a man enjoying an after-dinner cigar. 'It's like this. What you should do is tell him to fuck off. Then tell him to fuck off some more. And then to fuck off a bit more still. And then to keep on fucking off until he gets back where he started. Then you can tell him to fuck off again.' He paused. 'Is that clear?'

Carlisle blinked. 'Crystal, sir. I mean, boss. Thank you.'

'Always glad to be of assistance. Door's always open.' McKay gestured towards the door in question, in a manner clearly intended to indicate the meeting was over. Carlisle took the hint and rose to take his leave, stopping as he saw DCI Helena Grant standing in the doorway. She was a slightly stocky woman of no more than average height, but like most of his colleagues Carlisle found her more intimidating than any of her male counterparts. She was gazing at them now with the air of a teacher watching two over-excited schoolboys.

'Alec giving you one of his motivational team talks?'

'Something like that.' Carlisle shuffled past her and, with visible relief, made his escape.

'Good lad,' McKay said. 'Will go far.'

'As far as possible from you if he's any sense. What was that about?'

'Some scrote of an informant looking to screw a few more quid out of us.'

'Fair enough. In that case, I fully endorse your proposed approach.' She lowered herself on to the chair opposite McKay's desk. The building was too old to accommodate the open-plan offices now commonplace in most of their locations, and McKay shared this room only with his DS, Ginny Horton. Grant assumed it was Horton who kept the office in order, although McKay could be surprisingly domesticated when it suited him. 'How are you doing with the burglaries?' There had been a spate of apparently linked house-breakings in the estates off Glenurquhart Road.

'Ach. You know. Making progress.'

'Is that McKay-speak for getting nowhere?'

'It's McKay-speak for working our balls off but apparently still not doing enough to get your arse off the line. With respect,' he added.

Grant didn't rise to the bait. She and McKay went back a long way, and despite McKay's best efforts they'd always managed to maintain a more or less effective working relationship. 'I'm here because we've just had a big one called in.' She smiled. 'But don't worry if you're too busy. I can find someone else.'

For the first time, McKay looked genuinely interested. 'A big one?'

'Murder, looks like. Body up on the Black Isle. Bit strange.'

'Aye, well, they're an odd lot up there.'

'You know the Clootie Well, up by Munlochy?'

'You've proved my point. Worshipping the fairies. That where they found the body?'

'In the woods there. Shallow grave. Young woman, not yet identified. From the state of decomposition, it looks like she's not been there long. A few days.'

'I like my corpses fresh,' McKay said. 'So what's strange about it?'

'The grave was marked. Candles and vases of red roses. The sort of flowers you take home to Chrissie when you've something to apologise for.'

'In her dreams. Who the fuck murders someone and then sticks flowers on the grave?'

'Someone who cares about the victim? I don't know. That'll be your job.'

'Oh, Christ, I knew that was coming. You want me to be SIO?'

She laughed. 'Come off it, Alec. You'd be pissed as hell if I gave the job to anyone else.'

'Aye, well. Maybe. But you know how stretched we are.'

She sighed. 'I'll see what I can do.'

'Aw, thanks, pet,' he said. 'In that case, your wish is my command.' He paused. 'Or at least it will be if you give those sodding burglaries to some other poor bastard.'

***

McKay was a short wiry man. With his close-cropped greying hair and generally belligerent expression, he looked like a textbook illustration of a chippy Scotsman. He knew that and made a point of living up to the image whenever he thought it might be useful. He was a Dundonian by background, but most people assumed he was a ned from Glasgow. He didn't bother to disabuse them of the idea. Better be thought a streetwise metropolitan than a turnip-eating provincial. He had a university education, too, but didn't advertise the fact. On the whole, people underestimated Alec McKay and he was happy to keep it that way.

He and DS Ginny Horton made a disconcerting couple, but again McKay liked it like that. Horton was English—*fucking* English, to use McKay's standard phraseology—small, neat, anonymously pretty, with tidily bobbed dark hair and an amicable smile. Someone who, in McKay's words, looked as if butter wouldn't melt in her arse. He knew from experience that that wasn't the whole picture, either.

'I don't take the Munlochy turn, then?' He'd asked her to drive so he could relax and concentrate on making disparaging remarks about how badly she was doing it.

McKay shook his head. 'No. Best carry on up the A9 to the Tore roundabout, then take the Black Isle road from there. It's before you get to Munlochy. On the right.'

She knew the area fairly well by now. At the weekend, she and her partner would sometimes drive over to Cromarty or

Rosemarkie for a walk by the sea or to grab a bite at one of the cafes. But she normally took the more southerly route up through Munlochy, and the Clootie Well was a new one to her. 'What is this place?'

'Somewhere people go to worship the old gods.' He winced at what he saw as the endless gullibility of humankind. 'It's a stream, basically. People hang up bits of cloth belonging to sick relatives so they'll recover.'

She allowed him to finish his diatribe. 'You think there's any significance to the body being left there?'

'I don't imagine the killer thought she'd recover through the healing power of the well, if that's what you mean. Maybe the body was intended as some kind of offering. Perhaps that's the significance of the roses. Or maybe Helena's right and the killer did care about the victim. Placed the body there to make some kind of amends.'

'Must have gone to some trouble with the roses and candles,' Horton said. 'If you were burying a body, you'd think you'd want to get it done with as quickly as possible.'

'From what they've said, it's a fair way from the road. You could bank on not being interrupted if you were doing it overnight. I'm not aware the doggers have taken to hanging out at the Clootie Well just yet, and I can't think of anyone else likely to drop by. And this time of year it's not even dark for that long, so you could see what you were doing. But, aye, it shows a certain dedication.'

They were heading down the A832, the main road into the Black Isle. The place was, as the locals said, neither black nor an isle. It was a peninsular protruding out into the North Sea, north of Inverness, bordered on three sides by the Moray, Beauly and Cromarty Firths. No-one seemed to know why it had been called 'black'. Possibly because of its mild local climate which left the area relatively snow and frost free compared with its Highland neighbours. McKay preferred to think it was on account of the unenlightened heathens who inhabited the place.

After a mile or so, McKay gestured for Horton to slow down, pointing out the turning for the Clootie Well. The entrance was draped with police tape, a more formal echo of the festoons of fabric on the trees beyond. As they turned in, an ambulance was pulling out, presumably taking the body off to the mortuary.

Horton slowed to greet the uniformed officer controlling the entrance, waving her warrant card out of the window. 'DS Horton and DI McKay,' she said.

McKay leaned across from the passenger seat. 'Morning, Murray. You're not planning to delay us, are you?'

The police officer squinted into the car. 'Alec, I wouldn't delay *you* if my life depended on it. Which it probably would.' He unhooked the tape and waved them past.

Horton parked next to the white scene of crime van, and they climbed out into the late-morning sunshine. There was a marked car closer to the roadside, which presumably belonged to Murray and his colleague. McKay noted that the car was occupied, and he walked over and tapped on the window.

The passenger seat was occupied by another PC, a red-faced, slightly overweight figure who gazed benignly up at McKay. 'You've copped this one, then, Alec? Thought you would.'

'Just lucky, I guess, Russ. Who's in the back seat?'

Russ twisted in his seat and looked at the young couple sitting awkwardly in the rear of the car. 'The two poor wee buggers who stumbled across the body. I thought you'd want to talk to them before they left, and they graciously agreed to hang around. That right, kids?'

'You listen to Uncle Russ,' McKay said, peering into the interior of the car. 'Thanks for staying, you two. Not that Russ will have given you a choice. We'll need to take formal statements from you in due course, but in the meantime I'd appreciate an informal chat while your memories are still fresh.' He noted the paleness of their skin, the blank look in their eyes. 'I'm sure it's been a shock,' he added. 'I need to take a look at the site first, but I'll be as quick as I can.'

'You sounded almost human there,' Horton said, a few minutes later, as they were tramping through the woodland.

'Aye, well. Don't tell anyone, will you?'

Up ahead, through the trees, they could see the two white-suited crime scene examiners walking back towards the car park. McKay waved, and one of them walked over. 'Morning, Alec. Why am I not surprised to see your ugly mug here?'

'Because there's a job that needs doing properly, I'm guessing. How it's going?'

'All done. Trust you to turn up when the party's over.' Jock Henderson was a tall, angular man who looked as if his centre of gravity was too far from the ground. McKay wondered where they found protective suits to fit him. He had a slightly shambolic air, but was good enough at his job.

'Just in time to pick up the bill,' McKay agreed. 'Story of my fucking life. So what's the story?'

'Young girl. I'd say early to mid twenties, but the doc will no doubt confirm. No obvious signs of physical trauma, but I'd say she'd been asphyxiated. Suffocated, maybe. Dark hair. Five three. Slim built to the point of being skinny. Couple of tattoos which might be of use to you, though they look like fairly off-the-shelf designs to me. A dove and some sort of butterfly design.'

'Any other ID?'

'Nothing. She was naked. No other possessions as far as we can find. We'll have to see if her fingerprints or DNA are on the database.'

'How long you reckon she'd been here?'

'Not long, I'd say. Few days. There were some signs of decomposition, but not a great deal. Mind you, the weather's been bloody chilly at night, so you'll have to wait on the doc for a definite view.'

'What about these candles and roses, then?'

'Christ knows. There are some funny bastards about, right enough. We've bagged them up and stuck them in the van as evidence. God knows what we'll get from them.'

'Greenfly, probably. Still, you can take a bunch home to the missus, Jock. Save having to stop off at the petrol station next time you fuck up.'

'You're still as funny as a turd in a single malt, Alec. But we love you that way.'

'Aye, so I understand. How long for the report?'

'As soon as possible, Alec. You know that.'

'Quicker than that, Jock. You know me.'

Henderson gave a mock bow. 'Your wish is my command, oh mighty one. Now piss off and let me get on.'

McKay laughed and continued past Henderson up the track towards the woodland, Horton following behind. A few moments later, they reached the spot where the body had been found. It was a clearing, with relatively thick woodland surrounding it. The turf had been lifted and piled in one corner, and the hollow of the burial place was exposed.

'What do you reckon?' McKay asked without turning round.

'It's remote enough, I suppose,' Horton said. 'Can't imagine there'd be much risk of being disturbed here overnight. Would have taken a while to remove the turf, but not that long to dig the grave itself.' She crouched down by the hollow, running a trickle of earth through her fingers. 'Ground's dry and pretty loose. Wouldn't have taken long to dig this out. Take it from a gardener.'

'I'll bow to your superior knowledge.' He looked around. 'Assume the killer wanted the body to be found?'

'The roses suggest it wasn't intended to be hidden for long, anyway,' she said. 'Plenty of people go walking round here. It was likely that someone would spot it. Although it would have been less conspicuous once the roses died.'

'And why here? It all looks very carefully planned. Just a conveniently remote spot, or does it have some significance?'

'I saw the strips of cloth as we drove in,' Horton said. 'Weird.'

'Very weird,' McKay agreed. 'But it's just superstition. And if people are desperate enough—if their loved ones are ill or dying—they'll give anything a shot.'

'Careful, Alec,' she said. 'You're in danger of sounding human again.'

'Aye, you're right. The place must be getting to me. Let's go back and have a blether with those two youngsters instead.'

CHAPTER FIVE

'I've really got to go soon,' Jo said, conscious she was already struggling to form the words.

'You can't go yet,' Dave—or was it Pete?—said. 'Thought we were set to make a night of it.' He looked genuinely downcast, but she knew that was because he'd had more on his mind than just heading off to a nightclub. She wondered momentarily whether she should invite him back with her now, just to put him out of his misery. But, drunk as she was, she took another look at his doughy overweight face and rejected the idea as quickly as it had entered her head. She didn't even fancy him. He was just a bit of company, part of a group she'd latched on to, the way she often did when she was out on the town these days. She'd fancied Pete—or was it Dave?— more, but Jade had copped off with him, so she was sitting here with the leftovers.

The pub was open till midnight and had become busier than ever in the last half-hour. The punters were young enough to make her feel old, and most looked more successful than she'd ever be. Not just wealthier—though they were probably that—but more settled, more relaxed, with partners or groups of friends. Like they might have real homes to go back to.

That was one reason she hated coming into Manchester. She preferred just hanging around her local in Brinnington. It didn't have much to recommend it, but it was friendly and the clientele was old enough to make her feel like a teenager. She knew a few people—not exactly friends, but people she could spend an evening getting pissed with. Most of them were in the same boat, one way or another. Divorced, unmarried, or saddoes who'd never had a real relationship in their lives. Some had kids they wanted to get away from, some just had empty bedsits they didn't want to go back to. Most, unlike Jo, were locals who'd spent their lives in this nondescript suburb. She could understand pretty much everything else, but not that. Why would you want to stay there? For that matter, why would you want to stay anywhere without a good reason?

'Go on,' Dave said. She was pretty sure this one was Dave. 'Just a bit longer. Have another drink.' He was a brickie, she thought, or a plasterer. Something like that. He'd told her earlier. They were southerners—real southerners, that was, from Surrey or Sussex or somewhere, up here working on a job. She'd thought all southerners were rolling in money, and there were jobs down there for the asking. Dave had said no, it wasn't like that, not any more. 'First it was the recession, then it was the bloody immigrants. Bloody Poles and Czechs and Romanians, undercutting us and taking all the work—' He'd stopped, conscious of the way she was looking at him. She didn't like that talk. People should be able to go where they liked, work where they wanted, that was what she thought. If the likes of Dave weren't good enough to compete, well, that was their tough luck, wasn't it?

'Anyway,' Dave had gone on, 'if you want to make decent money, you've got to go where the work is, haven't you? That's why we're up here. Loads of new builds, and we can get a good rate. I mean, that must be why you're down here, isn't it?' He didn't appear to see any contradiction between this and what he'd been saying about immigrants, but Jo couldn't be bothered to point it out. She knew Dave's type well enough. If he was working up here, it was because no-one down south would have him.

Dave and his mates had latched on to her and Jade as soon as they'd walked in the pub. It had been all right at first—they were a lively enough bunch—but as the evening wore on most of them had peeled off for one reason or other, mostly in pursuit of another bunch of females. Now she was sitting here, in this noisy pub, stuck with builder Dave and his fascinating array of small-talk. Once he'd got beyond 'fucking Mancs' and 'fucking Scousers', along with a related set of negative views about the local football clubs, there wasn't a lot left.

'Just one more,' he insisted again. 'What can I get you?'

She shook her head. 'Really can't—' She'd almost called him Dave, but she still wasn't sure this actually was Dave, so she hurried on. 'Need to go now so I can get the last train.'

'Can't be time for the last train yet. Just another glass of wine.'

Jo shook her head, more insistently this time. 'I've got to walk up to Piccadilly,' she said. 'I'll be OK if I go now, but I'll only just make it.'

'What about your mate there?' Dave pointed out. 'She doesn't look like she's ready to leave.'

'She looks like she's ready for something,' Jo said. 'I'm sure I can leave her in your friend's safe hands.'

'Look, just stay a bit longer. Tell me about yourself.' This was a desperate ploy. Dave had shown no previous interest in finding out anything about her.

She shrugged. 'I'm from Scotland. It's a dump. That's why I left. All you need to know.' She pushed herself to her feet. 'And now I'm going. Been nice to meet you, Dave. Till the next time.' She grabbed her coat and, with an unacknowledged wave in Jade's direction, stumbled towards the door. Behind her, she heard: 'For Christ's sake, I'm *Pete*. That's Dave. Stupid fucking cow—' but she was already out of the door and into the chill night air.

It was supposed to be summer, but the last few days had offered nothing but heavy cloud and showers. Tonight, while she'd been in the pub, a fine drizzle had set in. She was hardly dressed for a wet night, but she'd lived in Manchester long enough to come prepared. She fumbled in her shoulder-bag for her foldaway umbrella, then, brandishing it in front of her to keep off the worst of the rain, she began to make her way back through to Portland Street.

The damp air had partially sobered her up, and all she wanted now was to reach the shelter of the station. She always found the layout of the city centre confusing, and it took her a few seconds to work out which way to turn at the next junction. Despite the rain, the streets were busy with revellers, many of them even drunker than Jo.

She was walking past the southern edge of Chinatown, the ornate archway looming to her left, when she heard the voice calling. 'Jo? It is Jo, isn't it?'

She turned, startled, assuming the speaker was calling to some other Jo in the street behind her. There was a figure in a heavy-looking anorak, head bowed against the drizzle, peering at her. 'Christ, it is you, isn't it? How about that?'

Baffled, Jo took another step towards the figure. 'Sorry, pal. I think you must have the wrong person—'

The figure suddenly threw back the hood. 'Jo, it's me. Don't you remember? I mean, what are the chances?'

It took her a few seconds. The figure was partially silhouetted against the smeared neon of the rows of Chinese restaurants. The face was a little older and not a face she'd ever have expected to see here. But there was no doubt.

'Jesus,' Jo said, 'what the hell are you doing here?'

'It's a long story. You in a hurry?'

Jo glanced at her watch. 'I'm heading home. Last train. Shit, I'm already cutting it fine.'

'We should catch up. Look, do you want a lift? I'm parked just round the corner.'

'To the station? That would be great.' She could feel the cold rain dripping down her neck.

'No problem. We can arrange to meet up properly sometime. Have a good catch-up.'

'You living down here, then?' She followed the hunched figure down one of the side-streets, past vehicles parked on ignored double-yellows.

'Another long story, but I'm around for a couple of weeks, so, yeah, let's get together. This is me.' It was a battered-looking van. 'A bit clapped out, but it should get us up to Piccadilly safe and sound.'

'Better than walking.' Jo pulled open the passenger door and climbed inside. The interior of the van was a bit of a mess—empty Coke bottles, discarded parking tickets—but at least it was dry.

'Seat belt's a bit dodgy. Here, let me—' The hand reached into the van as if to pull on the seat belt. Then, unexpectedly, it was in front of her face, and she was trying to identify the piercing scent burning the back of her throat.

The wet cloth was clamped across her mouth, and she realised she was struggling to breathe. She kicked out furiously, trying to free herself from the confined space of the van, but the hand pressed more firmly. She felt dizziness, the throbbing of a headache behind her eyes, a burning on her skin, the taste of raw acid. She clutched at the wrist pressing hard against her mouth, desperately trying to loosen its pressure. But she was already losing control of her senses, the evening's alcohol combining with whatever she was inhaling. Her grip loosening, she looked up, terrified, to see that familiar face looming down towards her. It seemed to remain there for long minutes, staring down at her. And then, almost as a relief, she felt and saw nothing more.

Two minutes later, the van pulled out, completed a rapid U-turn, and wound its way through the one-way system towards Salford and the motorway.

CHAPTER SIX

'So what do we know now?' Helena Grant said. She wasn't keen on inviting McKay to her office because he tended to wander round the room, poking his nose into files that were none of his business and sniffing disapprovingly at what he found there. She knew he did it only to wind her up, but that didn't stop her being wound up. On the whole, it was easier to deal with McKay on his own territory, but she had the comms team on her back wanting a line on the Clootie Well killing, as the local media had inevitably dubbed it.

'A few things,' McKay said. 'We've got the path report. Seems there's evidence of poisoning by inhalation. Good old fashioned chloroform, would you believe?'

'I thought chloroform didn't work,' Grant said. 'All those old whodunits where the villain holds a handkerchief to the victim's mouth and the poor wee thing drifts off into la-la land.'

'According to Doc Green, it certainly doesn't work like that,' McKay said. Dr Jacquie Green was the senior forensic pathologist the local force used for its post-mortems. 'Bloody nasty stuff. You're more likely to kill the victim than just knock them out. Liver damage, the lot.'

'And in this case?'

'She thinks the dosage might have been fatal in itself. But looks like the killer also made a point of suffocating the presumably unconscious victim, just to make sure. Kept the chloroform-soaked cloth, or whatever it was, pressed over the poor lassie's mouth for as long as it took. There's burning to the skin around the mouth. Jockie Henderson missed that.' The last said with some degree of satisfaction.

'So what's this telling us?'

'We're dealing with a killer. Chloroform suggests pre-meditation and serious intent. If the aim was just to render the victim unconscious, there are easier and less risky ways of doing that.'

'What else do we have?'

'Doc reckons the body had been in the ground for maybe four or five days before it was found. Death probably occurred within the forty-eight hours before that. So the time of death in within the last week or so. She can't be much more precise than that. The body was moved after death, but that doesn't tell us much, given we know she wasn't killed where she was found. Could have been moved one mile or several hundred.'

'No ID yet?' Grant asked.

'Not yet. There are no recent local missing persons that fit the bill. We identified a couple of other recent possibles in Scotland, but neither panned out. There are a few other UK cases we're following up, but nothing very promising. We're still waiting on fingerprints and DNA.'

'What about the flowers and candles?'

'Nothing much. None of the local florists has any recollection of any unusual purchases, so it looks like they were just bought piecemeal from supermarkets and the like, as we thought. The vases are a bog-standard cheap model sold by various garden centres and DIY stores. Same with the candles and candlesticks.'

'Anything else?'

'Not so's you'd notice,' McKay said, gloomily. 'We've considered the tattoos, but again they're just standard off-the-shelf designs. We've checked with a couple of the local tattoo parlours and they reckon they could have been done anywhere. There's nothing traceable.'

'OK,' Grant said, 'so where from here?'

'If the DNA and fingerprints can't help us, I reckon we need a media appeal. Unless we know who the victim is, we can't make much progress.'

'The other question,' Grant said, 'is why the Clootie Well. Did it have some significance? And if the killer's not local, how did they know about it?'

'That place attracts nutters,' McKay said, 'like crap attracts journalists. But, aye, you're right. The place isn't exactly world famous. Suggests some local knowledge. But could just be someone who's been up here on holiday. I've heard tell there are people who do that.'

'OK, I'll agree some sort of holding line with comms. There's a lot of media interest in this, so we need to give them something soon. Let's hope we can get an ID.'

McKay nodded. 'Aye. Ideally one that means we can throw the whole case in some other bastard's direction.'

'You don't fool me, McKay,' Grant said. 'That's the last bloody thing you want.'

***

Ginny Horton slowed to a halt and took a deep breath. Not bad, she thought. A good five miles at a decent pace, and she was barely short of breath. She was never going to break any speed records, but she had the endurance and tenacity to keep going for as long as it took. Story of her life, really. Lately, she'd been upping the pace on these shorter runs. At first, she'd been surprised by how much it took out of her. Now, after a few months' practice, she was getting to the point where she could combine speed and a reasonable distance without undue effort.

It was a glorious early summer's evening, the sky clear, the waters of the Moray Firth a rare deep blue. She had no great expectations of the weather up here, which seemed to operate to its own, unique meteorological laws, but she tried to make the most of whatever decent weather they did get. Last summer hadn't been too bad. Maybe they'd be lucky again.

She walked over to one of the benches on the shoreline, and sat down to watch the play of the water on the rocks below. She'd been adamant, when they'd decided to move up here, that she wanted to live near the sea. They'd ended up here in Ardersier on the southern side of the Moray Firth. It was convenient for them both in terms of getting into Inverness, and handy for the airport when Isla had to make one of her frequent work trips south. It was a pretty enough little village with its mix of stone and white-rendered cottages. Their own house was small but comfortable, exactly the kind of place that Ginny had dreamed of living during her painful adolescence in red-brick Surrey suburbia.

Best of all, she could enjoy this regular run along the waterside between the village and the army barracks at Fort George. Fort George was typical of this place, she thought. A fortification built in the eighteenth century to strengthen control of the Highlands after the Jacobite rising, but still a working army barracks. She would run alongside the towering orange stonework, marvelling at its sheer presence in the landscape.

The evening was mild rather than warm, and the sweat on her body was beginning to cool her as she sat gazing out across the calm waters. Across the firth, she could see the southern edge of the Black Isle, the linked villages of Fortrose and Rosemarkie, the jutting tip of Chanonry Point. It wasn't unusual to see dolphins playing around the point, sometimes close to this shore, but she could see no sign of them today.

Time like this helped her clear her mind. She was happy to work whatever hours the job needed, but she wasn't one to bring her work home. At some point in the drive along the A96 from Inverness, she'd flick a mental switch and put it behind her, preparing for her evening with Isla.

But sometimes while she was running, her conscious mind virtually in neutral, she had ideas and insights that would never have come to her otherwise. Tonight, as she'd pounded along the shoreline, her thoughts had drifted unbidden to the Black Isle across the water and to the case she and McKay were currently investigating.

Her mind had somehow made a semi-conscious link with the missing person case they'd dealt with the previous summer over on the Black Isle. It had been something and nothing, that case, or at least that had been Horton's opinion. A woman with a history of doing a runner whenever life got on top of her appeared to have done another runner. There were circumstances that merited further investigation but no strong evidence that a crime had been committed. They'd looked into it, done their duty, but in the end the case had simply been left open, awaiting any reason to close it or take it further.

McKay, though, had seemed uncharacteristically affected by it. He'd maintained his usual persona of bluff cynicism but she could tell he was taking it more seriously than she'd expected. He hadn't delegated the work but interviewed potential witnesses himself, taking the time to visit the father in Inverness. It had gone nowhere, of course. But when they finally decided to suspend the investigation, McKay seemed genuinely upset. He'd raised no real objections— there was no justification for throwing more of their scarce resources at it—but she could tell that, if left to him alone, the decision might have been different.

She didn't know what made her think about that now. She'd run along this coast, night after night, autumn, winter and spring, never once recalling that case. Now, suddenly, the sight of Rosemarkie and Fortrose across the water had brought it back to her, and it was somehow linked in her mind with the body at the Clootie Well.

The individuals concerned were women of roughly the same age, she supposed, although that was where any physical similarity ended. There was a small possibility that last summer's misper might have ended up in the same condition, lying, so far undiscovered, in some shallow grave in a Highland woodland. But, as far as she could see, that was where any similarities ended.

Mostly the insights that bubbled up into her conscious mind as she ran were worthless. Even so, she'd learned not to disregard them because from time to time they resulted in something that blossomed into a genuine lead, a new avenue for investigation, some possibility that would never otherwise have occurred to her.

She made a mental note to bear it in mind, maybe even risk raising it with McKay in the morning. McKay respected her enough to listen to what she had to say, however off-the-wall.

After a moment, she set off again, initially jogging along the waterfront, then picking up speed as she thought about getting back to supper, to a glass of wine and to Isla.

CHAPTER SEVEN

'Bingo,' McKay said.

'Bingo?' Horton was sitting at her desk, ploughing assiduously through mind-numbing paperwork.

'Bingo. We've got an ID.'

She sat up. 'For the Clootie Well? Who?'

'Katherine Scott,' McKay said. 'Known as Katy. Last known residence an address in Manchester. On the file for a couple of minor drugs offences and one count of shoplifting, both in her late teens. She'd have been twenty-eight—no, twenty-nine now.'

'Bit older than we thought then?'

'Doc reckoned mid-twenties. But hard to be sure. She'd not looked after herself. Heavy drinker. Smoker.' McKay ostentatiously pulled out another strip of gum and began to chew.

'Manchester?' Horton said. 'So does that mean we can hand it over to GMP?'

'Last known address was in Manchester, but that was four years ago. There's no information on where she's been living since.' He paused. 'She's a local lass. Born in Inverness, brought up in Culbokie. Hung around in Inverness till her early twenties then buggered off south to convert the heathens.'

'And ended up in a shallow grave back in the same neck of the woods,' Horton said. 'Interesting.'

'Wherever and whyever she was killed,' McKay said, 'we have to assume she was buried up here for a reason. Either she was killed locally and it was just a conveniently remote spot to dispose of the body. Or she was killed somewhere else, and the killer made the effort to bring the body back to bury it within a few miles of her home town. Either way, it means that the case is still ours.'

'You're preparing your arguments for Helena, aren't you?' Horton said. 'You know she'll be only too keen for someone else to take responsibility, given the pressures on resources.'

'Not my problem,' McKay said. 'Well, only partially my problem. I'm just interested in truth and justice.'

'And not being bored.'

'That too.'

'Anything else on Scott?'

'They've just sent the basics. I'll see what I can get off the PNC though our last contact with her was more than ten years ago, so I'm not hopeful there'll be much. Probably worth doing some digging. Birth certificate and any other documentation we can find. Any relatives locally. Anything we might have on file. Assume she probably went to the Academy. We can see if they've got any details on her family and so on.'

Horton smiled. 'This is what you live for, isn't it, Alec? The chance to get your teeth into a proper case.'

'Too right, lass, too right. Better than some wee scrote stealing knickers off the line in the backstreets of Inverness.' He leaned forward in his chair, chewing enthusiastically on his gum. 'My advice is to make the most of it.'

***

'So what about that woman last year?'

'What woman?'

They were in the small garden at the side of the Plough Inn in Rosemarkie, trying gamely to make two Cokes last the afternoon. Greg was eighteen now and so in theory could have had a beer, but he was driving, and these days there was no point in risking even the smallest amount of alcohol. She'd be eighteen in just a few more days, and generally got away with ordering alcohol when she was with Greg. But the truth was that both of them actually still preferred Coke though Greg would never have admitted this to any of his male friends.

'You know the one. The one who went missing. She did some cleaning for your dad.' Greg's dad was a farmer and owned a stretch of land between here and Cromarty. He still did some dairy farming but there was no money in that anymore, so he'd gradually diversified. He'd built a cluster of upmarket holiday chalets on the hillside with views over the Firth and then more recently had opened a farm shop selling produce from other local farmers. One way or another, he managed to make a decent living for himself. 'We chatted to her a few times.'

'What about her?'

'Well, she went missing. Maybe it was her.'

'Maybe what was her?'

'Christ, Greg, you can be thick sometimes. I mean, maybe it was her up at the Clootie Well.'

'It wasn't. I saw her face, remember?' Greg blinked and took a sip of his Coke, his expression suggesting that, for his own part, he'd rather forget.

'I know. But dead people look different, don't they?' She thought she'd read that somewhere. It sounded the kind of thing that could be true.

'Do they? I don't know. But I'm sure it wasn't her. Anyway, the police are bound to have followed that up, aren't they? They were all over it at the time.'

'They don't know what they're doing,' Kelly said. 'Probably wouldn't even have occurred to them to link the two.'

Greg batted away a huge seagull intent on stealing any scraps of discarded food that might be lying around. The cawing of the gulls was an unremitting backdrop to their conversation. 'Anyway, it wasn't her.'

'Well, maybe she's another one then. Maybe we've a serial killer on our hands.'

'What was her name, anyway?' Greg asked, partly to change the subject. He still hadn't quite recovered from the shock of stumbling across the body. The word had got out among their mates over the last couple of days as the story hit the media. Both he and Kelly had been interviewed, briefly and over the phone, by some local journalist. Neither had had much to say but that hadn't stopped the journalist making up some suitably juicy quotes. The two had become minor celebrities among their circle of friends, but Greg was hoping the glamour would soon fade.

'Lizzie something, wasn't it?' She paused, thinking. 'Hamilton? I liked her. She was a good laugh.'

'My dad thought she did a runner because she owed people money.'

'Did she?'

'I don't know. It was just a theory. But the police didn't seem all that interested. They must have thought she'd just buggered off as well.'

'Yes, but they—'

'I know. They know nothing. But it is their job.'

They sat in silence for a few minutes, enjoying the afternoon sunshine, the breeze blowing in from the sea, the relentless chorus of the gulls. They were both conscious that this was a golden time—the brief few months with Highers out of the way and university still to come. They wanted to make the most of it, even if that involved little more than drinking Coke in the garden of an old pub. Greg was working part-time for his dad over the summer, and Kelly was helping out in the store in Cromarty, so they had a few quid to spend. Finally Kelly said: 'But adults don't do that. They don't just run away.'

'Yes, they do. I've got a cousin, or a second-cousin or something. His wife just pushed off one day, left him with a baby. I've heard my dad talk about it.'

'I suppose.' She watched a cluster of gulls squabbling over some titbit. The garden was tucked away at the side of the old pub building and provided a comfortable sun-trap at the right time of day. There'd been another couple enjoying lunch out here earlier, but now Kelly and Greg were alone. 'But adults get murdered sometimes too.'

'Give it a rest, eh, Kelly? She wasn't murdered.'

'How do you know?' She paused, thinking. 'What about Denny Gorman?'

'Who's Denny Gorman? Another "murder victim"?' The quote-marks were clearly audible.

'No, you numpty. The landlord at the Caledonian. He's a creep.'

'Is he? I don't know him.'

'Well, he looks like one. You know the guy. Greasy hair. Comb-over. Stubble. Always looks like he's slept in his clothes.'

'I've never been in the Caley. If we go up that way, we go to the Anderson or the Union.'

'You'll have seen him around, though. Shambling through the town. He's an old lech.'

'Is he?'

'I reckon so. I've seen him eyeing up the girls in the Co-op.'

'That proves it then. He must be a murderer.' Greg finally finished off his Coke. 'Another? I've just about got enough on me.'

'Let's go for a walk instead. Makes you think, though, doesn't it?'

'What does?'

'Well, finding that body. If we hadn't stumbled along there, it might have stayed hidden.'

'The roses were pretty conspicuous.'

'For a while. But I don't imagine many people go wandering into those woods. If we hadn't found it when we did, that body might never have been discovered.'

'Well done us, then.' Greg was zipping up his rucksack. They'd brought down a couple of books to read on the beach and a towel in case they decided to go into the water. 'Shall we head down to the sea?'

'Yeah, why not?' She rose to follow him. 'But that's not what I meant. I meant that there might be others. Other bodies buried that have never been discovered. Lizzie Hamilton might be one of them.'

'Kelly—'

'I'm just saying. She could still be out there somewhere. Undiscovered. Up in Fairy Glen. Or by the burn up there behind us—'

'Kelly, just give it a rest. OK.'

The sharpness of his tone took her by surprise. It suddenly struck her how much this had affected them both. Much more, she thought, than either had been able, or had wanted, to articulate. She was coping by blethering on about murders and missing persons and shallow graves. Greg was coping by trying to forget it all.

'Sorry, Greg,' she said, after a pause. 'Just ignore me. You know what I'm like.'

'Aye,' he said. 'You're grand. I'm just a bit distracted, that's all.'

'I know,' she said. 'Come on. Let's go for a paddle.'

CHAPTER EIGHT

McKay took a breath and glanced at Horton. 'Here we go then.' He leaned forward and pressed the bell.

For a few minutes there was no sign of life from within the bungalow. He was about to press the bell a second time when he caught a glimpse of movement through the frosted glass in the front-door. There was a rattling of locks before the door finally opened a few centimetres, held by a chain.

'Yes?' A woman peered back at them through the door. She was perhaps in her early sixties, but looked older, her hair white, her face lined and worried-looking. She was dressed smartly, in a tweed skirt and white blouse.

'Mrs Scott?'

'Who's asking?' she said, suspiciously. 'Didn't you see the notice?'

McKay glanced at the sticker in the upper frame in the door. 'No hawkers, cold callers or circulars.' When was the last time anyone was bothered by a hawker?

He held out his warrant card. 'Police. DI McKay. DS Horton.'

'Is this about the break-ins? We've had no problems, but next door's said that their shed—'

'No, Mrs Scott. It's not about the burglaries. May we come in? I'm afraid we have some bad news.'

'Bad news? Well, you'd better—' The door closed, and they heard the sound of the chain being removed. Then Mrs Scott opened it fully and led them into the narrow hallway.

The inside of the small bungalow was as McKay had envisaged it. There was a sitting room off to the right, a kitchen straight ahead of them and a row of closed doors on the left. The interior was scrupulously tidy, the decor fussy and old-fashioned.

There were shelves lined with porcelain figurines and similar knick-knacks.

'Is your husband at home, Mrs Scott?'

'He's in the sitting room. We were just sitting down to watch *Countdown*. Ronnie's retired now, you know?' She spoke as if McKay was an old acquaintance who might have failed to keep up with the latest news. 'Would you like some tea?'

'I think you'd better come and sit down, Mrs Scott.' Before Mrs Scott could object further, McKay led the way into the sitting room, Horton following behind. Mr Scott, who had obviously been semi-dozing in front of the television, started up in surprise.

'I'm very sorry to disturb you, Mr Scott—' McKay began.

From behind him, Mrs Scott said: 'It's the police, Ronnie. They say they've got some bad news.'

Scott pushed himself slowly to his feet, looking startled and slightly bewildered. He looked older than his wife, probably late sixties, with slightly unkempt grey hair and eyes that blinked at the world through thick glasses. He was wearing an open-necked shirt and slacks, but looked as if he'd have been more at home in a suit. McKay suspected that retirement wasn't suiting the man. He could empathise with that.

'Police?' Scott repeated, as if he hadn't quite understood. He was staring at McKay as if expecting to be arrested himself. 'You'd better sit down.'

McKay sat himself in one of the two armchairs, while Mrs Scott perched beside her husband on the sofa, reaching for the remote to mute the sound of the television.

'As I told your wife, Mr Scott, I'm afraid I've come bearing some bad news. It's about your daughter.' Ever since they'd confirmed that Katy Scott's parents were still alive and resident in Culbokie, McKay had been mentally preparing this conversation. He'd been in this position numerous times, and it never became any easier.

Scott glanced at his wife, then back at McKay. 'Katy? What about her?'

'I'm afraid she's dead, Mr Scott. I'm very sorry.'

He wasn't sure what reaction he'd been expecting. In his experience, responses to that kind of news varied dramatically and often unpredictably. Loving, close parents sat in apparent calm, while supposedly estranged mothers and fathers threw themselves into unstoppable paroxysms of grief.

The Scotts seemed closer to the former camp. Scott was looking at his wife, as if expecting her to take the lead. 'My God,' he said, finally. 'Well, that's a shock.' It sounded like the response to the death of a family pet rather than his own daughter. 'What—what were the circumstances?'

'It's rather complicated, Mr Scott. If it's not too intrusive, can I ask when you last saw your daughter?'

McKay was trying to decipher Scott's expression. It wasn't grief, or even quite surprise. It was something that felt wrong in the context, some emotion with no place here, but McKay couldn't quite pin it down.

After a moment, Mrs Scott said: 'There's no point in lying to you, Mr McKay. We've haven't seen her in a good few years. She was a rather—difficult girl.'

'That's one way of putting it,' Scott said. 'She was a nightmare. Especially after Emma passed on.'

'Ronnie—'

'Well, it's true, isn't it? While she was here, she made our lives a complete misery.'

McKay nodded, unsure how to respond. 'I'm sorry to broach this just at the moment, but we'll need one or both of you to identify the body, I'm afraid. We'll take every step to ensure it's not too distressing.'

Mrs Scott looked up as she absorbed his words. 'Is there any doubt, then?'

'I'm afraid not, Mrs Scott. We identified her through her DNA and fingerprints. But, if it's possible, we need a relative to confirm for the records.'

'DNA and fingerprints?' Mr Scott said. 'She had a police record then?'

'A minor one,' Horton said. 'From some years ago.'

'I see.' Mr Scott looked as if he didn't believe this. 'I'm not surprised. She was a bad one.' His wife looked as if about to interrupt him again, but he went on. 'I'm only telling the truth, Megs. These people need to know.' He looked up at McKay. 'You said it was complicated?'

'We believe she was murdered, Mr Scott. Her body was discovered—well, relatively close to here. We don't yet know the circumstances of her death.'

Mrs Scott was staring at him. 'It's that body, isn't it? At Munlochy. That was our Katy. My God—'

It was inevitable they would join the dots. The finding of the body had been widely reported in the local media despite the best efforts of Grant and the media team to keep it low-key. The details had not yet been made public. 'Yes, I'm afraid so.'

Scott looked disbelieving. 'But why would she be up here?' he said. 'She hasn't been back in years. It's the last place she wanted to be.'

And the last place she'd ended up, McKay thought. 'You were telling me about when you'd last seen your daughter, Mr Scott.'

'Not for years,' Scott said bluntly. 'I mean, real years. Ten, at least.'

'Did you have a falling-out?'

'No more than usual. We argued constantly while she was living here. I never knew what we did wrong. We'd brought her up in a good, Christian lifestyle—'

Well, there's your answer, McKay thought. What sort of child would want that? He looked around the room, spotting the large leather-bound Bible on the shelf below the television set. 'I'm sure you did.' He paused, his mind tracking back over the previous conversation. 'You mentioned an—Emma?'

'Our first daughter,' Mrs Scott said. 'We lost her too.'

'I'm sorry,' McKay said. McKay knew what it was like to lose a daughter. He couldn't imagine what it must be like to have lost two. 'I didn't realise.'

Mrs Scott looked at her husband as if seeking his permission to speak. After a moment, Scott said: 'It was cancer. Leukaemia. She'd never been a healthy child, and it was diagnosed too late.'

'She and Katy had been close,' Mrs Scott said. 'It hit her hard.'

'God's judgement,' Scott said bluntly. 'Ours not to reason why. But we tried to look after Katy. Tried to do our best for her. We never had a lot of money, but what we had we spent on her. She threw it back in our faces.'

'In what way?'

'Everything,' Scott said. 'Drink, boys, even drugs, I think, though we never caught her at that. We caught her at most other things. We tried everything.'

'Why did she leave finally?' McKay asked. He caught Horton's eye, recognising that he was perhaps pushing things too far.

But Scott responded without hesitation. 'You tell me. It just happened one day. She was eighteen so there was nothing we could do. We'd both been at work—Megs worked part-time—and we got home to find her gone. Clothes and everything. Not to mention a few quid that Megs had got stashed away in the kitchen for housekeeping.' He made it sound as if that was the real loss.

'There was nothing that particularly prompted her to go? Just then, I mean.'

'Not that I'm aware of. There was a boy. She went off to live with him.'

'You don't remember his name?'

'Haven't a clue.' Scott looked across to his wife. 'Megs is better at that sort of thing.'

Mrs Scott frowned. 'It's a long time ago,' she said. 'Denny something. No, Danny. Danny Reynolds, I think.' There was something about the way she said the name that made McKay suspect the hesitation had been feigned. Perhaps she'd kept in touch after the daughter had left home. McKay made a mental note that, when it came to taking formal statements, they should interview the Scotts separately.

'Do you know where he lived?'

There was an almost imperceptible hesitation before Mrs Scott responded. 'Katy might have sent us an address for forwarding mail.'

McKay could see from Scott's expression that this was news to him. 'Any information you do have would be useful to us.' He shuffled forward on his chair. 'And you've neither of you had any contact with her in the last few years? You've no knowledge of where she was living?' He avoided catching Mrs Scott's eye.

Scott shook his head. 'We've heard nothing from her since she left.'

'I understand.' McKay pushed himself to his feet. 'Well, we won't trouble you further for now. We appreciate this must be a dreadful shock. I don't know if you'd like us to contact a neighbour—'

'We'll be fine,' Scott said, brusquely. 'Thank you.'

'We'll be in touch about the formal identification. And we'll need to take formal statements from you both. Just for the record, you understand.'

Scott looked as if he might object, but his wife intervened. 'We understand. Mr McKay. We want to know what happened to Katy.' McKay had the sense that she was only just keeping her emotions under control.

'Thank you, Mrs Scott,' he said. 'I promise you, we'll do our best to find out.' This time, he realised, he was avoiding meeting her husband's eyes.

***

'I'll get you another ice-cream later,' Craig Fairlie said. 'We'll get some real food soon. It's nearly lunchtime.'

Fraser looked up. He was engaged in the creation of some highly extended sand edifice. Castle, Craig reflected, was too limited a word for what his son was building. Fraser never did anything by halves. He had already built an array of towers and battlements stretching over several square metres, and had now moved on to constructing a network of working moats. He was trying to deflect the flow of one of the streams that ran down the beach from the woodlands behind them. It was painstaking work, because the water had a habit of reverting to its preferred routes, but Fraser did seem to be making some progress.

Craig could see it would be heartbreaking for the boy to leave all this behind, knowing the overnight tides would simply wash it all away. He also knew Fraser well enough to be confident the despair would be short-lived. By the time they'd sat down to fish fingers and ice-cream, he'd be ready to move on to the next thing, whatever that might be.

'Anyway,' Fraser said, not looking up from his work, 'I've already had lunch.'

'Oh, really?' Craig said. 'And what did you have?'

Fraser was silent for a moment, digging away at a bank of sand. 'Chicken nuggets. And beans.'

'Right. So where did you have those?'

'The cafe,' Fraser said without hesitation.

'Which cafe?'

'The one where they do chicken nuggets and beans.'

Silly question, Craig acknowledged. Fraser was four years old, nearly five, and, as far as Craig could recall, this was the first time he'd told an outright lie. His mother might know differently, of course. Perhaps this was some significant point of development, a rite of passage to be celebrated. Certainly, it was likely to be the first of many, and Fraser would no doubt become more adept at ensuring their credibility.

While Fraser played, Craig lay back enjoying the sun on his face. It was good to get a spell of decent weather, and it was lucky they'd been able to take advantage of this one. Craig had been owed a couple of days in lieu after working some evenings. He'd been hoping Jules could take the time off too but that hadn't worked out, so he'd come up here with Fraser on his own. Jules's mother had been pleased to be relieved of childcare for a day or two, and Craig himself had welcomed the opportunity for what he'd jokingly told Jules was 'father and son bonding'. 'Bond all you want,' she'd said, 'as long as you don't spend a fortune. I know you. You'll spoil him rotten given half a chance.'

The truth was that he rarely got even half a chance. He was having to work every hour just to make ends meet. They'd already laid off a few people this year. Craig was probably safe enough, given the time he'd been with the firm. But you never knew. They said that the economy was recovering—but they'd been saying that for years and it didn't feel like it up here.

So he wanted to make the most of today. They'd brought Fraser up here a few times at weekends for a day out. It was a place Craig remembered from his childhood. The big suspension bridge had only just opened in those days, and it was a novelty to be able to get over to the Black Isle without having to take the ferry or traipse the long way round through Beauly.

Even now, he thought of it as a slightly magical place. There was the long stretch of unspoiled beach around the bay, backed at the eastern end by woodland and crumbling cliffs. On a clear day like today, the firth was a rich blue, stretching from the open sea in the east to the jutting headland of Chanonry Point.

Craig knew that if he tried simply to drag Fraser away from his sandcastle there was bound to be a scene. He'd no desire to end up as the stereotypical father unable to calm his screaming son. The trick, he'd found, was to distract Fraser with some other, potentially more attractive option.

'Wondered if you fancied a walk along the beach?' he asked, casually.

'Doing a sandcastle,' Fraser said, still carefully digging away at one of his trenches.

'It's very impressive. I just thought we might go and look at the secret cave.'

Fraser's attention was caught. 'Secret cave?'

'Up there at the far end of the beach.' He held a finger to his lips. 'But don't tell anyone.'

'Can we go and see?' Fraser was already on his feet.

'Well, it's very secret. I'm not supposed to let anyone else know where it is.'

'Show me!'

Craig began, with apparent reluctance, to stand up. 'Well, as long as you promise not to tell anyone—'

'I won't! Promise!'

Which was probably Fraser's second lie, Craig reflected. 'OK, then. Let's go see.'

They collected their possessions, including Fraser's precious bucket and spade, and stuffed them into Craig's rucksack. Fraser seemed already to have forgotten about his sandcastle.

As they walked east, the beach became rougher, with more rocks and stretches of shingle. Woodland rose up the hillside to their left. At high tide, this area was reduced to a barely passable strip, but the sea was currently far out and they had no difficulty in walking further round the bay.

The walk to the cave was longer than Craig remembered, but he kept Fraser entertained with searches for sea-creatures in the rock pools. They still had time to reach the cave and get back in time for lunch.

In due course, the woodland gave way to a line of rough sandstone cliffs, slowly being eroded by the weather and the tides. Craig had once found a small ammonite fossil among the rocks here, and he knew that more serious fossil hunters visited the Eathie cliffs further up the coast. Maybe that was something he should do with Fraser when the boy was older.

He didn't really know the history of their destination, Caird's Cave, except that, according to the exhibit in the beachside cafe, it had been the source of various prehistoric finds and that, remarkably, it had been used as a dwelling until the early part of the twentieth-century. It was difficult to imagine what it would be like living in such an exposed location, yards from the roaring sea.

The cave itself was set back from the beach, its entrance a broad archway in the cliff-side set among the surrounding undergrowth. As Craig recalled, there wasn't actually a great deal to the place, but he knew that, with a few judicious stories, he could make it seem exciting enough for Fraser.

As Craig led the way up the narrow footpath towards the entrance, Fraser clutched his hand nervously, gazing up at the dark space beyond.

'A home for smugglers and pirates,' Craig said, in what he intended loosely to be a pirate voice. 'Let's see if we can find any of their buried booty, landlubber—' He stopped. He couldn't fully make out what he was seeing at first but it was sufficiently disturbing for him, almost involuntarily, to move Fraser behind him. But it was, of course, too late.

'What's that, dad? Is it booty?'

'Look, just wait there a sec while I check. I don't want us to get captured by pirates.' He prised himself free of Fraser's clutching hand and took another few steps forward. He could sense that Fraser was reluctant to be left behind, but Craig wanted to be sure.

He crouched and peered into the gloom and, as his eyes adjusted to the dim light, he could see four black candlesticks, complete with unlit candles, and four black vases of red roses, set in a rectangle. Between the candles and roses, there was a dark elongated bundle, something wrapped in a heavy sheet or tarpaulin. Craig already had little doubt what it was.

He turned back to where Fraser was still standing, hanging back nervously from the cave entrance.

'The pirates have already been, Fraser,' Craig said, his mouth dry. 'I think we'd better call the police.'

***

It was only once the front door had closed behind them that McKay realised how tense he'd been feeling. 'Jesus fucking Christ. No wonder she left home.'

Horton watched in amusement as he unwrapped a stick of gum, pushed it into his mouth and began to chew furiously. She could see what he wanted more than anything, at that moment, was a cigarette.

'Cut them some slack,' she said. 'You can never tell how people will respond to news like that.'

'Ach.' He stomped down the garden path. 'That old bastard couldn't give a bugger about the poor lass. *Either* of the poor lassies. We were just interrupting his viewing of *Countdown*.'

'I'm not sure that's entirely fair—' The Scotts' bungalow was on a slightly bleak residential estate just outside the village. Horton could almost feel the net curtains twitching as they returned to the car.

'Bloody God-botherer,' McKay continued. 'God's fucking judgement, for Christ's sake.'

'OK, I get the point.' Horton looked at McKay across the roof of the car. 'What about the wife, though? What did you make of her?'

McKay took a breath. 'Aye, that was interesting. She knew a few things the old man didn't.'

'That was my impression. As if she'd been in touch with her daughter more recently than she was letting on.'

'My guess is Scott won't be keen on us talking to them separately. But I think we should.'

They climbed into the car. McKay was fiddling with his phone, checking e-mails and texts. 'Oh, Christ.'

'What?'

'You should stop off back at the Scotts so I can ask him just what the fuck his God thinks he's up to.'

'What is it?'

'You need to head back out to the Black Isle. We've another one.'

CHAPTER NINE

'**H**ow the fuck did she get out here?'

Even the police had had problems reaching the spot. In the end, they'd brought a 4x4 down through the farmland at the rear of the beach. Even so, they could get only to within fifty or so metres of the cave itself. A couple of officers would have to carry the body back up in due course

'We think pretty much the same way we got down here,' DC Mary Graham said. She'd been delegated down here by Grant to hold the fort for CID until McKay and Horton arrived. Graham cut an imposing figure, tall and with a main of thick blonde hair around an angular face that suggested a Viking ancestry. McKay knew she'd have taken no nonsense, ensuring the scene was properly protected until the examiners arrived and organising one of the uniforms to keep people away from this part of the beach.

'They wouldn't have come through the farm, though?'

'There's another entrance to the fields a quarter of a mile or so before then. I haven't had chance to check it yet but the most likely route would be through there and across the fields. You can get pretty close to the beach.' Graham was a local, who'd spent her early years in Fortrose.

'Still be conspicuous to bring a vehicle over there at night, wouldn't it?' Horton asked. 'Not exactly a bustling metropolis here.'

'I don't know,' McKay said. 'Modern 4x4s are pretty quiet. These farmers tend to be early to bed and early to rise types. It would be a risk, but not a huge one.'

'But why take it at all? Why bring a body down here, of all places?'

'Christ knows,' McKay said.

The three of them were standing outside the cordon that had been erected around the cave. Two white-suited examiners were busy inside. 'How long's old Jock Henderson going to be?' McKay asked.

'Not long, he reckoned. Fifteen, twenty minutes.'

Across the firth, they could see the orange walls of the fortress at Fort George. A couple of boats were heading out towards the open sea. 'What the fuck is this?' McKay asked, after a pause. He sounded as if he genuinely wanted an answer. 'Who the fuck kills two young lasses, and then lays the bodies out like some kind of sodding state funeral?'

'A lunatic?' Horton offered. She turned to Graham. 'Who was it found the body?'

'A bloke and his young son. They'd walked out here so he could show the son the cave. I took a statement from them and got their details.'

'You didn't hold on to them?' McKay asked.

'Well, no,' Graham said. 'He looked shaken and the boy was upset. They'd been intending to grab some lunch so I let them go. Sorry. '

McKay had felt a momentary irritation at Graham's actions but knew he was being unreasonable. Graham was a good reliable copper. She'd have taken a decent statement. She'd have got the man's contact details and made sure his footprints could be eliminated from any others that might be found outside the cave. There was probably nothing more the man could tell them. 'Ignore me. Ginny will tell you I'm not in the best of the moods.'

'It's his time of the month,' Horton said. 'Runs from the first through to the thirtieth or thirty-first. Shorter in February, for which we're all grateful.'

'Very funny,' McKay growled. 'No, you did good,' he said to Graham.

She shuffled uncomfortably on the damp sand. 'I'll go and see how the examiners are getting along,' she said.

'What is it, Alec?' Horton said when Graham had walked off.

'What's what?'

'You've been like a bear with a sore arse ever since we left Culbokie.'

'Ach, I don't know. That bastard Scott, I suppose. Fucking Christian hypocrite. Loves our Jesus Christ, but can't bring himself to love his own fucking daughter.'

'People show their love in different ways.'

'And he showed his by throwing her out of the fucking house?'

'She walked out.'

'Because he made her. Because his own morality was more important than his love for his daughter. Who knows what he did to the poor lass.'

'You don't, for a start. And neither do I. And you don't know what he's going through now. Not inside.'

McKay made no response, but stood, chewing rhythmically, staring at the open sea. Finally, he turned and said: 'Let's go see whether Jock Henderson's finally got his act together.'

They arrived back at the cave as the two examiners were emerging. Henderson pulled back his white hood and stood blinking in the noonday sun.

'What's the matter, Jock?' McKay asked. 'Don't they normally let you out in daylight?'

'Just the shock of seeing your ugly mug, Alec.'

'What have we got?'

'Young girl. Similar age to the last one. Maybe mid-twenties. Death from asphyxiation, again, I'd say.'

'Any signs of chloroform?' McKay tried, not entirely successfully, to keep a note of mockery from his voice.

'Aye. Burns round the mouth. Same MO as the last one, I'd say. Though I think this one might have been more difficult for the killer. Looks like she might have vomited. Maybe choked on her vomit, with her mouth held firmly shut. Imagine the doc will confirm.'

'Any ID?'

'She was naked like the last one. A few more tattoos this time, so you might have some luck with those. I'll get the photos over to you. Dyed blonde hair. Skinny little thing.'

'And roses and candles again?'

'Aye. Like up at Munlochy. The body wasn't buried this time. Ground in there's too hard to make it feasible. It was wrapped in plastic sheeting. We'll have a look at that and see if we can get anything from it.'

'How long's she been here?'

'I'm pretty sure she was placed here last night. In this kind of weather people walk up here to explore the caves, so if she'd been here longer she'd have been spotted. I'd say she'd been dead for maybe three or four days before that.'

'Anything else?'

'Might be a bit more chance than there was last time of getting some DNA traces, given the body's not been here long and it's been under cover.'

'If there's any on there, other than the victim's.'

'As you say. No sign of any fingerprints, certainly. But you wouldn't expect someone who goes to these lengths to be that stupid.'

'You reckon this is likely to be the same killer?'

'Well, I'd say so, wouldn't you? You haven't released any details of how the first victim died, so it's not a copy-cat killing.'

'So we've got a random multiple killer on our hands,' McKay said. 'Helena Grant's going to be so pleased.'

'More your problem than mine, pal.' Henderson sounded more pleased than any man who'd just finished examining a murdered corpse had a right to be. 'The report will be with you in due course.'

'As always, quicker than that,' McKay said. 'Much quicker.' He turned away, then looked back over his shoulder. 'Pal.'

***

McKay dropped Horton off back at Divisional Headquarters and continued back through the city to his house on the outskirts. He expected to be pulling a late one tonight—and possibly for the foreseeable future—so he wanted to square things with Chrissie in person, rather than trying to do it over the phone. It probably wouldn't help but it was worth a shot. In any case, the journey would give him a bit of time to himself and he felt he needed that just at the moment.

Chrissie was in the kitchen when he arrived, preparing something for their suppers. Not the most auspicious of starts. 'Jesus,' she said, 'you made me jump. What the hell are you doing back at this time? Have they finally sacked you?'

Lovely to see you too, dear, he thought. 'They've still not found me out. But I'll need to work late tonight. So I thought I'd pop in on my way past.'

She took it better than he'd expected. 'I saw the latest on the lunchtime news,' she said. 'Sounds like another one?'

'Looks that way,' he said. 'Which isn't good news for anyone.'

'Least of all us,' Chrissie said. She looked at the casserole dish into which she had been carefully dicing vegetables. 'I'm just doing a stew,' she said. 'It'll keep till you get back. Whenever that is.' She allowed just the faintest edge of bitterness to creep into her tone.

'Aye, I know, Chrissie. Look, I'm sorry—'

'I know you're sorry, Alec. You're always sorry. It doesn't help.'

'I know—'

She held up a hand as if stopping traffic. 'Don't, Alec. We've been through it. It doesn't go anywhere. There's no point in having another argument.'

As if I'd been the one trying to provoke it, he thought. He could feel his irritation rising. The anger and despair he'd felt when speaking to that bastard up in Culbokie came back into his throat like bile. This was how it always seemed to be these days. As if she wanted to needle him just enough and then stamp the lid firmly back if he tried to respond. In his more rational moments, he knew he did the same. It was like probing a loose tooth. You could never stop yourself until the damn thing dropped out.

'No,' he said, finally, 'you're right. There's no point. Everything's been said. It doesn't help us to keep saying it.'

She looked, for a moment, as if she were about to argue after all. 'No, you're right. It doesn't.'

'I'll give you a call when I'm on my way back. I hope it won't be too late.'

'No, well. I know it's important. Those poor wee lassies. It's frightening just to think about it.'

'Whoever's doing this is a mad bastard, right enough.'

'Look, Alec, I'm not trying to be difficult. I'm a cantankerous old bitch, just like you're a miserable old bastard. But at the end of the day we're on the same side. We're having to deal with the same things. We're both suffering. We need to help each other.'

'Aye, you're right,' he said, finally. 'I've had a bad time today. Went up to see the parents of the first victim—we've managed to ID her now. God-bothering old bugger up in Culbokie. Cared more about his precious Bible than he did about his murdered daughter.'

'Alec—'

'Aye, I know. Get a bit of perspective. But bastards like that don't deserve any perspective.' He paused. 'And then we got the call about the second body. They found her in this bloody cave just up from Rosemarkie. I watched as they carried her body away. She was just a poor wee slip of a thing—' He could feel, embarrassingly, the tears welling behind his eyes.

Chrissie took his hand in hers. He couldn't remember the last time she'd made a gesture like that. She was still the same woman he'd married, he thought, the fiery redhead who used to drag him on to the dance-floor and made damn sure he had a good time, whether he wanted to or not. But she looked shrunken now, her shoulders stooped, streaks of grey in that copper hair. 'Alec. I *know*. I understand,' she said. 'Nobody else does. Nobody else can. But I do. I'm there as well, you know?'

He wanted to say it wasn't a fucking competition. But he knew that hadn't been what she'd meant. She meant, he thought, that they were both burning in the same hell. But at least they were there together. For what that was worth.

'Aye, pet, I know,' he said. 'We struggle on, eh? That's all we can do.'

'That's all we can do.'

He released her hand and, giving her a kiss on the lips that felt more perfunctory than he'd intended, he turned and left her standing in the kitchen. He felt as if he should stay longer, do something for her. Above all, he felt as if there should be more words, but he hadn't a clue what they might be.

CHAPTER TEN

'**P**enny for them,' Horton said. They were driving through town to visit Danny Reynolds, Katy Scott's one-time boyfriend. Horton was at the wheel. They'd hit what passed for rush hour up here, and the traffic was clogged and slow-moving. McKay had never been able to work out how the Highland traffic authorities could contrive so many tail-backs from such a small population.

As it had turned out, it hadn't taken them long to track Reynolds down. He was still on the PNC, with a recorded caution for possession, the best part of ten years before. The address had been out of date, but Horton had identified three Daniel Reynolds on the electoral role. A couple of telephone calls later, and they'd pinned down the correct one.

'They're not even worth a penny.' McKay was conscious he'd been staring blankly out of the passenger window for the last ten minutes or so. He'd been thinking, with no real focus, about Katy Scott, about her father, and then about Chrissie and about his own life. That way, he knew, lay nothing but self-pity or worse.

'This is the place,' Horton said. 'Next left.'

It was a respectable looking new-build. Neat semi-detached houses with tidy, low-maintenance front gardens, most with at least one new car sitting on the drive. The sort of place that would attract young professionals with a half-decent joint salary. Somewhere you could trade up, step by step, from a tiny starter home to a five-bedroom villa without moving off the estate. The Reynolds were on one of the lower rungs of that ladder, but doing all right.

Horton pulled into the curb. 'Number eleven.'

The houses along this stretch were largely identical, differentiated only by the colour of the paintwork and the efforts made to personalise individual properties—window boxes, garden furniture and ornaments, decorative door-knockers. All looked neat and well-maintained.

As they entered the front garden, McKay gestured towards a football lying at the edge of the lawn. 'Patter of tiny feet,' he said.

The front door was opened before he'd pressed the bell. A young woman, slim with pale blonde hair, was standing inside the doorway. 'Can I help you?' she asked, in a tone that suggested it was unlikely.

'Police,' McKay said, holding his warrant card steadily before her face. 'DI McKay and DS Horton. Mrs Reynolds?'

'Yes?'

'We'd like a word with your husband, if he's in.' McKay gave a smile unlikely to provide any reassurance. 'Just a routine enquiry, in connection with an ongoing investigation. Nothing to worry about.'

'You'd better come in.' She ushered them into the house, leading them into a small sitting room. 'I'm sorry everything's a bit of a mess. I'll go and get Danny.'

The room seemed tidy enough to McKay, except for a small pile of children's toys next to the television. Exactly what he would have expected. Neat modern furniture purchased from some chain store. Large screen TV and a stack of DVDs. A handful of paperbacks on a bookshelf largely occupied by random ornaments. Aspirational was probably the word.

After a few minutes, an anxious-looking man appeared. He was probably around thirty, ginger hair already slightly receding, dressed in a tee-shirt and jeans, his watery blue eyes blinking nervously at them. 'Danny Reynolds,' he said. 'Was it you phoned earlier? I don't know why you'd want to speak to me.' He sat himself down in the middle of the sofa. McKay and Horton had occupied the two armchairs.

'As I told your wife, Mr Reynolds, it's just a routine enquiry—'

'Isn't that what you say just before you arrest someone?' Reynolds laughed. It wasn't entirely clear whether he was joking.

'We're enquiring about someone we believe was a past acquaintance of yours. A Katy Scott.'

For a moment, Reynolds looked baffled. 'Jeez. Katy. Haven't seen her for years.'

'But you did know her?'

'Oh, aye. A long time ago. Is she in trouble?'

'In a manner of speaking. I'd appreciate if you'd keep this confidential at present, Mr Reynolds, as we haven't had formal confirmation of identity from the next of kin.'

Reynolds jolted upright. 'Next of kin?'

'You'll have seen the news reports about the discovery of a body in the woods up near Munlochy?'

'Up on the Isle, aye. Christ, you mean that's Katy?'

'We've reason to believe so, yes.'

'My God. You never expect—' He shook his head, as if trying to deny what he'd just heard. 'Not someone you know.'

'Can I ask how you knew Ms Scott?'

'She was—well, just one of the crowd, you know? We're talking ten years ago.'

'You weren't particularly close to her?'

Reynolds looked up in surprise. 'You mean were we an item? Christ, no.' He sounded unexpectedly vehement. 'Is that what you thought?' He looked nervously towards the door, as if concerned his wife might be eavesdropping.

'Her parents seemed to have that impression.'

'Is that why you're here? Because her dad fingered me. It wouldn't surprise me. But, no, we weren't an item. She was just a friend. Hardly even that.'

'Did your wife know her too?' Horton asked.

'Zoe?' For a second, Reynolds looked uneasy. 'Yes, a bit. Like I say, we were all part of one crowd. You know what it's like at that age.'

McKay could barely remember. 'How did you meet her?'

'I've no idea, really. Probably with some others in a pub. She was just *there*, you know? I'm not sure there's much I can tell you. It's been a long time.'

'At this stage, we're just after background. Trying to find out what sort of a woman she was.'

'Well, she was—difficult, let's say. She was always a handful. I mean, sometimes in a good way. She could be fun. But then she'd go too far. She'd go a bit off the rails.'

McKay decided to take a punt. 'You've a police record for possession?'

Reynolds sat back heavily on the sofa. 'Oh, Christ, I suppose it's still on the record, isn't it? It was only a bloody caution. Possession of a bit of grass. But, yes, that was her.'

'In what way?'

'We were coming back from the pub one night. Quite late. All a bit pissed. We got stopped by a couple of your colleagues in the city centre. It should have been nothing. We'd done nothing wrong, except had a few too many drinks. They'd probably just have given us a ticking off for being rowdy. But Katy starts making a big play about what I've got in my pocket, like I'm trying to hide something. I've no idea what she's on about, but eventually the cops start taking it seriously. They ask me to empty my pockets, and when I do there's this little packet I've never seen before. Turns out to be grass.'

'She planted it on you?'

'Her idea of a joke. I think she was a bit pissed off with me for some reason. Something I'd said or done earlier in the evening. Can't remember what. But obviously the cops have to take it seriously then, so they haul me off to the station. And I end up with a caution and a record on your bloody system.' He glanced nervously towards the door. It was evident this was a story he'd never shared with his wife. 'Which, fortunately, hasn't affected my career so far.'

'I don't think you need to worry about that now, Mr Reynolds.'

'You never know. I work for a US company. They're a bit puritanical.'

'That was typical, was it? Of the way she behaved?'

'That was one of the more extreme examples. Let's just say that it didn't pay to get on the wrong side of her. And she was a daredevil. Did things for the hell of it. I remember her sitting on the fencing at Kessock Bridge, drunk as a lord. We thought she was going to topple off. Scared the hell out of us. But she was just laughing.'

'When she moved out of her parents' place in Culbokie, they had the impression she moved in with you. Wasn't that the case?'

'Only in a manner of speaking. I was living in a shared house, a big Edwardian place. The landlord had inherited it and was trying to scrape together the cash to do it up properly. So he let the rooms to pull in some money. There were eight of us living in there. When Katy decided to move out of her parents' place, there was a spare room so she moved in. A couple of us went to help her move. That's probably why her dad got the idea she'd moved in with me. She didn't stay long. Just a few months, then she went off to live with some girlfriend who'd got a spare place in a council flat.'

'I don't suppose you're still in touch with the girlfriend?'

'Not for years. I can't even remember her name off the top of my head. Kirsty something? I've no idea what she's up to now.'

'What about Katy? Did you keep in touch with her?'

'She was still part of the crowd. It was a mixed bunch. We were all local. Most of us had been at school together in Inverness, but there were others—like Katy—who'd got to know people and started tagging along. We were late teens, early twenties. I was doing an apprenticeship. A few of us were students. Some were working. One or two were on the dole.'

'What about Katy?'

'A mix as far as I remember. Did bar-work, waitressing, that kind of stuff. She was on the dole a bit when she could get away with it. Never stuck with anything for long.' He hesitated, as if not quite sure how to articulate what he had to say. 'If you want my real impression of Katy Scott, I'd say she was damaged goods.'

'How do you mean?'

'Ach, it's hard to describe. There was something not quite right, you know what I mean. Not quite balanced. I've told you about the daredevil stuff, the trouble-making. But there was something—I don't know—something *darker* about her.' He stopped, his expression suggesting he'd said too much. 'I don't want to badmouth her. Not after what's happened. But somehow I'm not surprised she's ended up like that. You always felt she was destined for a bad end, somehow.'

'Aye, I know people like that,' McKay said. 'Why do you think she was like that?'

Another hesitation. 'You met her parents?'

'Aye,' McKay said. 'Not my type, if I'm honest.'

'It was her dad,' Reynolds said. 'I mean, he was a right bastard, that goes without saying. He was a bully, a nasty piece of work. But there was something creepy about him as well. Something about the way he treated Katy. Something about the way he behaved to any young woman, from what I saw.'

'You think he abused her?' Horton said.

Reynolds shifted uncomfortably. 'Look, I've no reason to think so. Katy never said anything. Not in so many words, anyway.'

'Not in so many words?'

'She'd talk about—you know, home being hellish. About wanting to get away from her dad. I thought it was just the religious thing, the discipline. But it seemed more than that. Then I thought maybe he hit her. But then, when I met him, when I saw him and Katy together—'

'Aye?'

'I mean he always had—well, like his hands on her somehow. I can't really explain it any other way.'

McKay nodded. 'I get the picture.'

'But even if there is something in that, what would it have to do with her death? You're not suggesting her dad killed her?'

'Jesus, no, son. Get that out your head. All we're trying to do is build a picture of Katy Scott. Her life. Who she was. Where she went. Who she knew.'

'The thing is,' Horton added, 'abusers tend to be very manipulative. They're very skilled at shifting the responsibility on to their victims. They condition the victim to think it's their fault they're being abused. That they deserve it. The victim comes to believe it, and they can end up drifting from one abusive relationship to another.'

Reynolds nodded. 'I can see that with Katy. She was always attracted to the wrong blokes, the ones who treated her badly. I thought it was the danger she was after. But she was always self-destructive.'

'So if she was abused by her father,' Horton went on, 'apart from the fact that we'd want to bring any abuser to justice, it might help give us a lead on Katy's death.'

'When you last saw Katy, was she still living in Inverness?' McKay asked.

'Yes, I think so.' Reynolds stopped and frowned. 'Actually, that's not quite right. I ran into her again, a couple of years later. I'd forgotten.'

'In Inverness?'

'Yes, but she'd moved on by then. It was just before Christmas—two, maybe even three years since I'd last seen her. Maybe six or seven years ago.'

'Where was this?'

'A pub in the city centre. The old crowd had pretty much broken up by this point. I was going out with Zoe. A couple of others had got married. One or two had moved away. Anyway, it was a Friday night. Zoe and I had arranged to meet some friends for a couple of drinks after work.' He gestured towards the pile of toys. 'We used to do that sort of stuff before the young ball and chain turned up. We were in the pub and Katy came in with a bunch of other women. She spotted me and made a bee-line over. She didn't look great. She was looking worn, you know? Skinny, cheap clothes, looking a bit older than she really was. I thought it was probably just because the rest of us had moved on. We'd got ourselves decent jobs, reasonable places to live. We'd put the teenage stuff behind us, but she was still in the same place.'

'You think it might have been more than that?'

'She just struck me as being in a bad way. We chatted for a bit. She reckoned things had been going pretty well for her. She'd found some counsellor who'd been helpful, had begun to help her deal with things. But of course being Katy she couldn't be content with that. She'd taken up with some new bloke and they'd moved down south, and it wasn't really working out.' He paused. 'I'm trying to remember what she said. I didn't really take it in at the time. It was just Katy, blethering on about her troubles. Manchester, I think. She was living in Manchester. Can't remember any more than that. It didn't mean much to me.'

'She didn't tell you the name of the guy she was with?'

'If she did I've forgotten. It was no-one I knew.'

McKay sat back on the sofa. 'Well, many thanks, Mr Reynolds. That's been very useful.'

'I don't feel I've been able to tell you anything.'

'You've given us plenty to chew on. As I say, we'd appreciate if you could keep all this confidential until we've confirmed Katy Scott's identity. We expect to do that tomorrow.'

'Can I tell Zoe what this was about? She'll be worried about why you were here.'

'Yes, of course. Just don't go thinking you can earn yourself a few quid by leaking this to the local press. If it gets out, I'll know where it's come from and I might have to start telling your puritanical US employer about your unfortunate police record. You get my drift, son?'

'I get it.'

'Good lad. There's one more thing you could do for us, and then we shouldn't need to trouble you again. Have a think about the people who would have known Katy when you were hanging around together. Anyone you can remember with whatever information you might have about them. Addresses, phone numbers, whatever. Doesn't matter if they're well out of date. They might give us a start.'

'I've lost touch with most of them, but I can remember some names. I might have some old contact details. I'll see what I can dig out.'

McKay slid a business card across the coffee table between them. 'Whatever you've got, call me or e-mail. Like I say, with this one, we need all the help we can get.'

CHAPTER ELEVEN

'**H**_ow_ old?' Denny Gorman asked again, his voice still sceptical.

'Eighteen,' Kelly repeated. 'Only just, but definitely eighteen. I wouldn't forget my own birthday. Even if everyone else does.' She knew she was talking too much, but she couldn't do much about that.

'Aye.' He ran his eyes appraisingly from her face down the length of her body. She knew she wasn't unattractive, but she'd never thought of her looks as anything special. She was just your typical Scottish girl, she thought—short dark hair, green eyes, Celtic features, a slim build. Today she'd made a point of dressing in a neat white blouse and a mid-length black skirt. Not exactly provocative to the majority of the male sex. Even so, she was beginning to wish she'd picked a boiler-suit instead.

'You don't look eighteen,' he said, finally. 'Got ID?'

She fumbled in her handbag, conscious that Gorman would be taking the opportunity to give her body another perusal, then slid her passport across the sticky top of the table. 'There you go.'

After a few moments, he looked up at her, apparently satisfied. 'OK,' he said. 'You're eighteen. That's a good start.' He smiled, giving her the full benefit of his yellowing, tobacco-stained teeth. 'So what are you looking for?' He paused, his expression suggesting he might have intended some double entendre in his question. 'Hours, I mean.'

'Your ad in the window said you were looking for someone to do lunchtimes. I'm available to do that for the next couple of months. As much as you like.'

'Student, are you?'

'Finished at the Academy. Going to uni in the autumn, so I'm free over the rest of the summer.'

He nodded, slowly, still watching her intently with his bloodshot eyes. He really was an unprepossessing creature, she thought, with his thinning comb-over and unkempt stubble. He was wearing a stained black tee-shirt with the logo of a heavy metal band, which struggled to contain his sagging beer-belly. His faded jeans looked like he might have been wearing them for a couple of weeks. Why the hell had she come in here?

She knew fine well why, of course. Curiosity. The previous day, she'd stopped off in Fortrose to pick up some meat for her mother from Munro's. Walking past the Caley Bar, she'd noticed a hand-scrawled note in the window advertising for lunchtime bar-staff. On a whim, she'd called the number given and spoken to Denny Gorman. He'd asked her to pop in after the lunchtime session the next day.

It was mid-afternoon and the place was deserted, except for Gorman himself. Even the hardened drinkers who prop up the bar for most of the day had temporarily absented themselves, maybe to catch a few rays of the unaccustomed sunshine or an afternoon nap before resuming their dogged glass-emptying. Gorman had been behind the bar, totting up the lunchtime takings.

The bar wasn't much more attractive than Gorman himself. The two other pubs in town, the Union and the Anderson, had character in their different ways. The Caley just had gloom and a pervading smell of damp. It attracted a particular type of clientele, mainly barely-functioning alcoholics. Or so Greg had told her. Not that he had ever frequented the place.

'References?' Gorman asked.

'I've been working in the stores in Cromarty. They'll give me a reference if I ask.'

'Ever worked in a bar before?'

She shook her head. 'I've done shop work. And some waitressing last summer holidays.'

'You'll soon pick it up. Know how to pull a pint?'

'I'm not sure.'

He pushed himself up from the table. 'I'll show you. We've only got one beer on cask. The rest are all keg, so it's straightforward enough.'

She hadn't a clue what he was talking about but followed him through the narrow opening behind the bar. Gorman picked up a pint glass and held it out to her, gesturing towards the hand-pump. 'Have a go.'

Greg had told her how to pour beer. Tilt the glass, he'd said, and pour down the side so that you don't end up with too much of a head. She held the glass carefully and began to pull down on the hand-pump. It was harder than she expected and she had to step back slightly to gain more leverage. As she did so, she realised how close Gorman was standing.

'That's it,' he said. 'A nice long slow steady movement. Keep pulling.' She continued filling the glass and finally placed the pint on the bar, conscious all the time of Gorman's proximity. She could almost feel his breath on her neck and was sure that, at any moment, he would reach round her to demonstrate how the task should be carried out. 'Not bad for a first effort,' he said. 'You've definitely got the knack, lass.' Without hesitation, he picked up the glass and swallowed a good third of the beer. 'Aye. Decent pint, that.' He'd moved away and took the opportunity to peruse her body again. 'I think you'll do, if you want the job.'

Her good sense was telling her to get out and never come back. But her curiosity was more piqued than ever. Gorman was every bit the creep and lech she'd expected. She could easily imagine him trying it on with Lizzie Hamilton. And she could imagine how, a few pints to the worse, he might have behaved if Hamilton had rebuffed him.

She'd said nothing more to Greg because she'd seen how their conversation had disturbed him. But she'd searched for Hamilton's name on the internet and dug out various local news stories from the time of her disappearance. There'd been a small flurry of reports before the media had lost interest. Kelly didn't really even know why she was interested. She'd met Hamilton briefly just a few times up at Greg's dad's place and had found her pleasant and lively. After what they'd found in the woods, she felt disturbed that someone like that could simply disappear.

'Well?' Gorman said.

'I think so,' she said, finally. 'What would you be paying?'

He quoted a rate slightly lower than she was earning in the shop, saying he could probably do with a couple of hours each weekday lunchtime.

'OK,' she said, finally. 'I can fit that round the shop work. When do you want me to start?'

'Tomorrow, if you can,' he said.

'Why not? Twelve?'

'Aye. That'll be grand.' He gave her one final examination, his eyes moving slowly downwards from her face. 'I'll look forward to working with you, lass. We're not a bad crowd in here.'

It was only when she emerged into the bright sunlight of the High Street that she realised how claustrophobic she'd been feeling. What the hell had she just done? Christ knew what Greg would say when she broke the news.

She was on the bus, heading back along the coast to Cromarty, before she had chance to check her texts. There were a couple from Greg, inevitably. The first was just confirming the time for them to meet that evening. They were going to see some film Greg was keen on at Eden Court in Inverness.

The second text was longer. It said: 'Have u heard the news? Another body. Caird's Cave in Rosemarkie.'

She sat staring at the text, as the bus trundled through Rosemarkie, turning the corner past The Plough Inn, up past the woodland entrance to Fairy Glen, then over the bridge towards Cromarty. Caird's Cave was just a short distance away, further up the coast.

Jesus, Kelly thought, what the hell is this?

She thought of Denny Gorman standing centimetres behind her, his breath almost on the back of her neck, his eyes no doubt still mentally undressing her.

What was she letting herself in for?

CHAPTER TWELVE

D C Josh Carlisle was hovering by the door, hopping gently from foot to foot. He looked, even more than usual, liked a nervous schoolboy who'd been summoned to see the head.

'Got something to tell us, Josh?' McKay asked. 'Or just desperate for a piss?'

Carlisle took cautious step into the room. 'I just thought better let you know. We've been checking on Katy Scott as a potential misper and we've hit the jackpot. Greater Manchester. Looks like she's only been reported formally in the last couple of days.'

'Have we got details?'

'We've got an address.' Carlisle glanced at the print-out in his hand. 'Chorlton, apparently. Unmarried. Seems to have been living alone. Reported missing by a neighbour—looks like she lives in a flat—and then by the landlord.'

'No relatives?'

'None mentioned. Imagine that's why it took so long to be reported.'

'What about work? Anything on what she did for a living?'

'Nothing on the file.'

'Have we got a contact in GMP?'

'Couple of names given. A DS Mortimer and a DI Warren.' Carlisle looked pleased with himself.

'OK. Leave me the details and I'll give Warren a call. It might perk him up a bit to find it's a murder enquiry.'

'They might want to take it over if she was killed on their patch,' Horton pointed out.

'Not a million years. Buggers down there are even more stretched than we are. Last thing they'll want is a high profile murder enquiry on their hands. Anyway, I'll have him wrapped round my little finger. You know what I'm like when I turn on the charm.'

'I've read historical accounts of the phenomenon,' she said. 'Well done, though, Josh. That's a real breakthrough.'

Carlisle looked, as he generally did in McKay's company, as if all he wanted was to be somewhere else as quickly as decency might allow. 'I just did what you asked,' he said.

'Well done, lad,' McKay said. 'You have my permission to have a celebratory cigarette in the outside lavvy.' This was McKay's term for the smoking shelter at the rear of the building. Since he'd given up himself, McKay made a point of highlighting those of his colleagues who were, in his words, 'still unfortunate slaves to the demon weed.'

Josh gratefully made his escape, no doubt to do just as McKay had enjoined. McKay turned to Horton, rubbing his hands. 'Now we're getting somewhere. Easier than we'd feared.'

Horton looked up at the clock. 'Speaking of Katy Scott, we're due to meet the parents in half an hour.'

'What are the arrangements?'

'I've sent Mary Graham to collect them. Thought it was only right if they're coming to do the ID. Arranged to meet them at the Raigmore, so we can get that out of the way. Then we'll bring them here to get statements.'

'You reckon they'll both want to be involved in the ID?'

'Who knows? The father will want to show he's boss, and the mother will want to see her daughter for the last time, I'm guessing.'

'Then we interview them separately.'

'You think they'll agree?'

'I'm not planning on giving them a choice. I don't want to make this any harder for the mother than we have to.' He paused. 'But if he doesn't agree, I'll rip his fucking balls off.'

***

The Scotts were already waiting inside the main entrance of the Raigmore Hospital, Mary Graham valiantly trying to make small talk. They were blank-faced and pale. Mrs Scott looked as if she might not have slept. Her husband was dressed more smartly than he had been the previous day. McKay guessed that he'd dug out an old work suit for the occasion.

'I'm sorry to put you through this,' McKay said. 'But better to get a personal identification if we can. Then everything is put beyond any doubt.'

Scott nodded sceptically. 'Let's just get it over with.'

McKay looked at Mrs Scott. 'We only need one of you for identification purposes. If you'd prefer to wait here, my colleagues can take you for a coffee.' He gestured towards the cafe area.

'If it is Katy,' Mrs Scott said firmly, 'I want to see her.'

Leaving Horton and Graham in the cafe, he led the way to the mortuary at the rear of the hospital. They were greeted at the entrance by a taciturn young man in a white coat who led them silently into the bleak, chilly room. He produced a bunch of keys and, carefully checking the reference, took them to one end of the row of cabinets.

'You're sure you both want to go through with this?'

'I'm sure,' Mrs Scott said. Her husband grunted his assent. The assistant swung open the drawer in a practised movement. McKay gestured for the Scotts to take a look.

Scott nodded. 'That's her. She'd lost weight.' He sounded as if she'd returned from a long holiday or university.

Mrs Scott leaned forward to gain a closer look. 'Katy,' she said, softly. 'Katy.' After a moment she turned away, her shoulders hunched, sobbing. Her husband made no move to comfort her.

McKay gestured to the assistant to close the drawer. 'Thank you,' he said. 'I'm assuming you'll want to make arrangements for the funeral. If you let us know what would suit you, we can organise the release. We've completed all the examinations we need.'

Scott nodded, though McKay suspected that he was thinking about nothing beyond the unexpected expense. Well, tough luck, buddy, McKay thought.

'Are you ready to go back out now?' he asked Mrs Scott.

She raised her face to his, her eyes red-stained. 'Thank you, yes. I'll be all right in a moment.'

'We'll get you a cup of tea,' he said. 'I'm sure it's been an ordeal.'

'I wanted to see her,' she said. 'I needed to be sure.'

'I understand,' McKay said.

Perhaps more than anyone, he added to himself.

***

McKay had offered the Scotts the opportunity to delay giving their statements, recognising the vulnerability of Mrs Scott's condition. Scott had responded, very firmly, that they just wanted to get it over with. And be back in time for *Countdown*, McKay glossed to himself.

'If you're sure,' McKay said. 'If you come with me, Mr Scott, and your wife goes with DS Horton, we'll get it sorted as quickly as we can.'

Mr Scott eyed him suspiciously. 'I'd assumed we'd do this together.'

'We need a statement from each of you,' McKay said, blandly. 'That's how it has to be done. It won't take long.'

Horton was already beginning to usher Mrs Scott out of the room. 'I'll take good care of your wife, Mr Scott,' she said. Before either of the Scotts could respond, she had swept Mrs Scott out of the room, taking her down the corridor to another of the small interview rooms.

Horton completed the formal interview with Mrs Scott quickly enough, tapping the details into her laptop so she could print off a copy for Mrs Scott. Mrs Scott's responses confirmed only what she'd said the previous day. Horton could sense, though, that Mrs Scott was growing more anxious with each question. She was sitting with her handbag clutched on her lap, her fingers toying anxiously with the handles.

Horton finished typing and closed the lid of the laptop. She sat back and smiled at the older woman. 'I'm sorry we've had to put you through all this. I realise it must be a strain.'

'You've got to do your job.' Mrs Scott's words sounded stilted, as if she'd been coached by her husband. 'We want to give you every help we can to catch whoever was responsible.'

'May I ask you one further question, Mrs Scott?'

She could almost see Mrs Scott stiffen. 'Of course.'

'When we were talking yesterday, I had the sense that you might have kept in touch with your daughter after she left home. Is that right?'

Mrs Scott hesitated a moment too long. 'I don't know what made you think that.'

'There are two things I should remind you of, Mrs Scott. First, we're trying to identify the person who killed your daughter. Anything you can tell us might help us in that task.' She stopped. 'The second, and I'm sorry to have to put it in these terms, is that we're conducting a murder enquiry. If you obstruct us in that, whatever your reasons, then potentially you're committing a serious criminal offence. We've found a second body. Another young woman. It's possible we're dealing with a multiple killer. This isn't just about your daughter, Mrs Scott.'

There was a long silence. Finally, Mrs Scott said: 'I'm scared.'

'What are you scared of? Your husband?'

Mrs Scott nodded, the merest tremor of her head.

'Is he a violent man?'

'He's— He has been, at times, yes. Not for a while. He used to get—so angry.'

'With you or with your daughter?'

'Both. But after she went—'

'We can take action about that. If you want us to.'

Mrs Scott held up her hands. 'No, I don't want that. Not now. It's been a long while since—well, since the last time. I need him. We need each other.'

'But you're still afraid of what he might do? If you tell me about your contact with Katy.'

'Yesterday, after you'd gone, he was angry in a way that he hasn't been for years. He had a minor heart attack a couple of years ago. I thought he wasn't like that anymore. It was almost as if Katy had come back into the house. Behaving like she used to. Winding him up.'

'All I can do, Mrs Scott, is stress that anything you say to me will be treated as confidential. You husband need never know what we've discussed.'

'Honestly, there's not a lot I can really tell you. You're right. I kept in touch with Katy after she left home. Not frequently. She wasn't the kind of girl for that, even with me.'

'But she kept in contact?'

'Every month or so. She'd send me a text, asking me to call her when I could so that Ronnie wouldn't know. The mobile's one of the few things I keep to myself. I pray he never finds it. She had pay as you go phones, so the numbers were always changing.'

'She was living in Manchester at the time of her death. Did you know that?'

'Yes. It's probably only five or six weeks since I last spoke to her. She'd just moved flats—'

'We understand she was living in the Chorlton area of Manchester. Is that what she told you?'

'It didn't mean much to me. She said she'd text me the new address but she never got round to it.'

'You had her previous addresses?'

'Some. She was always on the move. She gave me the address if she wanted me to send her something.'

'Money?'

Mrs Scott blushed. 'Usually. A few pounds to dig her out of a hole. I couldn't send her a lot without Ronnie finding out.' She looked up at Horton and, for the first time, gave a thin smile. 'When Ronnie said Katy stole my housekeeping money, he was wrong. I gave it to her, as much as I could. I thought Ronnie wouldn't realise but he noticed it had gone. So—' She shrugged. 'You know how it is.'

'If you've got the previous addresses, and any details of friends or acquaintances she might have mentioned, even if it's just first names, it would be useful to have that information.'

Mrs Scott picked up her handbag. It took Horton a moment to realise that the older woman had re-stitched the lining of the handbag to create a concealed pocket. Jesus, how scared must this woman be?

Looking nervously towards the door, Mrs Scott produced a mobile phone. 'This is the one Katy used to text me on. I've kept all the texts for the last couple of years. You can pick out anything you think is likely to be useful. There aren't a huge number.' She switched on the phone and thumbed through to the text menu. 'There.'

Horton flicked carefully through the texts. They made poignant reading, a distillation of two wasted lives. It was clear to Horton that Katy had contacted her mother only when she wanted something. Mostly, it was a request for money—a few quid to tide her over till next payday or her next benefit payment or the next job. Horton noted down any substantive information—addresses, names of friends she'd mentioned in passing. There was little likely to be of use to them.

Horton held out the phone. 'Many thanks for letting me look at this.'

Mrs Scott took the phone and then, hesitating for a moment, pushed it back across the table. 'You might as well hold on to it. The information might be useful to you.'

'But—'

'I don't need it anymore.' Her eyes were darting towards the door, as if she expected her husband to burst in at any moment.

'If you're sure. I can hold on to it as potential evidence.'

'I won't want it back.'

Horton took the phone from the table and slipped it into her pocket. 'I'm very grateful for what you've told me, Mrs Scott.'

'And you won't—?'

'Not in a million years, Mrs Scott. Trust me, not in a million years.'

CHAPTER THIRTEEN

McKay's interview with Scott was less productive. Scott had made it clear that he had no interest in being there. The fact that his contribution might assist in the identification of his daughter's killer seemed of little interest for him. He'd seemed more concerned about the fact that he and his wife were being interviewed separately.

'What was Katy like as a child?' McKay had asked early on.

'Is that relevant?'

'We're trying to gain an understanding of what your daughter was like, Mr Scott. It all helps.'

'Well, she was—' Scott stopped, as if trying to find the right words. His eyes blinked behind his thick spectacles. 'She was the apple of my eye,' he said, finally.

McKay hadn't been sure what he'd been expecting, but not that. Whatever the real nature of Scott's relationship with his daughter, McKay had been expecting nothing more than the same contempt and dismissal they'd heard the previous day.

'You were close, then?' McKay said. 'When she was smaller?'

Scott looked up at him, his eyes clear and unblinking. 'Aye, we were close,' he said. 'Two of a kind. You know what it's like between fathers and daughters.'

McKay gazed back at him, trying to fathom this man. *I know what it was like between me and my daughter,* he thought. *But I can't begin to imagine what it might have been like between you and yours.*

'She was different then,' Scott went on. For the first time, there was a note of genuine loss in his voice. It was as if his real daughter, the daughter he'd really wanted, had died a long time ago. 'She'd do anything for me. She'd do whatever I said. She was—well, she was mine.'

'How do you mean?'

'She was an obedient child, that's all I mean. She did her schoolwork, dressed smartly. Went to church with us. Went to bed when we told her to. She was the kind of daughter any man would want.' The smile grew wider, though with no evident warmth. 'Her sister Emma was the difficult one.' He leaned forward and stared at McKay. 'It was God's will she was taken, just as it's God's will that Katy's been taken now.'

The words were unexpectedly chilling. It was then that McKay recognised the emotion he'd read in the man's face when they'd broken the news of Katy's death. Not surprise or shock. Not despair or anguish.

Relief.

That was what it had been. Relief that, finally, his daughter would not be there to expose him. That now there was no danger that, one day, two police officers might turn up on his doorstep for a very different reason. He recalled Scott's apparent shock when he'd first introduced himself, and how, if anything, the man had seemed calmer once they'd broken the news. Scott had his wife firmly under his thumb. His only potential vulnerability had been his daughter, out there in the wide world. And now she was gone.

If McKay's speculations were correct—and, increasingly, despite the absence of anything approaching substantive evidence, he was beginning to believe they were— Scott had a motive for his daughter's killing. It was possible, McKay supposed. Perhaps he'd invited her up here on the basis of—what? A reconciliation? A confession? It was difficult to imagine Katy would have willingly agreed to a meeting. But abusers were always expert manipulators. Scott might have told her anything.

Would Scott have had the strength and stamina to have killed her and dispose of the body? It seemed unlikely, looking at the frail elderly man in front of him, and it would surely have been impossible for Scott to have involved any accomplice. But a desperate man might be capable of more than you could imagine. If Scott were responsible, it would perhaps explain the candles and roses. A final tribute to the young daughter who had been lost to him many years before her death.

All of this might be conceivable if it weren't for the second body. Scott might have had reason to kill his daughter. It was harder to imagine why he might have killed again. A second victim? Someone his daughter had told? Looking at the man before him, any scenario stretched increasingly into the realms of fantasy.

'You say you were close to your daughter when she was younger,' McKay said. 'When did that change?'

Scott shrugged. 'Emma's death made a difference. Katy changed after that. But mainly it was just growing older. Becoming a teenager. She became more rebellious, disobedient. Began to hang out with the wrong crowd. We tried everything but it just made her worse. Emma had been just the same.'

'What age are we talking?'

'Thirteen, fourteen. After she went to the Academy. It was a gradual thing. We didn't notice at first. She began bunking off school. Getting into trouble.'

'With the police? There's nothing on the record.'

'It never went that far. It was petty shoplifting. Stupid vandalism. That sort of stuff. And she started dressing up like—well, I don't know what. Punk, that sort of thing.'

And so it went on. McKay sat through the recital of Scott's grievances against his daughter for as long as his patience would allow. He elicited little in the way of substantive information—Scott claimed, unsurprisingly, to have no knowledge of his daughter's friends or associates during that period—but he felt an increasing certainty that Danny Reynolds's suspicions had been correct.

'What prompted your daughter to leave home, Mr Scott? In the end, I mean. Was there some specific incident?'

'Not that I'm aware. She'd threatened to before. But she'd had no money, nowhere to go.'

'But this time she did?'

'Someone was stupid enough to take her in.'

'She took some money from you?'

'From Megs. Not a fortune. But not pennies either.'

'You didn't know where she'd gone?'

'She left a note saying she was going to stay in Inverness. She didn't say who with.'

'Your wife mentioned this Daniel Reynolds?'

'There was a boy. Probably more than one. I don't recollect their names.'

McKay sat back. 'OK, Mr Scott, that's all from me. Is there anything else you can tell us you think might be useful? Anything that might give us an insight into Katy's life or character?'

'I've told you everything I can. I can't imagine any of it being particularly useful to you, but that's your business.'

'As you say, Mr Scott. I'm sorry we've had to put you through this. But it is necessary, I'm afraid.'

'If you say so. I'm assuming we won't need to be involved any further?'

'I hope not, but it's really too early to say.'

'I hope so too, then. I've better things to do.'

'We appreciate that, Mr Scott,' McKay said, his voice emollient. 'We'll trouble you only if we have real cause.' He waited for Scott to look him in the eye before adding: 'Whatever that might be.'

***

Leaving Horton to take the Scotts down to rendezvous with Mary Graham, who'd been detailed to drive them back to Culbokie, McKay returned to his desk and dug out the details Carlisle had given him on DI Warren of Greater Manchester Police. It took a few minutes chasing round the switchboard to track Warren down.

'Jesus,' Warren said, when McKay had explained the reason for his call. 'I saw that on the news. She's our misper?'

'Looks like it,' McKay said. 'We've got her last address in Chorlton and we know she moved to Manchester when she first moved down from Inverness. We've tracked down a couple of addresses for the period in between so it looks as if she's been living in and around Manchester since she moved south.'

'I'll see what else we can dig out,' Warren said, in a tone that suggested it wouldn't be top of his priority list. 'Where do you reckon she was killed?'

'We don't know for sure. But we've now got a second body up here. Similar circumstances and MO.'

'Suggests that the link's at your end, then?' McKay could almost hear the relief in Warren's voice. No doubt he was as hard pressed as all coppers these days. 'Look, I'll send you whatever we've got. I know we took statements from the neighbour who reported her missing and from her landlord. We had difficulties tracking down anyone else who knew her, other than a couple of work colleagues who couldn't shed much light.'

'Where did she work?'

'Mishmash of waitressing and bar-work. You know Chorlton at all?'

'Probably as well as you know Culbokie.'

'It's what you might call up and coming. Or up and come, really, these days. Full of bijou delis and cafes and bars. So there's lots of that kind of work going.' He paused. 'We wondered whether she might be on the game, but there was no evidence for that. I think she was just what she seemed to be. A bit of a drifter. Lost soul.'

'That would fit with what we know of her background.'

'I'll send you all the info we've got. Give us a shout if there's anything else you need.' Warren wasn't exactly being obstructive, but McKay had the impression he wouldn't be contorting himself backwards to help either.

'And if we wanted to talk to anyone in your neck of the woods?' McKay asked. 'The neighbour or the landlord, for example?'

'Just let us know. We're not precious.'

'Just one more thing—'

'Go on.'

'It's a long shot. But if there is a consistent MO here, it might be worth double-checking whether our second victim could also be one of your mispers. We've not identified her yet—DNA and fingerprints have produced nothing—so we're working in the dark.'

'You've no reason to think she might be from Manchester, though?'

'Just thought it might be worth trying. We've looked on the national list, but can't find anyone that looks a match. You might have more recent cases worth looking at.'

'Happy to check,' Warren said. 'You never know.'

'Thanks,' McKay said, making a mental note to chase Warren in a few days if they'd heard nothing. 'Been good to talk to you.'

When Horton reappeared a few minutes later, McKay filled her in on the conversation with Warren. 'How were Darby and Joan?'

'Usual bundle of laughs. He grumbled all the way downstairs about the inconvenience. Being dragged all this way just to identify his daughter's remains.'

'He didn't say that?'

'It's what he meant.'

'And how was she?'

'Quiet,' Horton said. 'Nervous-looking. What you'd expect.'

'We need to keep an eye on them,' McKay said. 'He'll try to find out what she said to you.'

'My instinct is that she's learned to be a very good liar.'

'Jesus, the lives people lead.'

'Well,' Horton responded sagely, 'in my experience, there'll always be enough utter bastards out there to make life miserable for the rest of us.'

'You know what, Ginny,' McKay said, expertly flicking out another strip of gum, 'you may never have spoken a truer word.'

CHAPTER FOURTEEN

Greg reacted exactly as Kelly had predicted he would. He'd borrowed his mum's car to drive them into Inverness to see the film, and they were heading along the coastal stretch between Rosemarkie and Fortrose when she broke the news.

'You've done what?'

She was looking out across the fields towards the blue waters of the Firth. It was another glorious evening and the early evening sun was stretching shadows across the pastureland. 'Just a couple of hours a day. At lunchtime.'

'Yeah, but the Caley. That dive.'

'You've never been in there. How do you know it's so bad?'

'I don't need to catch Ebola to know I wouldn't like it. Couldn't you find something at the Anderson or the Union?'

'They weren't advertising. And where's the harm? It'll help me get a few more quid together before uni.'

They drove into Fortrose, passing the Anderson Hotel on the left and the Union Tavern on the right, before they reached the unprepossessing frontage of the Caledonian Bar. An elderly man was standing outside the door, enthusiastically sucking on a cigarette. 'There's your clientele. They won't be able to keep their hands off you.'

'You're just jealous.'

'You said yourself the landlord's a creep.' Once they were through Fortrose, the road ran close to the sea. Outside the harbour, small boats bobbed on the sunlit water. 'That's what this is all about, isn't it? Lizzie whatsherface.'

'Hamilton,' she said. 'I liked her. I'm just curious to know what happened to her.'

'Nothing happened to her,' Greg said. 'She did a runner.'

She didn't want to get into that argument again. 'I'm sure you're right.'

'But that's why you've taken this job at the Caley, isn't it?'

'No. It's just a job. And how hard can it be at lunchtime?'

'Not very, I suppose,' Greg conceded. 'Three old blokes smoking Woodbines and knocking back the Mackeson would be my guess.'

'There you are, then,' she said. 'Money for old rope.'

He laughed. 'Money for old grope, more like. Fending off their wandering hands. Bet you won't last a day.'

She'd been determined to prove him wrong, and the following lunchtime she walked into the Caledonian Bar at eleven-fifty. She'd selected clothes which, while smart, were as unprovocative as she could make them—a dark blouse and a skirt that was longer than anything she usually wore. There'd be plenty of time for feminist principles later, she'd reasoned. For the moment, her primary concern was self-preservation.

The bar was almost as quiet as the previous day. Two elderly looking men whom she vaguely recognised were sitting in the corner, blethering over a couple of pints. Gorman was sitting at the customer side of the bar flicking through a copy of *The Scottish Sun*. As she entered, he nodded and smiled, gesturing her to take her place behind the bar. 'You didn't chicken out, then?' he said. 'Bit quiet so far. Will give you chance to get settled in.' He pushed himself to his feet and followed her behind the bar. 'I'll show you the ropes and then off you go.'

It soon became evident why Gorman wanted assistance even though the bar was largely deserted. As far as Kelly could judge, he had little inclination to do anything himself. After spending a desultory few minutes explaining how the cash register worked and showing her where various items were stored, he poured himself a pint and returned to his perch at the bar. 'If you need any help, just shout,' he said. 'If a barrel needs changing, I'll show you how to do it.' He allowed his gaze to progress the length of her body. 'Word of advice. Maybe don't dress quite so smart tomorrow. It gets dusty down in that cellar.'

The bar became slightly more lively over the next hour. Most of the customers were, as Greg had predicted, elderly men in search of company. Most drank pints of lager, with the odd pint of heavy interspersed here and there. A couple asked for whisky chasers. They greeted her cheerfully, saying it was nice to see a pretty young face in the place. 'Makes a change from Denny's miserable mug,' one said, chortling away at his own joke. Just after one, there was a noisy influx of half a dozen young men from a building site nearby. There was more banter from them as they crowded round the bar, but it was amiable enough. So far, the work had been straightforward and none of her worst fears had been realised. Gorman sat on his bar-stool working his way steadily through his third or fourth pint, watching her approvingly.

By one forty-five the bar had quietened again. The young men had finished their pints of lager and returned to work. Four or five of the older blokes were still chuntering away over a card game in the corner. Gorman pushed his pint glass back across the bar and gestured for her to refill it. 'You've done well, lass,' he said. 'Reckon them builder lads will be back in, now they've seen your pretty face.' He grinned, in a way that was only just the right side of a leer. 'Word'll get around.'

She began to refill his glass, but the stream of lager spluttered and died. 'Looks like the barrel needs changing,' she said.

Gorman sighed wearily. 'Aye, it does that. Right, lassie, come with me and I'll give you a wee lesson.' He made his way back behind the bar, leading her through the doorway into the rear of the pub. There was a further door which presumably led into Gorman's own living accommodation, and a passage to the right which led down a flight of stone steps into the cellar. He clicked on a light-switch, and took her down into the gloomy space beneath the bar.

He'd been right about the dust. Kelly made a mental note that, if she was expected to come down here frequently, jeans and a sweat-shirt would be more appropriate. The place looked as if it had never been cleaned. Piles of unidentifiable junk were scattered in the dark corners, and there were thick cobwebs across the couple of skylights intended to allow some natural light into the place. Barrels and kegs were distributed randomly around the room.

Gorman walked her across to the row of pumps, and demonstrated how to identify the empty barrel and how to detach and reattach the piping. 'Not difficult,' he said. 'But the kegs are under pressure so take a wee bit of care.' He gestured for her to have a go.

She managed the task without difficulty, conscious again of Gorman standing only centimetres behind her. At one point, he leaned around her to guide her hand, and her body tensed at his proximity. She could smell the acrid scent of beer on his breath.

'Well done.' He took a step back. 'So now you know.'

He retreated a few metres and stood smiling, his arms folded. As before, his gaze swept the length of her body. She felt like a piece of livestock being assessed by a butcher. 'Aye, you'll do nicely, lass.'

'Thank you,' she said. 'It's been fine so far.'

'You know what you're about. And you'll go down well with the lads upstairs. They've missed a pretty face about the place.'

'Do you usually have barmaids working here?'

'When I can find someone. Brings in the customers. No-one comes to see my face.' He laughed. 'Difficult to hang on to good people, though.'

'Where do they go?' More than anything, she wanted to get past him and out of this dank place. But Gorman was showing no sign of moving out of her way.

'No-one stays in this kind of work for very long,' Gorman said. 'Either they're temps, like you, doing it to raise a bit of cash before they go off to do something else. Or they get a better offer.' He shrugged. 'Some of them just bugger off.'

It was as good an opportunity as she was likely to get. 'Lizzie Hamilton,' she said. 'She worked here for a bit, didn't she?'

He was partly silhouetted against one of the two bulbs that illuminated the cellar, and she couldn't read his expression or body-language. 'You knew Lizzie?'

'Sort of,' she lied. 'I met her a few times.'

'She didn't have many friends,' Gorman said.

'She did some work for my boyfriend's dad. She seemed nice enough.'

She could see he'd registered her reference to a boyfriend. 'Aye, well. She was one who buggered off, all right.'

'You don't know what happened to her?'

'No-one knows. Probably did a runner.' He began to turn, as if now keen to bring the conversation to an end.

'You don't think something might have happened to her?'

'What could have happened to her? She just left. Simple as that. Just left.'

'But—'

'She just left.' The voice was harder this time. He was already making his way back towards the stairs.

She hurried after him, suddenly struck by an irrational fear that, when he reached the top, he would shut the door and lock her in. But of course he didn't. By the time she reached the bar, he was already striding back towards his customary seat.

She finished pouring him the pint and slid the glass across the bar. He took it with a nod of thanks. She thought there might be a new wariness in his bloodshot eyes, but it was impossible to be sure. Behind him, the elderly blokes were still engrossed in their card game, apparently oblivious to anything else.

Just after two, Gorman glanced at his watch. 'Aye, that's you then, right enough.' He jerked his thumb over his shoulder. 'If that lot want more, I'll deal with them. But they'll be packing up soon.'

'Thanks,' she said. 'Same time tomorrow?'

'Long as you're up for it.'

The brief exchange in the cellar had left her uneasy, but had also aroused her curiosity. She couldn't seriously see Gorman as a threat. But there'd definitely been something odd about his response. 'Yeah, I'm up for it.'

'Don't suppose you fancy a few evenings as well. Got a young bloke who comes in, but—well, he doesn't have your assets, shall we say?'

She ignored that. 'I'll give it some thought. I've got some other commitments so it may not be possible.' Even if she could manage the transport, the prospect of being here with Gorman after last orders was hardly enticing.

'Well, the offer's there.'

She grabbed her coat and handbag and made for the door. She could almost feel Gorman staring after her, but she resisted the urge to look back.

She just left, Kelly thought as she pushed open the door, blinking at the unexpectedly bright sunshine. She just left.

But where did she go?

CHAPTER FIFTEEN

It was starting to rain again as she scurried from the bus stop on Princess Road through the backstreets of Hulme. It was warmer down here, but it seemed always to be raining. The Mancs reckoned that was all a myth, and they'd quote you chapter and verse about the average rainfall levels of the city compared with Barcelona or some such. But it was all bollocks. The sky was almost permanently iron-grey, and if it wasn't actually raining it was about to.

Not that she minded, most of the time. She wasn't exactly the type to sit outside sunning herself. She was Scottish, for a start, with red hair, pale skin and freckles. Ten minutes in the sun, and she looked like an embarrassed beetroot. Anyway, the rain was the least of her problems.

Another mind-numbingly dull day in the shop, serving customers who couldn't even be bothered to pass the time of day. Another day of being bawled out by her psychopathic halfwit of a boss for no reason other than that's what he thought management was about. Then, at the end of it, all of them being handed redundancy notices because the shop's owners—some national chain owned by an anonymous overseas equity company—had decided to 'rationalise their network'. Which, as far as she could understand it, meant shutting all but a handful of shops in the south-east. The only consolation had been that the idiot boss was in the same boat and had been as much in the dark as rest of them. He'd found out only when the head office bod had arrived at four-thirty and taken him into the back. Ten minutes later, they'd all received their letters.

So that was that. Another sodding job up the spout. She hadn't even been there long enough to get redundancy pay. Back to the Job Centre, back to all the balls-ache of trying to claim Jobseeker's Allowance, and back to frantically applying for any job she could find. She still had a few hours of bar-work each week, but there didn't seem any prospect of expanding that, even if she could do so without tripping over the benefits threshold. She was no scrounger. She'd always tried to be self-reliant and was happy to take on any work she could find. But it was getting harder and harder. She wasn't getting any younger, and employers were starting to look at her employment record and wonder why it was so patchy. Some of that was her fault, of course. For a start, she had a criminal record. A couple of convictions for shoplifting, and the second time she'd been given a short custodial sentence. It was long spent, but she'd got the sack from her job at the time and had found it hard to get work afterwards. From then on, it had been dead-end stuff. Many employers weren't prepared to offer anything more than short-term or zero-hours contracts these days, and even when she'd found what was supposedly a permanent role, as with the shop, it had generally ended in being laid off as soon as they found half an excuse.

Every month she struggled with the rent and the bills. She'd been lucky there in that she'd found a house-share in a decent housing association place, but she wasn't entirely sure of the legality of the arrangement. Apart from the difficulty of scraping the money together each month, she had a fear the whole set-up would fall apart. She'd spent weeks sofa-surfing on a couple of previous occasions and didn't want to end up doing it again. It was a good way to lose what few friends she still had.

On top of all that it was, as always, pissing down. She'd lost her umbrella somewhere, and she had only a thin coat and hood to ward off the rain for the fifteen-minute walk between her bus stop and the place that, for the moment, she was able to call home. She hunched her shoulders and began the trek.

Hulme was decent enough these days. She'd heard people talk about the old days of the Hulme Crescents, the medium-rise estates that had been a disaster almost from the days they were built. By the 1980s, the council had more or less abandoned them and they became a haunt for drugged-up criminals and every kind of weirdo you could imagine. There was something oddly romantic about that, she thought. A derelict estate taken over by people from the fringes of society. But maybe it had been less romantic if you had to live there.

It was different now. There were still areas you steered clear of but most of it was neat rows of housing, well-maintained by the council and housing associations. The university area was adjacent, and the student population meant there was a decent selection of pubs and bars and a few interesting shops. It was only a short bus-ride into the city centre. The place would be perfect, if only she could afford to live here. Or to live anywhere for that matter.

From time to time she wondered if she'd be better returning back up north. But it was too late for that. She'd eventually put all that behind her. It was still there, lurking in the darkest recesses of her mind, and every now and then she'd wake from an unremembered nightmare, knowing it had seeped back into her consciousness like a toxic gas. But it was dealt with. She'd moved on. Maybe not far and in no clear direction. But away from all that. She had no intention of doing anything to risk bringing any of that back to the surface.

The rain was coming harder, clattering off the roofs of parked cars and the grimy pavements. She broke into a semi-run, hoping to reach the shelter of the house before she was completely soaked.

She turned into the cul-de-sac where she lived, still with her head down, and almost ran headlong into the figure standing outside the shared house.

'Oh, Jesus, sorry. Didn't see you there—' She looked up, and took a breath.

It was almost as if her thoughts had conjured this up. The figure was standing, motionless, head tipped forward, clad in a heavy-duty black cagoule. She could barely make out the features in the shadow of the hood, but she'd known as soon as she raised her head.

'Christ, what the hell are you doing here?' she said.

'Waiting for you.' As if it was the most obvious thing in the world. As if it wasn't so many years.

'But how the hell did you know—?'

'Where you lived? I was just lucky. Came across it.'

'But—' She couldn't make sense of it. She might have expected a call or maybe a friend request on Facebook. Not this.

'I didn't have any way of contacting you beforehand. Just the address. So I thought I'd come out on the off-chance you might be around.'

'You'd better come in,' she said, aware she sounded grudging. All this would do was stir it up again, bring out those same demons from the corners of her head. 'You must be soaked.'

'I'm OK inside this. It's designed for Manchester weather. Look, I don't want to intrude. Wondered if you fancied grabbing a bite to eat somewhere. My treat. We can chat. Catch up. Then I'll bugger off and leave you alone.'

She'd realised, even as she made the offer, that she really didn't want to go into the house. It was as if it would bring everything, all that history, inside. That it wouldn't be a refuge, but just another place contaminated by the past. Anyway, it wasn't every day that someone offered to take her for dinner. The way things were going, it would be a long while before she could afford to eat out herself. She raised her rain-drenched face. 'I'm not exactly dressed to go out,' she said, 'unless the drowned rat look became fashionable when I wasn't looking.'

'I wasn't thinking of anywhere posh. Just a pub or something.'

'We'll get even wetter walking there.'

'I'm parked just round the corner. I can drive us somewhere then drop you off back here when we're done.'

'Aye, why not? Like you say, we should catch up. It's been a hell of a long time.'

'It has that. All kinds of stuff gone on. I'll tell you about it. Let's get on before you get any wetter. Car's only a minute or two away. Follow me.'

'But what the hell are you doing down here?' she called.

'Long story.' There was a parked van, with the passenger door standing open. 'Here, get out of the wet.'

For a moment, unexpectedly, she felt a shiver of unease, a cold finger down her spine that had nothing to do with the rain leaking into her thin overcoat. But she could think of no reason to refuse.

She climbed into the car, relieved to be out of the driving rain.

***

It was nearly eight when McKay finally left the office. Helena Grant had managed to beg, steal and borrow resources from every part of the division. They had a decent-sized team now, working out of the MIR and a couple of overflow rooms, camped on the phones, taking statements, collating intelligence, crunching data. Most of it was routine stuff, trawling through the list of addresses and contacts that Mrs Scott had left for them, calling individuals who had known Katy Scott during her time in Culbokie and Inverness.

Scott's identity had been announced to the media that evening, along with a couple of the most recent photographs they'd been able to obtain. Since the story had appeared on the local news, they'd had a steady trickle of calls from people claiming to have information. Most were nothing more than attention seekers, old school-friends or past acquaintances who had some vague half-memory of having encountered Katy. Little of this was likely to be of real value, but it was the necessary leg-work. McKay had similarly been liaising with the communications team at Greater Manchester Police to organise an appeal for information on the local news there.

They'd still made no progress in identifying the second victim. She hadn't shown up on the police databases. They'd found a few possible matches on the national missing persons database, but so far those had led nowhere. They'd issued a description, complete with reference to the distinctive tattoos, and had received a few calls but none yet sounded promising.

They were still at that relatively early stage in the investigation when you can sense a genuine buzz of enthusiasm among the team. It was hard and monotonous work, but they still felt that, sooner or later, some real lead would emerge. But he knew this energy could be sustained only for so long. Within a few days, if they still seemed to be getting nowhere, the enthusiasm would start to wane. The leads would become less numerous and less promising;

the work would become routine; the team would start just going through the motions in the vague hope that something would turn up. If they reached that point, McKay's challenge would be to lead them through it, keep the promised land in sight as they trudged through the investigatory desert. It wasn't something he was looking forward to.

He spent the last half-hour tidying up various administrative loose ends and checking through his e-mails. McKay was happy to cultivate his reputation as a maverick, but he knew as well as anyone the importance of professionalism in this work. You could be as brilliant as Sherlock Holmes, but nobody would thank you if the prosecution fell apart because you'd screwed up the evidence or hadn't followed due procedure. By eight, he decided to call it a night. A couple of the team were still on the phones or tapping away at their keyboards, so he gestured that they should follow his example before long. It didn't do anyone any good to end up knackered on a case like this, where it looked like they were in it for the long haul.

At home, Chrissie was curled up on the sofa, watching a cookery show on the TV. A half-empty bottle of white wine was sitting on the floor. 'You're earlier than I expected,' she said, in a voice which suggested that this wasn't necessarily a welcome development.

'Done what I could,' he said.

'Stew's still in the oven. I had mine earlier. Potatoes in the saucepan on top. You'll need to heat them up.'

'Thanks. I'm starving.' Stews of various kinds were Chrissie's default supper these days. He couldn't blame her. His working days were as erratic as ever. A stew would sit in the oven without spoiling, or without spoiling too much, as long as he wasn't ridiculously late.

He'd told her not to bother cooking. He enjoyed cooking himself—he often did it at the weekends—and would have been content to rustle up something when he got in. But she insisted that this was her contribution. These days, she only worked a couple of mornings doing administration for a local medical centre so she had plenty of time, she said. In his worst moments, McKay felt it was simply another way of punishing him, a way of ensuring he owed her something, however trivial. A way of making him feel guilty on those nights when he arrived back too late and the food was dried out and inedible.

Tonight, it was fine. He reheated the boiled potatoes, spooned out a decent helping, and poured himself a glass of red wine from the resealed bottle on the side. There'd been a time, after it had happened, when both of them had been knocking back the booze too much. McKay had always been a serious drinker. It had been part of the role profile in his early days in the job—a few pints and chasers after work alongside the chain-smoking and the crap fast food. In his mid-thirties, McKay had realised he was well on the way to participating in the grand Caledonian tradition of a coronary before the age of forty, so he'd made an effort to knock it on the head. That was when he'd given up smoking, cut back heavily on the drinking, and started to think about eating some food that was green without being mouldy.

He'd more or less kept it up ever since. But both he and Chrissie had found their alcohol intake creeping up as they tried to come to terms with what had happened. McKay had reached the point where he could easily knock back half a bottle of Scotch in an evening without noticing. Chrissie had hit the wine. It had taken him a month or two to realise what was happening, and then he'd made the effort to stop. These days, he limited himself to no more than one or two glasses of wine. Chrissie, he thought, was still drinking too much, but he wasn't about to try to tell her so.

He slumped himself on the sofa next to her, the plate of food on his knee. On the television, a chunkily-built bald man was expressing doubts about the flavour combinations in the dish he was tasting.

'How's it going?' she said.

'Slowly, but we're making progress.' He rarely talked about his work with Chrissie, except at the most superficial level.

'I saw it mentioned on the news. Didn't say much, except that you'd identified the first victim.'

'Aye, some poor lass from Culbokie. Well, originally. She'd been living in Manchester.'

They both sat in silence for a few minutes. Chrissie's eyes were fixed on the TV screen where one of the contestants was struggling with an unsuccessful chocolate fondant. McKay munched through the stew and potatoes, occasionally pausing to take a sip of wine.

'What are we going to do, Alec?' Chrissie asked.

'How'd you mean?' Though he knew full well.

'About us. We can't go on this way.'

'Can't we?' He felt, already, as if he were being coerced into a row. His instinct was to clam up, play dumb, but he knew that would only make matters worse.

'Oh for Christ's sake, you know we can't. Every sodding night sitting in silence because neither of us knows what to say.'

'So what do you suggest?'

'We need to talk about it. We need to talk about what happened.'

'We've talked about it. Endlessly. We just go round in circles.' Except, he thought, that generally you end up blaming me, and I end up blaming you. And not even because we really do blame each other, probably, but just because we're each trying to offload our own guilt.

'Maybe it's time we thought about professional help.'

'Professional help?'

'You know, counselling. Couples counselling. That sort of thing.'

McKay felt himself bridling. Chrissie had suggested this before and he'd always resisted, maintaining it was all just woolly bollocks. But he knew, really, that he disliked the idea of someone, some stranger, sticking their nose into his head. Trying to tell what he was thinking. But that was maybe just because he was afraid of what that might be.

'If you like,' he said, now, grudgingly. He felt a tightening in his chest even at the prospect. 'We could give it a go.'

'It might help.'

'If it's what you want.'

She banged her glass on the coffee table, spilling wine on to the polished surface. 'For Christ's sake, Alec, it's not what I want. It's what might be good for us. For our marriage.'

'I've said I'll do it, haven't I?'

'Aye, in the same way that you might have agreed to having your bollocks removed without anaesthetic.'

'Well, what do you expect? I can't pretend to be comfortable with the idea. But if you think it's the right thing to do—'

'It's not what I think. It's what we both think.'

'I think it's time we faced facts, Chrissie. It wasn't either of our faults. It was just one of those things.'

'How can you say that? About your own daughter? "Just one of those things"?'

'Oh, Christ, you know what I mean. There's nothing either of us could have done.'

'We could have given her a reason to stay here. We could have stopped it ever happening.'

'For fuck's sake, Chrissie. She left home. She grew up and she flew the fucking nest. It's what children do.'

'Not if you give them a reason to stay. She walked out the first chance she got.'

'And could you blame her? The way we were. The way we still are.'

There was a prolonged silence, both of them conscious they were on the verge of saying things they were likely to regret.

Finally, Chrissie said: 'She *died*, Alec. She fucking killed herself because she wasn't here. Because she had no-one. Because she was on her own in a big city.'

'Oh, for God's sake, Chrissie. We don't know that. And even if she did, we can't begin to speculate why she did it. She suffered from depression. We knew that. We just didn't realise how serious it was.'

'We should have fucking realised,' she said. 'We should have known. We were her fucking parents, for Christ's sake. We should never have let it happen.'

'But—' There was no point, he thought. We both know, objectively, there was nothing we could have done. Not then. Not by the time it happened. What we don't know—what we can never know—is whether we could have done something before then. Whether we could have done more to help her. We tried. We did our best. But maybe, as it turned out, our best just wasn't anything like good enough. 'Look, you're right,' he said. 'Let's give it a go. Let's try the counselling.'

'And you think that'll do it, do you?' Chrissie said, bitterly. 'You really think that'll be enough to wash all this away?'

He held himself back from pointing out that it had been her idea, that just a few minutes before she'd been attacking him for his reluctance to accept it. This wasn't about reason. This was about working through fears and emotions that neither of them fully understood.

'No,' he said, finally. 'No, I don't think that. But we've nothing else, Chrissie. It's all we've fucking got.'

CHAPTER SIXTEEN

To McKay's surprise, early the next morning he received an e-mail from DI Warren of Greater Manchester Police. 'Everything I could track down,' it said, simply. 'Hope it's some use.'

There was a zip file attached containing a number of documents. McKay clicked on a couple. As far as he could see, Warren had sent, in scanned form, the full contents of Katy Scott's file. There wasn't a lot, and most of it related to her being reported as missing. Statements from her landlord and from the neighbour who'd first raised concerns about her absence. Statements from a couple of other neighbours in the same converted house. Nothing that, at first glance, seemed likely to shed much light on the case other than providing a few more contact names and addresses.

Still, it was good of Warren to take the trouble, particularly to do it personally. Given that the two forces were now liaising on the case at senior level, it was possible that some pressure had been placed on him to be co-operative. McKay didn't much care as long as it achieved the desired effect.

Helena Grant turned up later in the morning to do a walkabout among the troops. Afterwards, she sat herself down in McKay's office. Horton was out somewhere conducting an interview.

'You've a decent bunch there,' she said.

'Aye, I'm happy. Mostly your efforts, that. I can see you've pulled a few strings to get people released.'

'Called in a few favours,' she said. 'But people are usually keen to help in a case like this.'

'Must be causing a few jitters out there,' he said. 'Killer on the loose and all that.'

'Media are starting to stir it up a bit,' she agreed. 'And it won't get any better. We've set up a press conference for this afternoon. Update on progress.'

'You want me there?'

She considered. 'Plan is for the chief super and me to lead it,' she said. 'Some of that lot are very good at adding two and two together and getting twenty-five.'

'I'll stay out of it, then,' McKay said. 'You know me. Someone starts talking shite, I'm likely to tell them.'

'Aye, Alec,' she said. 'And that's why they've never made you chief media officer, I'm guessing.'

'I don't have the face for television,' he said. 'That's the only reason.'

They spent an hour or so working on the statement that she was going to make and brainstorming the questions that might be thrown at her. At the end of it, McKay said: 'Jesus, Helena, I'm awful glad you like doing this stuff. This is your game, not mine.'

'Horses for courses. If I can keep the media sweet—well, sweetish—I'm more than happy to do it. We want them onside in this one if we can. This is one where we really do need whatever information we can get from the public.'

'We've fuck all else at the moment, other than a few names and addresses.'

After Grant had gone, he went back to the material Warren had sent up. The statements from the landlord and neighbour were both pretty bland—largely 'she kept herself to herself' stuff. The neighbour had noticed she wasn't around because her mail had been building up and had mentioned it to the landlord. The landlord had been trying to gain access to the flat to conduct a maintenance check, and in the end had let himself in. He'd found the place deserted, but looking as if Scott hadn't expected to be away. There was food rotting in the fridge, a bottle of curdled milk left out in the kitchen, the bed left unmade. It was at that point he'd decided to report her absence to the police.

The police had checked through the mail, but, other than a couple of bills, it had been largely junk. The flat had been treated as a potential crime scene and examined thoroughly, but there were no clues as to where or why she might have gone. The landlord and neighbours had had little knowledge of Katy Scott's family or friends, and—until the discovery of her body—it had not been possible to track down her next of kin. They'd found some payslips from a couple of local bars where she'd been working, but the owners and staff there knew little about her personal life. She was friendly enough, they said. Occasionally went out for a drink with the other girls, but no-one had got to know her very well. She'd just drifted into the place, rubbed along well enough, and then drifted out again. When she hadn't turned up for work, nobody, including the bar managers, had thought much of it. It was that sort of job. People were here today and most likely gone tomorrow.

It struck McKay, as he read through the various documents, that there must be countless people out there living similarly isolated, rootless lives. Politicians banged on about hard-working families even while those traditional family structures dissolved around them. There was an army of young, and sometimes not so young, people moving from dead-end job to dead-end job with no family support and, in many cases, little in the way of real friendships. They held on, for the most part, made enough to survive, maybe even had an OK time. But if they fell off the grid, as Katy Scott seemed to have done, there was no-one to notice, let alone care.

Why were they there? Countless reasons, he supposed. He knew, or suspected, why Katy Scott had left home. It didn't have to be that extreme. Often, it was just because of the constraints of living with parents, or simply a question of money. His own daughter, Lizzie, had moved out because—well, who knew? Neither he nor Chrissie had ever really understood, which was one of the reasons why the guilt continued to gnaw at them. But theirs was just one instance among many.

McKay finished going through the files, highlighting any contact names or addresses he spotted though there were only a handful not already on their lists. He dutifully handed over the details to members of the team, and left them to it.

Mid-afternoon, as he and Ginny Horton were mapping out their next steps, Helena Grant poked her head round the door. 'Just finished the media conference,' she said. 'Bit of a scrum, so I cleared out as quickly as I could. Left the chief super to fend them off.'

'How was it?' McKay said.

'Not so bad, really. We had quite a national contingent there. BBC, Sky, various dailies. It's becoming a big story.'

'Oh, joy,' McKay commented sourly.

'Ach, it was OK. Most of them just wanted me to use the phrase "serial killer" so they could stick in their headlines. Needless to say, I played a straight bat. "Treating the cases as possibly linked but not making any assumptions" stuff.'

'How much have we released in terms of detail?' Horton asked.

'Just the bare bones. Two bodies. Treating them as murder. Nothing about the roses or candles. Nothing about the actual cause of death.'

'Wonder how long before some of that gets out,' McKay said. He jerked a thumb towards the wall, indicating the team working in the adjoining offices. 'They seem a decent bunch, but some of them are unknown quantities. Wouldn't be surprised if we get some leakage.'

Grant shrugged. 'We'll see. I put my trust in the innate goodness of my fellow man.'

'Aye, me too. Right up until they land me in the shite. Speaking of which, did the media buggers try to throw any in our direction? Shite, I mean.'

'They're keeping their powder dry,' Grant said. 'With a case like this, it's bad taste to start attacking the police too early. They'll wait till we mess something up or look as if we're getting nowhere.'

'May not have long to wait, then,' McKay said, gloomily. 'We're getting nowhere fast at the moment. Don't even have an ID for the second victim yet.'

'It'll come.' Grant exuded a confidence that McKay knew she didn't feel. That was one reason she was so good with the troops. She led from the front, unlike some of those above her. 'We gave the media a description of the second victim, including the tattoos. It'll go out nationwide. Let's hope that sparks something overnight.'

'Aye, let's hope,' McKay said, in a voice that suggested that, for him at least, that particular quality was currently in very short supply.

***

Once she'd passed the entrance to the military camp at Fort George, Ginny Horton took one of the left-hand tracks down to the sea. She was into a good rhythm now, feet pounding on the hard surface, breathing steady and in control. She was at the point where she felt she could run forever, keep going until she reached the ends of the earth.

The weather had held up for another day, and it was a glorious evening, the setting sun throwing shadows across the landscape. The sky was clear and the waters of the firth, now visible ahead of her, a rich blue. On an evening like this, you could almost fool yourself into thinking you were living somewhere warmer, more tropical.

She reached the point where the track petered out into scrubland, and then slowed. In front of her, across the scrub, there was a rough sandy beach, deserted except for the crowds of gulls that descended periodically in search of food. As she reached the top of the beach, she came to a halt, catching her breath and fumbling for her water bottle. She was doing well. Every night, she'd manage to shave a little off her time. She had no real objective with this, other than to keep doing it. Pushing herself as far as she could go.

The view was spectacular. Across the firth, to her left, she could see the small village of Rosemarkie, with its clustering of pastel coloured houses and church tower rising above a pale strip of beach.

Caird's Cave, where the second body had been discovered, was a short walk along the beach from Rosemarkie. She couldn't clearly make it out from here, although she could discern the point where the cliffs rose above the woodland to the east of the village. She wondered now, as she had when they'd first seen the body, what had prompted the killer to leave it just there, laid out surrounded by the roses and candles. It was bound to be discovered there, sooner rather than later. The first body, buried under turf at the Clootie Well, could conceivably have lain undiscovered for much longer if the young couple hadn't happened upon it. The roses would have lost their blossoms, and quite possibly no-one ventured far off the tracks into those woods for weeks or even months at a time. It was as if, the second time, the killer had chosen to increase the chances that the body would be found.

The received wisdom about multiple killers is that they want to get caught. That, with each killing, they take increasing risks or try to expose themselves. Horton remembered vaguely from her psychology training that this was seen as something of a myth—that the truth was, rather, that such killers simply became more confident with each successive murder. In this case, though, she wondered whether some message was being sent, consciously or not, by increasing the likelihood of the bodies being discovered. Could there be other bodies out there? Could the killer have struck previously, but made less effort to make the body conspicuous?

As she had previously when standing on this coastline, she thought back to the previous summer's case. Lizzie Hamilton. It was not dissimilar to their current cases. She had been a similar age, just a little older. She was a woman largely without close friends or available family, drifting aimlessly and rootlessly through life. Like Katy Scott she had simply vanished one day, with no sign that she was expecting to go. Like Scott, too, she had been a local, born and brought up in this part of the world.

Was that just coincidence? Or was it possible that Lizzie Hamilton's body was out there too, buried in a shallow grave somewhere in the wilds of the Black Isle? And, if so, might there be others?

Horton shivered, suddenly struck cold despite her recent exertions and the warmth of the evening sun. Just the breeze off the sea meeting her sweat-soaked tee-shirt, she thought. But the landscape opposite suddenly seemed much darker.

She turned, preparing to begin the run back home, when she felt her mobile phone buzzing in her belt. She pulled it out and looked at the screen. McKay's mobile.

'Alec?'

'Evening, Ginny. Caught you mid-run?'

'Something like that.' McKay didn't often call in the evening. He was one of those—rare in the force—who believed that leisure time was just that, and he made a point of not bothering his team outside work hours without good reason. By the same token, he gave the shortest of shift to anyone who called him without justification. One or two senior officers had discovered that over the years, and it was one of the numerous reasons why McKay's career had stalled. 'What can I do for you?'

'We have a development.' He intoned the last word with the air of a stage conjuror unveiling his latest miracle. 'Appeal for information went out on the national news this evening. Control room inundated with calls afterwards. Most of them bollocks, obviously. Usual procession of the halt and the lame. But we've got what sounds like it might be a credible ID for our second victim.'

'You're kidding.'

'Sounds like a match with the tattoos. And they were distinctive enough for us to take it seriously.' He paused, obviously consulting a note. 'Woman called Joanne Cameron. And get this. Greater Manchester again. Stockport somewhere. And a Scottish accent.'

'Sounds plausible,' Horton agreed. 'She wasn't on the mispers list?'

'Not been reported,' McKay said. 'Sounds like the usual story. No-one actually close enough to her to start worrying too much. Person who called in was one of her work colleagues. Someone called Jade Norris. She and Cameron went out on the lash together in Manchester. Sometime late in the evening Cameron went AWOL. Norris didn't think much of it. Just assumed that Cameron had copped off with someone. Reading between the lines, Norris ended up at some bloke's house, pissed as a rat, and thought that Cameron must have done the same.'

'Romantic,' Horton observed. 'So when did it occur to her to start worrying?'

'Cameron didn't turn up for work on the Monday. But that didn't seem to set off many alarm bells. She had a track-record of poor attendance, especially Monday morning sickies. None of her work-mates, including Norris, were particularly close to her. Was only on the Tuesday that anyone started to get concerned, and then they don't seem to have done much other than ring her mobile. Then someone caught the news broadcast and made the connection— Cameron was proud of her tattoos, apparently, so everyone knew about them—and called Norris. Who, bless her little cotton socks, took the trouble to call in and report it.'

'Probably wondering how soon she can sell her story to the tabloids,' Horton commented tartly. 'But, yes. Do you want me to come in?'

'There's not a lot more we can do tonight. I've asked our colleagues in GMP to follow up and get what information they can. We can take it from there tomorrow. Better get some rest and an early start, I think.'

'Be interesting to see if she has any local connections. If so, we may be starting to get somewhere.'

'Let's hope. I'll leave you to get back to your marathon.'

She ended the call and stood for a moment gazing out across the choppy blue waters. It was still a fine evening, but the sea breeze was growing stronger and a few clouds were gathering on the horizon. The forecast was for the weather to break tomorrow, which could easily mean they'd already had the best of the summer. Over the firth, the Black Isle was still caught by the setting sun, windows glinting gold. The woodland to the east was looking darker, more threatening.

She began to jog back towards home, picking up pace as she ran. Isla had been in London for the day, returning on the last flight and wouldn't be back until nearly eleven, so Horton would have only a ready meal and a glass of wine for company. It occurred to her now, pounding back along the sunlit waterfront, that this was how too many people had to live their lives. No-one at home and no-one ever coming home.

CHAPTER SEVENTEEN

Christ, he was running late tonight.

Jimmie Morton pulled into the car park at the rear of the building and parked as close as he could, trying to save a few seconds. It had been one of those evenings when anything that can go wrong, will. There'd been a problem with the alarm at his first call. Nothing serious—as far as he could see, the system just hadn't been maintained properly—but the device hadn't activated properly as he'd tried to leave. He'd been tempted to leave it—allow it to become someone else's problem—but if he did this was bound to be the night when there was a break-in and he'd get blamed for leaving the place unprotected. So he'd called out the maintenance team, who were supposed to treat alarm problems as a priority. But he knew enough about their ideas of priorities to make sure the call was properly logged, so if they couldn't be arsed to come out tonight at least it wouldn't be his fault.

At the next place he discovered that some kids had vandalised the rear of the building, painting graffiti slogans across a white-washed wall. At least, he assumed it was kids. One of the slogans was the independence slogan 'Still Yes' but there was little sign of reasoned political argument in the rest of it—just the usual obscenities and incomprehensible daubings. Again, he'd had to stop and phone it in so that in due course—probably six months or so— someone would come out and clear it up.

On top of that, there'd been a lengthy tailback on the A9 because some idiot lorry-driver had managed to lose control and blocked the northbound carriageway just before the Kessock Bridge. Morton had sat there long enough to be seriously considering taking the long way round to the Black Isle, if only he could find a way out of the tailback, but eventually the police had managed to clear a lane and get the traffic moving.

But he was at least a couple of hours late getting up here. He was tempted just to sack it off, but his van had a tracking device fitted so the bosses would know if he hadn't completed the round. Not that they'd pay him any overtime for finishing this late.

This was his least favourite stop at the best of times. The other sites were largely unoccupied shops or office premises. His remit was straightforward—carry out a basic security and maintenance check, deal with any routine maintenance problems himself where possible, and report back any more serious issues so that they could be dealt with as appropriate. Morton had trained as a joiner but it seemed increasingly hard to get proper chippy work these days, so he'd ended up in this half-arsed role. Jack of all trades, master of nothing and nobody at all.

On the whole, he didn't mind the work. The pay was OK, if not exactly spectacular for the hours he had to put in. Apart from the GPS system on the van, he was his own boss and could schedule his days as he thought best, as long as the full round of visits was completed. The actual activities were pretty routine. From time to time, he ended up doing some basic joinery to make a site secure or some plumbing to patch up a leak until it could be properly repaired. But anything more complicated was just reported in. Mostly it was just ensuring that the sites were safe, secure and adequately maintained.

The visits could really be done any time, but the security firm offered their clients the option—at a suitably increased fee, none of which found its way back to Morton and his colleagues—of an evening round. The clients liked that, because they thought it meant any scrotes who had their eyes on breaking into one of the unoccupied sites would see a physical security presence. Morton himself thought any half-decent scrote would soon work out that the physical presence was highly intermittent and, in his own case at least, comprised no more than a single overweight middle-aged man with a forty-a-day habit. But he did what he was told.

He supposed there was an element of risk in the job. His wife had occasionally expressed concern that he was expected to work unaccompanied. But there was little worth stealing in most of these sites. They were just empty shells. The biggest danger was that some down-and-out would break in and use the site as a place to sleep—and he'd found evidence of that from time to time. But that was more of an issue in the urban areas. Once you got out of the city, the only issue was petty vandalism. Local kids who couldn't think of anything better to do than spray paint any available blank wall.

This place, though, gave him the creeps even in the middle of the day. Out of curiosity, he'd dug about a bit on the internet to try to learn about the history of the building. It had originally been a private house, apparently, though he didn't know how much of the current building had been part of that original residence. Sometime around the turn of the twentieth century it had been converted into a hotel and had operated into the 1980s. Morton had a vague memory of that as a child, not that his parents could afford to go there. The hotel business had declined as people began to take their holidays overseas, and the building had eventually been transformed into a residential care home. Now, finally, it had ceased even to be that. Presumably, the costs of keeping up a large Victorian building like this had simply become prohibitive. The residents had been moved to other locations, the building had been put on the market, and now it was standing empty.

Morton could imagine the place would once have been warm and welcoming. In its heyday, it would have been an imposing place, a clear demonstration of social hierarchies with poorly-paid young maids from Stornoway waiting on wealthy holidaymakers up on golfing trips from the big cities. Now, it simply looked neglected and forbidding, a relic of another age. He didn't think of himself as particularly fanciful or fearful, but the place felt full of ghosts. Ghosts of the well-off customers who used to fill the hotel's lounges and dining room. Ghosts of the countless elderly folk who had lived and no doubt often died in its bedrooms.

Even in the full light of day, he was disconcerted by the building's empty spaces—the large reception rooms with their broad picture windows looking out on to the sea, the endless empty corridors. The sense that something was happening—or had just happened or was about to happen—whenever he looked away.

They'd only started looking after the place in the spring, so he hadn't often had reason to be here outside daylight hours. It was still far from fully dark outside, but the sun was setting over the hills behind the building, throwing long shadows across the landscape and the water. The front of the building, facing east out over the bay, was already lost in gloom.

Morton unlocked the side door he used to access the building, and made his way into the small foyer. He walked across to disable the alarm on the far side of the room, feeling his way cautiously in the half-light.

Even before he'd reached to turn on the lights, the indicators on the alarm unit had told him the system was inactive. Shit. He hurriedly thought back over his schedule for the previous days, trying to work out who'd been here last. Had he forgotten to reset it, or had it been one of his colleagues? He realised, with some relief, that the previous visit, two days before, had been on one of his rest-days. So someone else would have been responsible.

Although the other utilities had been disconnected, the owners had left the electricity operational to power the alarm system and other essentials. It probably also didn't do any harm to have a few lights showing from time to time. Even so, Morton carried his own flashlight and tended to use no more lights than he needed. If he accidentally left one burning, that would be another excuse to give him a bollocking.

His intention was to be in and out of here as quickly as possible tonight. He'd do a quick tour of the main reception areas and the upper corridors to make sure that there were no obvious signs of any problems. Then he'd make himself scarce.

The small inner foyer led through into what had previously been the main lobby, which in turn gave access to the various reception rooms. He turned on the lights in the lobby and walked through to the large area at the front of the hotel which he imagined had once been the main dining-room. The broad picture windows stretched the full length of the hotel frontage, giving a spectacular view of the bay and the firth. It wasn't difficult to envisage what this place would have been like in its prime—rows of white-starched table-cloths, silver cutlery, crystal glasses. Well-off guests eating substantial dinners while watching the spread of evening across the water.

Now it was just an empty space with worn carpets and peeling wallpaper. Morton walked over to the window. The setting sun threw the shadow of the building out across the grassed area at the front, down to the beach and the shoreline. Lights were coming on in some of the houses along the road below, and the sun was glinting gold in the windows of the houses on the far side of the firth. The sky was still largely clear, darkening in the west to a bruised mauve, though clouds were gathering on the far horizon where the firth opened into the North Sea. The last fine day for a while, according to the forecast.

In other circumstances, Morton would have found the view striking. Standing here, in this abandoned space, he simply felt unease at the gathering dark. Better do what he had to do, and get the hell out.

He turned, sensing again the illusion that something had been happening behind him, out of his sight, as he'd been staring out of the windows. But of course the place was as silent and undisturbed as ever. He scanned round the room to ensure there were no visible problems, no signs of leaks or breakages. Then he hurried through into the old kitchens, and checked the areas leading to the rear doors.

He completed his tour of the ground floor and climbed the wide stairway to the first floor. This was the part he disliked most. The upper floors were given over to what had been the hotel bedrooms. He had to patrol the long corridors checking the status of each room. When he'd made his first visit, some months before, he'd made a point of opening each bedroom door so that all he had to do subsequently was peer into each in passing and check there were no obvious problems. Nevertheless, it was a lengthy process, and something about the long empty corridors increased his unease. Even more than downstairs, he felt other presences. As if each room were reoccupied as soon as he had passed.

None of this was anything he'd ever admit to his wife or friends. He saw himself as a down-to-earth sort of bugger, not the sort who'd imagine ghosts and phantoms lurking behind every corner. But that was what this bloody place did to him.

He completed his round of the first and second floors without incident. The rooms were as he'd left them, silent and unlit, no signs of any problems. Finally, he began the slow climb to the third floor. The building had a lift roomy enough to take wheelchairs and hospital beds when the building had been transformed into a care home, but that had been disconnected and, in any case, Morton would have felt no inclination to trust himself to it.

The stairs up to the third floor were narrower and steeper than those on the floors below. There were only a few small bedrooms up here, intended for the servants in the building's original form and presumably later occupied by hotel staff. Even so, Morton had to give it a careful examination. It was up here that problems were most likely to arise—leaks from the roof or wildlife damage.

He stepped on to the landing and peered along the corridor. And stopped, holding his breath. There were five doors on the left hand side. The two nearer doors were wide open, as he'd left them, as were the two further doors.

The third door, the door in the middle, was closed.

He took a step forward, telling himself that, for some reason, the door must have been closed by whoever had carried out the patrol a couple of nights before. Morton had checked the log before he'd come out, as he always did, and there'd been no reports of any incidents or issues here, but maybe whoever was here had spotted something and thought it better to leave the door closed.

What, though?

As he stepped forward, Morton recalled the deactivated alarm downstairs. But if someone had broken in, why the hell would they wait till they got all the way up here before doing anything? Surely there would have been signs of an intruder elsewhere.

He fumbled in his pocket for the bunch of keys that included the skeleton key for the rooms. As he pressed the key into the lock, he realised, stupidly, that his hand was trembling.

It took him a moment to get the door open and press down the light-switch. And then he stood, staring blankly at what he saw.

He had no doubt what it was, even in that first moment. The room was otherwise empty, the furniture long removed. In the centre, spread out before the window, was a naked human body. A young female. Surrounding the body, as if in preparation for a funeral, there were six candle-holders each containing an unlit white candle. Between the candles, there were four vases of red roses.

Morton had taken all this in even before he had realised. Then, his breath caught in his lungs, he turned, sure somehow that whoever had prepared this scene would be standing behind him. But the corridor was empty.

Scarcely aware of what he was doing, he stumbled down the narrow stairway, almost losing his footing as he scrambled to get out of the place. Afterwards, he had no recollection of making his way down the final two staircases and out into the lobby. He was aware of nothing until he'd reached the chill of the evening air and was standing, only just able to recover his breath, his back pressed against the comforting solidity of his van, fumbling for his mobile phone.

As he dialled 999, he looked up and realised that the sky had already clouded over and that the first drops of rain were beginning to fall.

CHAPTER EIGHTEEN

For the first time in weeks, Helena Grant made it home in time to enjoy a half-decent evening. It wasn't generally like that these days. They were all overworked, but at times it felt as if she never stopped. As funding and resources were squeezed, the mantras were about getting 'more for less' and 'improving efficiency'. As far as Grant could see, that just meant that everyone worked longer hours without any more reward or recognition. They were also 'exploring partnership working with other agencies', which resulted in yet more unproductive meetings. The admin and paperwork got pushed outside normal work hours so she ended up staying late to complete it or, worse still, bringing it home so she could labour away into the night.

Mostly, she didn't mind too much. It wasn't exactly disrupting her active social life. She had no-one to come home to, and not much else to do once she got here. But occasionally, as tonight, she just felt weary of the whole thing. She wanted to stop and take a breath.

So this evening she'd made a point of leaving—well, not on time but at least not absurdly late. She'd exchanged the smart suit she'd worn for the press conference for jeans and a tee-shirt, and cooked herself a half-decent supper rather than the frozen meal for one that was her usual exhausted fall-back and poured herself a glass of a not-bad Rioja. Life, for once, was OK.

On an evening like this, she remembered why she'd moved into this place. For the first few months after Rory had died, she'd stayed put in the smart Edwardian villa they'd bought together, wanting to retain that connection. But as the weeks went by, she realised that the memories were more painful than comforting. There was too much of Rory in the place, too much of a sense that, at any moment, he might reappear, come jogging down the stairs or out of the kitchen the way he used to. And when that didn't happen, too much of a space where he used to be.

So she'd sold the villa in Inverness and brought herself a terraced house up here in North Kessock with ever-changing views out over the Firth. It was convenient for work, low maintenance and essentially anonymous, but that was what she needed. For the moment it was perfect, and it had left her with a few quid in the bank.

On nights like this, she could sit on the small balcony at the front of the house, sipping her glass of wine, watching as the twilight thickened over the water, thoughts of work temporarily suspended. She'd stayed out here even after the sky had clouded over and the first heavy drops of rain had begun to fall. She was sheltered as long as the wind wasn't too strong, and she enjoyed the chill, damp feel of the air against her skin. She was, by background, a natural west coast Scot. A few days of sun and warmth left her feeling uneasy, as if something wasn't quite right.

She was considering a second glass of wine when the phone call came. A sergeant from the contact centre. 'Thought you'd want to know straightaway,' he said. 'Looks like you've another one.'

It took her a moment to realise what he meant. 'Christ. You're kidding?'

'Don't imagine you'd forgive me if I was. We had a call out about half an hour ago. Body found up the other side of Rosemarkie. Officers just got up there and checked it out, and it sounds like another one.' They hadn't formally released any details of the first two bodies, even internally, but she didn't fool herself that word wouldn't have got around.

'Go on.'

'Roses and candles.'

'Shit. Where was this?'

'You're not going to believe this.'

'Trust me, I'll believe almost anything.'

'You know the old retirement home up between Rosemarkie and Cromarty? Used to be a big hotel.'

She didn't know that area well, but she recalled the large building set in its own grounds, just visible from the road, on the hills overlooking the firth. 'Vaguely.'

'In there. In one of the bedrooms on the top floor, would you believe? Laid out naked with the flowers and candles around her. Some security guy found her.'

'Her?'

'Youngish woman, apparently. That's all I know.'

'That's plenty, thanks. How's it been left?'

'Officers have secured the building. They're staying up there with the guy who found the body till CID gets there.'

'I'm on my way. I'll get things sorted.' She glanced at her watch. 'Imagine it'll be half an hour or so by the time we get up there.'

She ended the call standing at the open balcony windows listening to the rain falling softly on the trees. The air smelled of damp earth. So much, she thought, for suspending all thoughts of work. After a moment, she dialled McKay's number. 'Hi,' she said, when he answered. 'Hope you didn't have any plans for the evening.'

**

The car park was busy with blue-light vehicles. A couple of patrol cars and an ambulance, alongside the white van belonging to the crime scene examiners and some private vehicles. In the middle of the throng there was a van with a security company logo. McKay pulled in beside Helena Grant's car.

Jesus, he thought. Just when it looked as if they finally might be making some progress, the bastard pulls another one. It's like the bugger's playing with us.

It was still raining. McKay turned up his coat collar and made a dash for the brightly-lit entrance. Inside he found Grant and Horton, who'd clearly both just arrived, talking to one of the uniforms.

'What's the story?'

Grant gestured to the uniformed officer standing awkwardly beside her. 'PC Cowan here was just telling us.'

Cowan blinked nervously at McKay. Grant was the senior officer but McKay's reputation tended to go before him. To McKay's eyes Cowan, with his ill-combed blonde hair and baby-faced features, looked as if he ought to still be in school.

'Chap over there found her.' Cowan indicated a morose-looking middle-aged man in a badly fitting uniform. 'Does a security round, apparently. Body was on the top floor, laid out in one of the bedrooms. Young woman,' he added. 'White. That's about all I know.'

'Examiners have just started on the room,' Grant said, 'so I've left them to it. It looks the same. Body was naked. Carefully laid out. Roses and candles around.'

'And this one even more likely to be found quickly,' McKay commented.

'Looks that way, doesn't it? Unless the killer thought this place was just abandoned.'

'Can't imagine it. Any sign of a break in?'

'Not that we can see so far. Security guy reckoned the alarm was deactivated. He hadn't thought much of it, just assumed one of his colleagues had forgotten to turn it back on.'

'That would suggest someone who knew the place or knew what they were doing,' McKay said.

'The alarm's not new, apparently. They'd tried to persuade the owners to introduce a new system now the place is standing empty, but they hadn't got round to it. So the system was here when the place was a residential home. Someone who visited the place then might have been aware of it.'

'Doesn't narrow it down too much, then,' McKay said. 'Must have been countless people working and visiting here over the years.'

'Probably,' Grant agreed. 'Though a casual visitor wouldn't get chance to study the alarm.'

'Then there's the question of how they got in,' Horton added. 'If there wasn't a break in it suggests they might have had keys.'

'Again, the locks haven't been changed since the place became unoccupied,' Grant said, 'so there could be countless people with access to the keys.'

'If this bastard really does want to be caught, he's not making it easy,' McKay said. 'Handing himself into the nearest station would be a damn sight quicker.'

'They never do seem to want to make our jobs easier, Alec.'

'Aye. Bastards. Never any consideration for us, is there?' He smiled at Grant. Despite his words, he looked like a man who'd been saved from a night of domestic torture and brought back to life by this call to action. Anyone else might have been daunted by the prospect of a third corpse. McKay simply looked more motivated. 'OK, then,' he said, 'let's get this show on the road.'

CHAPTER NINETEEN

Kelly had survived the first few days and, in truth, was enjoying the work more than she'd expected. Sure, the place was a decrepit old shambles, and Denny Gorman even more of one. But the job was undemanding enough and the regulars seemed to have taken to her. During the lunchtime session, they were mostly elderly men who gathered to nurse their pints and stave off their solitude. One or two maybe had a drink problem—though nothing to match Gorman's—but most were there just for a blether and a game of cards or dominoes. They commented endlessly on how good it was to have a youngster about the place but their interest seemed grandfatherly rather than pervy. She enjoyed playing up to their compliments.

The young builders had also been back a couple of times. Word of her presence had got around and the group had grown larger: one or two young men working down by the harbour had joined it. The banter from this group was more pointed, and Gorman—with a typical landlord's hypocrisy—had had to ask them to tone down the language a few times. But the exchanges were good natured—young men showing off to their mates rather than anything more threatening.

After their odd exchange in the cellar, Gorman had largely been unobtrusive, spending most lunchtimes working through his newspaper and array of pints. Occasionally, he'd go out to deal with a delivery or phone through an order to a supplier but otherwise showed little inclination to involve himself in anything resembling work.

He hadn't asked her again about working in the evenings but she'd already decided to decline the offer if he raised it. Even though she was feeling more comfortable here, she wasn't attracted by the possibility of spending any time in Gorman's company outside daylight hours. There was still something about him that made her uneasy. It was partly the way he'd look at her as she moved about behind the bar. She'd turn back from pouring a drink or reaching for a packet of crisps to find him staring fixedly at her, even though his eyes seemed to be focused somewhere else.

A couple of days later she had to go back down to the cellar to change one of the lager casks. It took her a few moments to remember exactly what Gorman had told her, but she soon got the hang of it and found it easier than she'd expected. After the first day she'd turned up for work in jeans and a sweatshirt, so wasn't too fussed now about the dust and grime down here. She finished the task, made sure she'd tightened the connection properly, and took a step back in satisfaction.

Gorman was standing behind her. She felt the momentary touch of his body, smelled the sour beer-scented breath. 'Oh, Jesus,' she said, startled. 'Didn't realise you were there.'

He held his arms wide in a defenceless gesture. 'Didn't mean to make you jump. Just came to check you were getting on all right. Looks like you managed it OK?'

'Yes, think so. Maybe you should check it. Just to make sure.'

'Sure it's fine, but I can have a look.' He stepped forward, and peered cursorily at the cask. 'Looks OK to me. You've got the hang of it.'

'That's good. Look, I'd better get back upstairs. They'll be dying of thirst.' He was still standing between her and the cellar door.

'Aye,' he said, showing no signs of moving. 'Look, I just wanted to make sure you understood.'

'Understood what?'

'What I was saying the other day.'

'I don't—'

'About Lizzie. Lizzie Hamilton.'

'It's not—'

'I didn't want you to get any wrong ideas. You know what I mean? It's what happened. She just left. That's all. I don't know why. I don't know where she went. She just left.'

'I know. You said. Anyway, it's none of my business.' She took a step forward, hoping he would step aside.

'People do that.' He went on as if she hadn't spoken. 'They move on. That's what she did. I don't know why.'

'Look, I need—'

'Might have been all sorts of things. Money troubles. Who knows?' He sounded as if he'd almost forgotten that Kelly was there.

She took another couple of steps forward, determined this time not to give way. 'They'll be waiting up there.'

Slightly to her surprise, he stepped back, allowing her to pass. Relieved, she hurried towards the steps, just wanting to be away.

Behind her, she heard him repeat, as if uttering some form of mantra: 'She just left.'

***

'Tell me about Joanne Cameron,' McKay said. 'Whatever you've got.'

There was a pause at the other end of the line as DI Warren checked through his notes. 'We don't have a lot. She lived by herself in a flat in Brinnington, a suburb of Stockport. Not the most salubrious address. She worked in a credit control place.'

'Credit control?'

'Debt collection. Chasing unpaid bills, but business-to-business. Paid on commission. Hard work, I imagine.'

'And what's the story? Out on a bender in Manchester was what I heard.' 'We've spoken to this Jade Norris—the woman who responded to the TV appeal—this morning. She was a work colleague of Cameron's at the credit place. They went out last Friday night. Supposed to be some sort of girls' night out, apparently, but only the two of them turned up. They basically just got bladdered in various pubs around central Manchester. Norris copped off with some builder from Basingstoke. Cameron had been chatted up by one of his mates, so Norris assumed she'd done the same.'

'She didn't notice her friend had disappeared then?'

'Apparently not. Sounds like they were all pretty pissed by then. You know how it is on nights like that. You turn round and someone's buggered off. You don't necessarily think a lot of it.'

'Aye, I remember,' McKay said, with some feeling. 'Been a few years, though.'

'Me too.'

'What about these builders? You managed to track them down?'

'Give us a chance,' Warren said. 'I've only just got back from speaking to Norris. But she went back to the rented house some of them were sharing in Levenshulme and she's given us the address. Not sure whether the other guy lives there or not, but assume we won't have much difficulty finding him.'

'Norris hasn't kept in touch with her bloke, then?'

Warren laughed. 'I don't think it was that sort of relationship. From what she said, she buggered off first thing in the morning, hangover and all. Didn't even wait for breakfast.'

'You paint a touching scene,' McKay said. 'Anything else?'

'We've had the CSI out to look at her flat. No sign of any disturbance, but it looks like she's not been there for several days, which would tie in with her going missing on Friday. Also looks as if she wasn't planning to leave. Food going off in the fridge. Dishes in the sink. We spoke to a couple of neighbours, but it's the kind of place where nobody really talks to anyone else. Nobody had noticed she hadn't been around. Landlord knows nothing. Rent paid by standing order and not due for a couple of weeks.'

'This woman Norris told us that Cameron was Scottish. Any other info on that?'

'Not really. Norris confirmed that when we spoke to her this morning. She reckoned Cameron had a strong Scottish accent, but couldn't pin it down any further. Not like Billy Connolly seemed to be the best she could offer.'

'Aye, well, quite a few of us don't talk like Billy,' McKay said.

'She said she didn't think Cameron came from Glasgow or Edinburgh. Further north, she said. Maybe the Highlands, but she didn't know any more than that. Cameron had once told her where she was from, but it hadn't meant very much.'

'About as much as Brinnington and Levenshulme mean to me.' McKay finished scribbling down notes. 'That's great.'

'Don't imagine it's getting you very far.'

'It's a start. At least we've got a name.' He paused. 'Though we also have another victim.'

'Shit. You're kidding.'

'As of last night. Apparently the same MO. Young woman, same sort of age as the first two. As yet unidentified.'

'This really is one step forward, two steps back, isn't it?'

'That's the way it's feeling. But any step forward is welcome.'

'We'll get on to the builders this afternoon. I'll keep you posted.'

McKay ended the call and sat for a moment, staring blankly ahead of him. For the moment, they were keeping the third murder under wraps but they'd have to announce it to the media very shortly. Then the shit would really start to fly. That, he thought, was when Helena Grant would start to earn her keep.

'How're they doing?' McKay said to Horton. She'd just reappeared from the MIR where she'd been debriefing the team on the latest developments.

'You know. Plugging on.'

'All we can do. What's the word from Jock Henderson and his pals on our third lady?'

'MO the same as the first two. Chloroform burns around the mouth. Death by asphyxiation. Though obviously we'll have to wait on the post-mortem to confirm the details. Victim a white female aged probably late twenties. No particular distinguishing features other than a couple of minor scars and one off-the-shelf tattoo. We're doing the usual fingerprints and DNA stuff, but nothing back yet.'

'Fingers crossed she proves less difficult to ID than Joanne Cameron.' He filled her in on the conversation with DI Warren. 'We need to find out more about Cameron. I'll see if we can get access to her bank details and phone records. That might give us something. Even if it's only some of her former addresses. Her mate reckoned she'd said she was from the Highlands, but the mate was very fucking vague about any geography north of Preston.'

'Even if she was right, Highlands doesn't narrow it down much.'

'No, but if there is a pattern here, then maybe it's not coincidence she was brought back up here, alive or dead. Maybe she was a local girl.'

'There'll be a few Camerons up here, though, I imagine.'

'Aye, too right. We could maybe try the academies, though. See if any of them have a record of a Joanne Cameron of the right sort of age. We'll have to be discreet. We don't want word leaking out that she's our victim before we've announced it formally. And I'd like to find any next-of-kin before we do that.'

'Catch 22,' Horton said. 'If we announced the name of the victim, we'd find out if there was any next-of-kin soon enough.'

'Aye, but what a fucking way to find out your daughter or sister's been killed. It might come to that, but let's try anything else first.'

'You know your trouble, Alec,' she smiled. 'You're just a soft touch.'

'Aye,' he said, 'so I've been told. Now fuck off and make some fucking phone calls.'

CHAPTER TWENTY

Despite his earlier concerns, the afternoon proved much more fruitful than McKay had feared. The first sign of progress was a mid-afternoon call from Warren in Manchester.

'We've tracked down the builders,' he said. 'Easier than we expected. Checked out the address that Norris had given us. The two we wanted were at work but one of their mates was there. Off sick with the flu he claimed, but it looked to me like the flu you get after ten pints the night before. He told us where his mates were working and we tracked them down there.'

'Always good to catch them at work,' McKay observed. 'Makes them keener to tell you the truth so you bugger off before the boss loses his rag.'

'Too right. And I got the feeling that neither of them was exactly flavour of the month already. Lazy buggers, according to the site foreman.' Warren was obviously consulting his notes. 'Guy called Dave Bennett was the guy Norris was lucky enough to cop off with. Weaselly little toerag. Couldn't tell us much except to confirm what Norris had told us. Norris and Cameron had turned up at the pub together, already the worse for wear. Bennett spent the evening with his tongue in Norris's ear, and his mate Pete Graham spent the evening trying to get to first base with Cameron. Without much luck, apparently.'

'So what's Graham's version of events?'

'That around elevenish Norris announced she was heading home. Wanted to get the last train from Piccadilly. He tried to persuade her to stay longer, but no luck.'

'Any particular reason for her deciding to leave? Some fall-out with this guy Graham?'

'He reckons not. Said she'd been lukewarm all evening. Mind you, both these guys struck me as the opposite of irresistible. My guess is that Cameron just got sick of this oaf trying to paw her and decided to cut her losses.'

'She didn't bother to say goodbye to her mate?'

'Norris was otherwise engaged. And I'm guessing Cameron was feeling pissed off at the end of a miserable evening. She left her supposed mate to it and buggered off.'

'Sounds plausible enough. Graham didn't try to follow her?'

'Reckons not, and that sounds plausible too. It was pissing down. He stayed in the pub with various other mates who were still hanging about at the bar. Then when Bennett and Norris headed off for their night of passion, he went on to some nightclub with the others. They called over a couple of other guys who vouched for that. So I reckon Graham's telling the truth.'

'We don't know if Cameron ever got home that night?'

'Difficult to say. Her flat looks like she was expecting to go back there, but there's no way of knowing if she got back that night or if she went back and went missing sometime afterwards. The first might be more likely, but there's no way to be sure.'

'Neighbours have no recollection of her coming back?'

'Like I said, it's not that sort of place. No-one noticed anything, but I don't think they would have, whether or not she returned.'

'What about CCTV? Around the pub she was in? At the station? On that last train?'

'We can give it a go,' Warren said. 'But I suspect it'll be a waste of time. It was pissing with rain when she left the pub. You won't catch many faces on the street. As for the station—well, do you know Piccadilly? It's a big place and heaving on a Friday night. We might catch her face if she was passing, but the odds are against it.'

'And the train?'

'Can check. Some trains have CCTV. But that last train's always packed. Standing room only. Even if there was a camera on there, we'd be lucky to spot her.'

'And if we don't spot her, it proves nothing either way. Aye, I know,' McKay agreed morosely.

'We'll get them checked out anyway. You never know,' Warren said, in a voice that suggested you generally did. 'We've got her mobile phone number from Norris so we'll follow that up to see if there's any interesting call data. And the other news is that we've got the report back on the check we did on her flat.'

'Anything interesting?'

'Not much in itself. Like I said, there's no evidence of any crime scene there. So whatever happened to her, it didn't happen there. We didn't find much in the way of other information either. There was an old empty cheque book lying around, so we've got details of her bank account. We're in the process of contacting the bank to find out if there were any withdrawals after that Friday night, and anything else that might help us.'

'Previous addresses, too, if you can. Anything that will give us a clue where she came from.'

'Ah, well, I might have a tiny bit of information there.'

'Go on.'

'Like I say, there wasn't much in the flat. Not even a computer or a laptop. But one small thing we did find was a handful of books. Most of them just trashy paperbacks, but there were a couple of older hardbacks.' A pause, while Warren took another look at his notes. 'Little Women and the Catcher in the Rye, apparently.'

'Very literary. And?'

'Thing is, they were both old school editions. Books she'd presumably kept since she was at school herself. Both falling apart, so assume she'd kept them for sentimental reasons.'

'Come on then, you bastard,' McKay said. 'Don't string me along. What was the name of the school?'

Warren laughed. 'Place called Fortrose Academy. Mean anything to you?'

McKay took a breath. 'Oh, aye,' he said. 'That means something all right. A bit more than sodding Levenshulme, anyway.'

***

McKay began with a call directly through to the rector of Fortrose Academy, who fortunately was around and available, and explained the reasons for his call. He had little faith in the integrity of his fellow man, but he reasoned that, of all people, the rector of a local academy was unlikely to blab to the local media or anyone else. Particularly in this case when, as he'd stressed, the priority was to identify the next of kin.

The rector understood and instructed his secretary to help DI McKay obtain whatever information he needed. McKay asked for anything they had on one Joanne Cameron who would have left the school perhaps ten to fifteen years earlier. The next stage took slightly longer because the records pre-dated the school's current IT system. But within fifteen minutes the secretary had phoned back with the information requested.

'There you go,' McKay said to Horton. 'That's how to do it.'

'Yes, Alec. I do know how to use a phone. What have you got?'

'Last known address of Joanne Cameron's parents. Well, parent. Father was divorced. Interesting that he had custody. No details on the mother. Lived in Avoch.'

'We're sure this is the right Joanne Cameron?'

'Seems likely. She left the Academy twelve years ago. That would make her late twenties.'

'And if her father's no longer there?'

'May not be. But we've got some details. Thomas Cameron. Work contact details given as the BMW dealers in Inverness. Mechanic of some kind. If we get no joy in Avoch, at least we've some leads to follow up.' He rubbed his hands. 'It's a start, anyway. I'm heading on up to Avoch, then. Want to come?'

'Why not? I'm not making much progress here.'

The two of them were already heading out when DC Mary Graham poked her head around the door. 'Thought you'd want to know,' she said. 'We've just had some news.'

'I'm not sure how much excitement I can take in one day,' McKay said.

'Looks like we've identified the third victim.'

'Already?' Horton said. They were becoming accustomed to the glacial progress on this case to date. She'd almost forgotten this wasn't the norm. In most cases, you had everything you needed very quickly, often within the designated first 'golden hours' after the crime had been committed.

'She already had a record. Shoplifting in her late teens. Two months in prison. Name was Rhona Young. Last known address in Cromarty.'

'Funnily enough, we were just heading up to the Black Isle,' McKay said. 'Where all roads seem to be leading.'

CHAPTER TWENTY-ONE

The rain had fallen steadily since the previous night, and their journey up the A9 felt different from their previous visits. Then, just a few days before, spring had seemed to be turning into summer, promising days of sunshine and clear skies. McKay felt much more at home in this dense drizzling rain that suggested the brief summer was already past and all they had to look forward to was a protracted autumn before the inevitable return of winter. The Scottish year in all its glory.

The view from the Kessock Bridge was so restricted he could barely make out the grey waters of the firth below. As he turned off towards Munlochy, the surrounding fields were deep green, sodden from the pouring rain.

Avoch was the first village along the southern coast of the Black Isle. Historically, its economy had depended on fishing. The number and size of the boats had declined now, but there was still a fishing industry in the village, along with leisure boats taking the tourists out to see dolphins in the Moray Firth. It was mostly a working village rather than a destination for tourists, but an attractive enough place.

The address they were seeking was in a small estate at the western end of the village. It was a decent-looking bungalow, probably dating from the 1970s, with a wide-ranging view out over the Firth. It had been carefully maintained, with a neatly tended garden at the front. In the rainy late afternoon, the place looked unlit and deserted.

Without waiting for Horton to follow, McKay strode up the drive to the front door and pressed the bell, hearing the faint chime from somewhere within. There was no sign of any movement. As Horton joined him, he pressed the bell again, holding it for longer. 'If he's still working in Inverness we might well be too early,' commented McKay.

'Can I help you?'

The voice was from somewhere to their right. McKay straightened and looked around. An elderly man in a beige cardigan was peering at them from the doorway of the bungalow next door. The estate was sufficiently upmarket that the two houses were not identical.

'We're looking for Mr Cameron.'

'He won't be back yet. Doesn't get back till about five-thirty. From Inverness, you know.' The man seemed happy to share any detail he knew with this pair of strangers.

McKay took a step out of the porch and looked at the man, who was standing well back out of the rain. He looked to be in his late seventies, his wispy grey hair combed carefully over a largely bald head. 'He should be back later, then?' McKay asked.

'Should be,' the man agreed. 'Is his wife not there?'

'Seems to be no-one in.' Cameron had obviously re-married in the interim.

The man made a play of looking at his watch. 'She'll have gone out somewhere with the girls, then.'

'Girls?'

'Two daughters. Lovely girls. Very polite.'

'Aye, of course,' McKay said. 'The girls.'

'Anything I can do?' the man said.

'We really need to speak to Mr Cameron.'

'Can I take a message at all?'

'Thank you. But we'll call back later.'

'Shall I tell him you were here?'

McKay shook his head. 'There's really no need. It's not urgent.'

'Ah, no, well. I like to help if I can.'

McKay was already leading Horton back down the drive towards the car. The man was still gazing after them as they pulled away back down towards the main road.

'Nosy neighbour,' McKay said.

'He was just lonely. I'm assuming we're heading to Cromarty, by the way?'

'We might as well. Let's see if we have any more luck tracking down Rhona Young's family. By the time we've done that, we should be right to catch our friend on his return from work.'

On a fine day, the drive to Cromarty could be an inspirational trip through sunlit woodlands and golden fields. Today, it offered little more than a haze of grey. On the far side of Rosemarkie, they saw the police tape still blocking the tree-lined driveway down to the residential home where Rhona Young's body had been discovered. The examiners were still there, along with a couple of McKay's own team, working their way through the large building in the hope of finding some further leads.

Cromarty had always struck McKay as an odd place, even by the standards of the Black Isle. It was picturesque, full of multi-coloured houses and narrow, inviting streets that afforded a tantalising glimpse of private gardens and courtyards. There were the usual touristy cafes and bijou craft shops, and in summer the place was busy with holiday-makers from the surrounding areas.

But the view out over the Cromarty Firth was largely an industrial one, dominated by the oil platforms brought into dry dock at Nigg for repair or storage. There were facilities over there for oil processing and cargo handling, and it provided a thriving industrial centre. The effect should have been contradictory but was somehow complementary, the platforms adding their own austere beauty to the land- and seascape.

Their destination was an Edwardian terraced house on one of the narrow streets in the centre of the village. It was impossible to park outside, so Horton found a spot in a nearby side road and they both hurried across the street. 'Let's hope this bugger's in, then,' McKay muttered as he ducked his head against the ceaseless rain.

In fact, the door was answered almost immediately. A young man with a shaven head dressed in a checked shirt and jeans blinked at them through thick designer spectacles. The sort of arty type the place attracted, McKay thought. But this man was too young to have a daughter in her late twenties.

'We're looking for a Mr Young?'

'Not me, I'm afraid.' He frowned, thinking. 'He used to live here. But that was years ago. I'm afraid I can't really—'

McKay pulled out his warrant card and looked up at the heavy sky. 'May we come inside for a moment? Easier to talk out of the rain.'

'Of course. Though as I say—'

McKay brushed past him. 'I don't want to make a mess. Are we best in the kitchen?'

'Probably. Brewster. My name, I mean.'

'Good to meet you, Mr Brewster. Through here?' McKay, keen to get out of the wet, had already made his way into the kitchen and was warming himself by a radiator. The room was decorated with pictures of musicians—they were presumably musicians, since they were depicted playing an array of instruments. But the faces meant nothing to McKay.

'How can I help you?' Brewster asked.

'We're trying to track down Mr Young. We have this as the last address on our files. I don't suppose you have any information that might help us locate him?'

Brewster was looking confused. 'I think you're probably too late for that. I assumed—'

McKay caught Horton's eye. 'What do you mean?'

'Well—' Brewster stopped. 'I mean, I thought you'd have known.'

McKay sighed. 'I think you're going to have to start from the beginning. My colleague and I really have no idea what you're talking about. Which I suspect may be our failing.' He looked at Horton who shrugged her agreement.

'I just assumed—'

'That the police were a perfectly co-ordinated machine? Aye, it's an impression we like to give.'

'Well, I bought this place about five years ago. It was a real bargain, and I wasn't sure why at first. Then I got talking to some of the locals and found out the back-story.'

'Go on.'

'Archie Young. He was the previous owner—well, you know that. Apparently, he killed himself here.' Brewster pointed towards the kitchen door. 'In the sitting room. Overdose. Nothing gory.' He spoke as if that made all the difference.

McKay frowned. 'And you thought we should have known about that?'

'No, of course not. Not that in itself. But it was after his arrest that he committed suicide. He taught at one of the local primary schools. He was arrested for downloading child pornography.'

'Images of child abuse,' Horton corrected, softly. 'We don't treat it as pornography.'

'Well, he was arrested. From what I understand the investigation was still continuing, but then—'

'He killed himself,' McKay said. 'Which, I suppose, may or may not have been an admission of guilt. When would this have been? You bought the place five years ago?'

'It had been standing empty for a year or so before that. So probably six, seven years ago.'

McKay was wondering who deserved a bollocking for this. There should have been a flag on Rhona Young's file. Someone should have made a connection between father and daughter.

'What about his family?' Horton was asking.

'He was living alone, as far as I know,' Brewster said. 'There was some story about his wife having left him, but I don't know the details. Not really my business, you know?'

'We're very grateful for what you've been able to tell us, Mr Brewster,' Horton said. 'The full details will no doubt be on our files. We'll check on what you've told us but it's just a routine matter. Looks like we can scratch him from our list.'

***

They were still early for their intended meeting with Thomas Cameron, so Horton pulled off the main road in Rosemarkie and took the narrow road past the Plough Inn to the waterfront. She pulled into one of the parking spaces overlooking the sea and they sat—like an old married couple, McKay thought—staring out at the teeming rain. The tide was in, but it was impossible to see more than fifty or so metres across the leaden water. The far side of the Firth was invisible.

'What did you make of that?' she asked.

'Some bugger'll get my toe up his arse for failing to link the files,' McKay said. 'That's the first thing. Second thing is we do seem to be uncovering something of a pattern.'

'That was what was occurring to me. We need to check out Young's story. Sounds as if his wife had left him before all this happened. And presumably the daughter too?'

'Which raises the question of why the wife left. If Young really was downloading child abuse images, was he abusive himself?'

'It's a lot of ifs,' Horton said. 'And it doesn't explain how any of this links with the daughter's killing. Except that Young's no longer a suspect.'

'And there's no sign of any connection between our victims, other than that they came from this area and the first two ended up in Manchester. They don't seem to have known each other, up here or down there. So what's the link?'

They sat in silence watching the endless rain washing down the windscreen. In the previous days, the place would have been busy with holidaymakers, families playing on the beach, children eating ice-creams from the van at the end of the road. Today, except for a single hardy dog-walker, the seafront was deserted.

Eventually, Horton said: 'You remember that missing woman last year? In Fortrose?'

'Lizzie Hamilton,' McKay said without hesitation. 'What about her?'

'I don't know. There was something about that that seemed similar to these cases.'

McKay shrugged. 'We don't even know that anything happened to her. She wasn't local in the way these women are. She never ended up in Manchester, as far as we know. Doesn't seem much similarity to me.'

'She was a similar character,' Horton persisted. 'No close family ties. Estranged from her father. Rootless drifter type. Vanished in the same way, as if she hadn't been expecting to leave.'

'What are you suggesting? That her body's out there somewhere, surrounded by roses and candles?'

'I don't know. It just keeps coming back to me.'

'Aye, well. Me too, since you mention it. But I don't see how it helps.'

She turned on the ignition and switched the heater up to full-blast in an effort to clear the fogged windows. 'Time for us to give Cameron another try?'

'Why not? But do us a favour. Let's check there's a car in the drive before we stop. I don't want to find myself having another conversation with that bloody neighbour.'

***

As it turned out, there were two cars in the drive, a newish BMW 4x4 and an older Nissan. The door opened before they'd reached the porch and a middle-aged man peered at them suspiciously through the rain. 'Can I help you?'

McKay held out his warrant card. 'Police. Can we step inside?'

Cameron looked genuinely startled. Whoever he might have been expecting, McKay thought, we were the last people he wanted. 'Aye, yes, of course. Nasty afternoon…' He waved them past into the warmth of the house.

It was a decent place, well-furnished in expensive-looking taste, not that McKay was any judge. Cameron was a well-built man in his mid-fifties, with closely-cropped grey hair. He looked like someone who'd once been a sportsman but had now put on a few too many pounds. He was dressed in a slightly bulging back polo shirt and a pair of expensive-looking slacks.

'How can I help you? Old Morrie said someone had called round, but I didn't realise—' He ushered them through into the sitting-room. 'We can talk in here. My wife's in the kitchen with the girls.'

'It's about your daughter, Mr Cameron. Joanne, I mean.'

The colour had drained from Cameron's face. 'Joanne?'

'You might want to sit down,' McKay said. 'I'm afraid it's bad news.'

Cameron lowered himself on to the settee. 'Go on.'

'You may have seen the reports of the body found near Rosemarkie, Mr Cameron?'

'Aye, in the cave there.' He stopped. 'Christ. Joanne?'

'We think so,' McKay said. 'We'll need your help in confirming that. I'm sorry.'

Cameron had buried his face in his hands. But in the moment before McKay had seen his expression. There were echoes of the way that Scott had responded to the news of his daughter's death. After a moment, Cameron looked up. His eyes were dry. 'How did it happen?'

'We don't yet know the full story, Mr Cameron. Again, you may be able to help us in piecing it together.' He lowered himself into an armchair opposite Cameron. Horton did the same. 'Have you seen your daughter recently?'

Cameron looked up. 'Not for a few years.'

'Did you have some sort of falling out?'

'I don't know,' Cameron said. 'I mean, not as such. There was no grand argument. We just didn't get on.'

'Any particular reason?'

Cameron had dropped his head into his hands again. 'I was going to say you'd have to ask her. But you can't, can you?' He looked for a second as if he'd made a joke. 'Her mother left me. Twenty-odd years ago. Just walked out one day. I don't know where she went. She wouldn't give me an address.' He shrugged. 'She tried to get custody of Joanne. Came up with all kinds of lies about me. But I got the best lawyers I could and fought her every step of the way. And I *won*.' He spoke the last word with a bitterness that made McKay start. 'In the end, I won because she'd just walked out. No reason, no excuse. No word where she was going. I don't even know what she lived on. She didn't know how to work. She only knew how to sponge off me.'

'So you looked after your daughter as a single father?'

'Aye. I kept her. She was mine.'

'But then she left?'

'Ungrateful little bitch. Walked out one day when I was at work. Just like her mother.'

'How old was she then?'

'Seventeen. Eighteen, maybe. I forget.'

'Where did she go?'

'Inverness at first, apparently.'

'To her mother?'

'No. She had no idea where her mother was, any more than I did.'

McKay wondered whether that was true. Perhaps, like Mrs Scott, the mother had a closer connection with her daughter than her husband knew. 'Where was she staying?'

'Christ knows. With some friends. She wouldn't tell me who. Wouldn't give me her address.'

'Did you keep in contact?'

'Only for a week or two. She was after money at first. She'd just finished at school. Hadn't found a job. Wanted me to bail her out.' He shook his head. 'You can imagine my response.'

Only too well, McKay thought. 'And after that?'

'I tried to contact her a couple of times on the mobile number I had, but it was unobtainable. That was it.'

'You didn't contact the police?'

'What would you have done? She'd left home of her own free-will. She was nearly an adult.'

'And that was the last you saw of her?'

'Aye. Until you two turned up tonight, hadn't heard a word about her.'

'You didn't know she'd been living in Manchester?'

'News to me. But then she could have been living in Outer Mongolia for all I knew. Or cared.'

'You've remarried?' This was Horton.

Cameron looked at her as if he'd forgotten she was there. 'Aye, five years ago. Receptionist from the office. Divorcee. Two bonnie daughters.' Cameron stopped. 'Murdered, you reckon?'

'It looks that way,' McKay said. 'The investigation's continuing.'

'You've got two of them, haven't you? Bodies, I mean. So you reckon it's somebody local?'

'We're keeping an open mind,' Horton said. 'The first step is for us to confirm that this is your daughter. We'll need you to make a formal ID.'

'There likely to be any doubt?'

'We don't think so, I'm afraid. But we don't have definitive confirmation.'

'I see. So what do I need to do?'

'We'll make arrangements for you to view the body, Mr Cameron. It'll be at the Raigmore. You work in Inverness, I understand. Will you have any difficulty getting time off work? An hour or so is all we'll need. Tomorrow if possible.'

'Aye. Reckon they'll give me an hour off to view my own daughter's corpse, don't you?'

'Aye. I should think so.'

'Then what?'

'We'll need to take a statement from you, Mr Cameron. Background.'

'We could do that now. I've told you most of what I know already.'

'We'll do it properly, shall we? At Police HQ. Perhaps after you've completed the ID.'

Cameron was staring back at him. It was an expression that in a Glasgow bar might have suggested a fight was imminent. 'Fine by me,' he said.

'If you let DS Horton have a contact number, we'll call you first thing to confirm the arrangements,' McKay said. He pushed himself slowly to his feet. 'My sincere condolences on your loss, Mr Cameron. I appreciate this must be a shock.' He paused. 'Can I ask about Joanne's mother?'

'What about her?'

'Do you have any contact address for her now? We'll need to get in touch with her.'

'Last I heard she was in Edinburgh somewhere. But that was at the time of the divorce.'

'Do you still have that address?'

'Aye. Somewhere, probably. I'll dig it out.'

'I think she'd want to know, Mr Cameron, don't you?'

'Maybe. That's up to her.'

McKay stood for a moment, as if intending to offer some response. Finally, he said only: 'We won't disturb you any longer then, Mr Cameron. We'll be in touch in the morning.'

He and Horton didn't speak until they were heading back out of the estate on to the main road. McKay felt as if he'd been holding his breath for the last half-hour.

'He was a piece of fucking work, wasn't he?'

Horton had her eyes fixed on the wet road. 'Fits the pattern, though, doesn't he?'

'You reckon?'

'Respectable-looking household. Daughter has fall out with father. Walks out. Mother's already walked out.' She turned on the car headlights. It was almost as gloomy as a winter's evening. 'Question is why. Why'd the mother walk out? Why'd the daughter go?'

'I think we can guess the answer to that. Or part of it.' McKay shook his head and gave a theatrical shudder. 'What worries me is that new family of his. Jesus.'

'We need to get social services to check them out.,' Horton said. 'But we've no evidence. We don't know.'

McKay was staring out of the window, watching the rain-sodden fields of the Black Isle, the dark waters of Munlochy Bay visible to their left. 'We do, though, don't we?' he said, quietly. 'We do know.'

CHAPTER TWENTY-TWO

'I still think you should jack it in.'

'Give me one good reason.'

'Because he's a creep.'

'That's not a good reason. Plenty of people are creeps.'

They were sitting in the pub bar in The Anderson, engaged in what was as close as they ever came to a row. Kelly sometimes thought it might be easier if they just came out and shouted at each other, the way most couples seemed to. As it was, it often turned into this kind of low-level sniping, ostensibly good-natured but with each of them becoming more and more entrenched.

Jim Anderson, the American owner, was engaged in some activity behind the bar, no doubt trying to ignore the whispered exchanges in the far corner. He tolerated them ordering two Cokes rather than one of his specialist beers, given that they wouldn't actually be old enough to order alcohol in his native Philadelphia. Greg's dad was a regular here and was one of the few people who ever chose a Captain Beefheart track on the bar's typically idiosyncratic jukebox. 'You kids OK?' Jim called, mainly just to remind them he was still present.

Kelly waved back. 'We're fine. Just having an argument about creepy pub landlords. Present company definitely not included.'

'Well, that's a relief. You're the one working in The Caley, then?' He continued arranging bottles of some Belgian wheat beer with his back to them. Jim managed to combine the avuncular with the mildly acerbic, and Kelly was never sure how seriously to take him. But it was clear that, as ever in this small community, word had got around.

'Are you going to warn me off as well?'

'None of my business. You seem smart enough to make your own decisions.'

'There you are,' Kelly said to Greg. 'Not everyone lacks faith in me.'

'I don't lack faith in you. But you've said yourself that this Gorman guy's weird.'

'Nothing I can't handle.'

They'd met up today after her stint at the bar, and headed down to Chanonry Point to try to spot the dolphins. When you lived up here, it was easy to become blasé about the school of dolphins that lived in the Firth, but whenever she saw them Kelly felt surprised and cheered by their sheer playfulness. It was the kind of thing she needed after the gloom of the Caledonian Bar. In the event, the rain hadn't lessened and so they'd done little more than have a quick scurry along the beach, enjoying the driving rain on their skin and the blast of damp air from the Firth. They'd ended up sitting in the car, munching sandwiches from the Co-op, patiently watching for any signs of the elusive dolphins. On their way back they'd come into The Anderson, mainly seeking shelter and warmth. Its deliberately ramshackle charm was a world away from the seedy gloom of the Caledonian.

'That's what they all say,' Greg observed, 'right up to the point when the mad axe-murderer strikes. I've seen the films.'

'If you say so.' She contemplated the remains of her Coke. 'It's strange, though. The way he keeps insisting she just left. Like he's protesting a bit too much.'

'You think her body's interred just below the cask of Deuchars in the cellar?'

'No, of course not. I just get the sense that there's something he wants to say. Something he wants to talk about.'

'That he dismembered her body and left it in the lockers at Inverness Station?'

'It's not funny.' She knew he was joking only to cover his own anxieties. The police were being cagey about the bodies that had been found, but everyone was getting jittery. She'd heard there'd been police around the previous night outside Rosemarkie, blue lights up on the driveway to the old retirement home. Nobody knew what the story there was—probably just another break-in—but the lurid rumours were circulating already. Her own parents, normally paragons of good sense on such matters, were getting anxious about her being out and about on her own. For her own part, she wasn't worried in daylight hours, but she had no inclination to be out after dark without Greg.

'Don't try and make yourself his confidante, that's all. He'll get the wrong idea.'

'I'm not going to give him any opportunity to get any ideas at all, wrong or right.'

'If you say so,' he said. 'Shall we push the boat out and have another Coke?' The bar was starting to fill up with the dog-walkers who used their dogs as an excuse for an early evening pint. Given the rain, this evening's walk was likely to have been even more token than usual.

'Yeah, why not?' she said. 'You only live once.'

***

McKay arrived home around seven-thirty. He and Horton had finished off at the office on their return from the Black Isle. He'd worked through a trail of pointless e-mails, while Horton had trawled through the records trying to find information on Archie Young. The basic file hadn't been hard to find. As Brewster had said, Young had been a primary school teacher and, at the time of his arrest, acting head-teacher at one of the Isle schools. It was unclear why suspicion had initially fallen on Young, although some form of anonymous accusation had been sent to the school's parent council. Young's details had then been identified as part of a wider national investigation. Young had been arrested and his computer and laptop seized.

The investigation into Young had come to a halt following his suicide. Strictly speaking, particularly given Young's profession, Horton would have expected the enquiry to continue. If illegal material had been discovered on Young's systems, a key question would have been whether his proclivities had been confined to the downloaded material, or whether he'd acted on them in his day-today dealings with children. But that question—and indeed the initial question of whether any illegal materials had been present on the computers—had not been pursued. Horton's impression was that the investigation had been discreetly allowed to lapse. She didn't necessarily draw any sinister inferences from that. Most likely, it simply wouldn't have been a priority once Young was out of the picture. She could imagine that it might have been easier for all parties for the story simply to be airbrushed from history.

Frustratingly, there was nothing in the file about Young's wife or daughter. He was described in the notes as 'single', with no indication whether he might be divorced or separated. The next-of-kin was shown as Young's father, the address a retirement home in Inverness. Horton had followed that up, but the father had died several years earlier and the home had no other information. There was no mention of a daughter. This at least explained why no-one had made the link between Archie and Rhona Young. No doubt if the investigation had proceeded, this background would have been uncovered. As it was, they were left with an unhelpful dead-end. As with Cameron, the question was why and in what circumstances Young's wife had left him.

McKay agreed there was little more they could do that night. He'd initially been surprised he had no recollection of the Young case, but he could see now that it had barely surfaced long enough to reach the attention of anyone but the immediate investigating officers, even locally. 'We can do more digging tomorrow,' he told Horton. The investigating officer, then a DI, was still around, and had now apparently reached the dizzying heights of superintendent in Edinburgh. 'You can make him squirm by asking him why the fuck he let the case drop,' McKay pointed out helpfully.

He'd phoned ahead to let Chrissie know that, at least by his own standards, he was expecting to be home early. She'd greeted the news with limited enthusiasm, but said she'd have a cottage pie waiting. When he turned up only thirty or so minutes later than scheduled, she was in the kitchen checking the oven. As he entered, she made a visible point of checking her watch before pouring herself another glass of wine.

'Sorry,' he said. 'You know how it is.'

'Aye,' she said. 'I should do after all these years, shouldn't I?'

As so often, he felt as if she was spoiling for a fight, but tonight he determined to let it wash over him. He hadn't the energy or inclination for another slanging match. 'How's the pie?'

'Just waiting for it to brown. Peas?'

'Why not?' He pulled down a wine glass and poured himself a decent measure, wondering how much Chrissie had had before his return. This bottle was a third empty, but he suspected there might be another in the bin.

'How's it going?' she said.

'We're getting somewhere. But slowly.'

'There's a third body, then,' she said. They'd made the announcement late afternoon. Grant and the powers-that-be had decided they couldn't keep the news under wraps much longer. Otherwise, someone—the security guy who'd found the body, one of the paramedics who'd been on site—would leak it, deliberately or inadvertently. Then the media would be on to them for withholding information which might have an impact on public safety. Like the media cared a bugger for public safety. In the end, comms had issued a bald press release sufficiently late in the day that the media wouldn't have time to do much digging before the early evening news broadcasts. 'What did they say?'

'Just said a body had been discovered near Rosemarkie. That you were treating it as an unlawful killing. There was a bit of speculation as to whether it might be linked to the other cases, but they didn't make a lot of that.' She left the peas to boil and sat down next to him.

'They will, though,' McKay commented dourly. 'You wait for tomorrow's tabloids.'

They sat in silence until Chrissie rose to check the oven. 'Shall we eat in here?'

'Might as well.' McKay rose to fetch the plates and cutlery, setting two places opposite each other at the kitchen table. Chrissie carried out the steaming pie, and he watched while she doled out ladlefuls for each of them.

'Nice pie,' he said.

'Ach, it's tatties and mince, isn't it?' Not that there's anything wrong with that.'

There was more silence while McKay topped up their wine glasses. After a moment, she said: 'We can't go on like this, Alec. Dancing round each other. Walking on eggshells. Not daring to say anything for fear of saying the wrong thing. Both of us spoiling for a fight all the time, but doing our damnedest to avoid it because we know we'll say things we'll both regret.'

'Is that how you see it?'

'That's how we both see it, Alec. You just won't say it out loud.'

He had no response to that. He wasn't even sure she was right, not exactly. But there was enough truth for him not to want to engage with it. Which, he supposed, proved her point. 'What do you suggest?'

'What I've suggested before. Counselling. Couples counselling. You said we should give it a go.'

He felt the familiar tightening in his chest. He'd almost forgotten he'd agreed to her suggestion. That he'd actually said— God help him—that it was all they'd got left. 'Aye, if you say so.'

'You said so,' she insisted. 'So I've done it.'

He looked up, a forkful of pie halfway to his mouth. 'You've done what?'

'I've made an appointment for us. Tomorrow.'

'Jesus, Chrissie, you know how busy I am. I can't just go swanning off—'

'Six-thirty,' she said. 'He does early evening sessions.'

'Even so, I can't—'

'Do you want to make this work or not?' Her voice was threateningly even. 'Are you even prepared to give it a try?'

'For God's sake, Chrissie, that's not the point—'

'It's exactly the point, Alec. It's this or nothing.'

He slumped back in his chair, knowing he was defeated. 'Aye. OK. We'll give it a go. Who is this guy? Don't tell me you found him in the Yellow Pages.'

'I spoke to the GP. He recommended him. Does a lot of couples counselling work. But also has a specialism in working with troubled young people. Doctor thought he might also be able to give us some insights into— well, you know.'

'Aye,' McKay said, wearily. 'Anything's possible, I suppose.'

'Give it a go, Alec. A real go, I mean. Not just lip service.'

'I will. Look, I want this to work as much as you do. I don't want us rubbing along in pained silence. Always blaming each other to salve our own guilt.' He took her hand, conscious that he couldn't recall the last time he'd done that.

She looked back at him. 'Last chance saloon and all that. But, yes, let's give it a shot.'

CHAPTER TWENTY-THREE

McKay was in the office by seven-thirty the next morning, but Helena Grant was already waiting for him.

'Shit. Fan,' she said, succinctly, and tossed the *Daily Record* on to his desk. 'You seen this?'

The headline was 'Black Isle Killer.' McKay didn't bother to read the story. 'It was bound to come.'

'Aye, I know. But my phone's been ringing off the hook already. Chief. Deputy chief. Another deputy chief. Assistant chief. Assistant deputy chief. Chief super. Head of comms. You name it.'

'You talk to them so I don't have to,' McKay pointed out.

'Be thankful for small mercies. We need a breakthrough, though. Something. Anything.'

'Ach, it's like wading through treacle. We're building up a picture of these women's lives, but it's slow going. There's a definite pattern emerging.' He outlined the ideas that he and Horton had discussed after their interviews the previous day.

'You think this guy Cameron might be a suspect?'

'It's conceivable. He's the most likely candidate so far. Scott might have had a motive, but I can't see him coping physically with what was involved in these killings. Young's obviously out of the picture. Cameron's fit and able enough. There was clearly no love lost between him and his daughter, whatever the reasons. He drives a powerful-looking 4x4, so he wouldn't have had any difficulty getting the second body out to the shoreline...'

'But?'

'But why would he kill the other two? It's possible to come up with a scenario in which he might have killed his own daughter. Maybe she turned up out of the blue. Maybe threatened to expose him, if he is an abuser. Maybe threatened to tell his new wife, assuming that she hasn't already guessed. Something along those lines. And he decides the best thing to do is to silence her. I can buy that, probably. But why the other two?'

'Because he's off his head? You said he seemed odd.'

'Aye, there was definitely something not right about him. Especially the way he talked about his daughter. As if she was his property. He didn't seem able or willing to conceal that, even talking to us. But odd enough to kill two complete strangers? I don't know.'

'If they really were strangers,' Grant pointed out.

'We've found no evidence of any links so far. They seem to have lived fairly parallel lives, but there's no sign to date that they knew each other or even had any common acquaintances.'

'It's possible, though, surely? They all come from within a few miles of each other.'

'Of course it's possible. And if Cameron were predatory, it's conceivable they might all have been victims. But that's just speculation at the moment. Cameron's got no kind of record, any more than his daughter did.'

'So where next?'

'We'll interview Cameron after he's ID'd his daughter. Just to take a statement at this stage. We've no grounds to treat him as a suspect yet. We'll carry on plugging away at the backgrounds of the other two. We don't know where Rhona Young was living. We'll ask GMP to keep tabs on the misper lists in case she crops up there. We could do another request for info through the media.'

'Let's hold that back for the moment,' Grant said. 'We'll look a bunch of numpties if that's all we keep doing. People will think it's because we don't have a clue what to do otherwise.'

'Aye, well, we don't really, do we?'

'No, but don't let on. Christ knows where that would lead.'

'The other question,' McKay mused, 'is why Manchester? Is it just a coincidence that that's where the first two victims were living, or does it have some significance? If it turns out Young was living there too, we'll have to assume it's part of the pattern. But why?'

'God knows. It's one of the places you can fly to from Inverness? There aren't that many. London. Birmingham. Bristol, I think.'

'Bloody Stornoway and Kirkwall. But, yes, maybe.'

She pushed herself wearily to her feet. 'OK. Well, keep plugging away. I know you're doing your best—'

'And my best is bloody good,' McKay said, 'as you well know.'

'Aye, well, keep blowing your own trumpet, Alec, because no other bugger's going to blow it for you.' She stopped at the door and turned back with a smile. 'And, yes, it bloody well is. But we still need a miracle. As soon as you like.'

***

Thomas Cameron had confirmed that the body in the mortuary was indeed that of his daughter, Joanne. His interest in the matter seemed almost non-existent. It was as if he'd been asked to confirm some detail in a report or an item of expenditure in a bill.

Afterwards, Horton had driven him back to HQ so that she and McKay could take a statement. Although it was no more than a witness statement at this stage, McKay felt that both of them should be present in case anything more substantive should emerge. Given Cameron's taciturn demeanour, Horton wasn't hopeful. McKay had set up the meeting, as formally as possible, in one of the interview rooms.

'Can I ask you about your relationship with your daughter, Mr Cameron?' he began.

He could almost see Cameron tense. 'I don't see how that's relevant.'

'It may not be,' McKay said. 'At this stage, we're simply trying to build up as full a picture of your daughter as we can. We've very little information other than her address and occupation at the time of her death.'

'Then you're one up on me,' Cameron said.

'So it's helpful to gain some understanding of her background,' McKay persisted. 'You said she continued to live with you after her mother left?'

'Aye. I told you all this yesterday. Her mother walked out. We had a bastard of a fight in the courts. And I won.' Even now, he sounded smug. McKay had already noticed that Cameron seemed unwilling even to speak his ex-wife's name.

'Why didn't the court grant custody to Joanne's mother?'

'Because she was a waste of space. She'd always been unreliable. Had walked out a couple of times before. She was on anti-depressants and Christ knows what else. She'd had a couple of suicide attempts—'

'All while married to you?' Horton tried not to make the question sound too pointed.

Cameron laughed. 'Aye, I suppose. But she'd always been flaky. It wasn't hard for my lawyers to demonstrate she wasn't a fit mother.'

'You said yesterday she levelled accusations at you,' McKay said. 'What kinds of accusations?'

Cameron shifted uncomfortably on the hard plastic chair. 'Christ, you name it.'

'Did she claim you were abusive?'

'Among other things.'

'Towards her or your daughter?'

Cameron leaned across the table, jabbing a finger angrily towards McKay. 'What the fuck is this? What's this got to do with Joanne's death?'

'I don't know, Mr Cameron,' McKay said, patiently. 'I'm just trying to establish some background.'

'There's nothing to establish,' Cameron said. 'She just threw all kind of mud in the hope something would stick. Like I say, the court found in my favour, so you can draw your own conclusions.'

'And why did your wife leave you in the first place?'

'Like I say, she was a flake. Mad as a box of frogs. I didn't realise till it was too late.'

'And your daughter? She walked out as well?'

'She was as mad as her mother, in her own way. Two of a kind. Always had been. When Joanne was small, her mother used to take her off to have fucking fantasy tea parties at the beach, like two kids playing together. And it wasn't Joanne who took the fucking teddy-bears and dolls. Joanne ended up like her mother. Hadn't a clue what she wanted to do with her life. Eating disorders. Depression. You name it.'

'But you weren't concerned when she left?'

'Of course I was concerned. But there was nothing much I could do, was there? She was an adult. She could make her own decisions.'

'You didn't try to find her?'

'I thought she'd come crawling back eventually. Those first couple of weeks she kept calling and asking for money. I didn't think she'd be capable of looking after herself.'

'You don't know where she went? I mean, in those initial weeks.'

'She never told me. Just kept asking me to transfer money to her account. I told her where she could stick her account. I got the impression she was staying with a mate, but I don't know who.'

'Locally?'

'I'd guess so. She couldn't drive, so I can't see how she'd have got very far to start with.'

'But you've no ideas who she might have stayed with? No friends from those days? No-one she was particularly close to?'

'I never thought she had many friends. She was too screwed up. Always seemed a bit of a loner. But I suppose there must have been someone.'

McKay nodded. 'If you come up with any ideas, if you think of anyone, please let us know. Even if it's a name from years ago, it might give us a lead. We need to find out who her friends were, what kind of circles she moved in.'

'You'll be the first to know,' Cameron said.

'You've not kept anything of hers?' Horton suggested. 'Old diaries, notebooks, anything that might potentially be useful to us?'

'I cleared the whole place out when I remarried,' Cameron said. 'Burnt the lot.'

'What about Joanne's mother?' McKay said. 'Do you think she might have kept in touch with Joanne? Is it possible that's where Joanne went?'

'Your guess is as good as mine. She made no effort to keep in touch with me, but that's hardly surprising.'

'You've no recent contact details for your ex-wife?'

'Nothing.' Cameron fumbled in his jacket pocket. 'I've got the old address I promised you. Where she was living at the time of the divorce. Address in Edinburgh. She was staying with an old school friend who'd moved down there to work. But that's all I know.'

'Thank you,' McKay said. 'That may be a useful start for us.'

'Maybe,' Cameron said. 'I know she's no longer there. And her friend's long gone too. But good luck.'

'Anything else you can tell us about your daughter, Mr Cameron? Anything that might give us some sort of lead?'

'I don't think so. I've not seen her for ten years or more.'

'Can you think of any reason why anyone might want to kill her?'

'Could be a thousand reasons. She always struck me as the type who'd make a natural victim. You know what I mean?'

'Not really,' McKay said. 'For us, a victim is just that.'

'Aye, well. You never met her.' Cameron seemed to have switched off, as if the interview was already over. 'Anything else you want from me?'

McKay was tempted to string him along with further questions. But his sense was that they'd get no more out of Cameron for the moment. The man was an undoubted arsehole, and possibly an abusive one, but McKay wasn't convinced there was anything more to him than that. They needed something more if they were going to take this any further. 'No, that's fine for today, Mr Cameron. We'll probably need to talk to you again as the investigation proceeds. I take it that won't be a problem?'

'Talk away,' Cameron said. 'Just don't expect me to have any new answers.'

CHAPTER TWENTY-FOUR

'What do you reckon?' Horton said, once they'd offloaded Cameron. Josh Carlisle had offered to ferry him back to his place of work. Carlisle was something of a petrol-head, who'd welcome the chance to stroke the shiny new BMWs.

'I reckon we're getting nowhere,' McKay said.

'You don't think Cameron's our man?'

'Well, he *could* be. He's our best fit so far.'

'We could try for a warrant. Check his house. His car.'

'On what basis? We've nothing. Just a clear dislike for his ex-wife and a lack of interest in his estranged daughter. If we went with those, we'd have a thousand candidates.'

'He's an abuser.'

'We *think* he's an abuser. OK, we know he is, you and I, with our well-honed coppers' intuition. But we've no evidence for it. We haven't even met his second wife or his step-daughters. I can't see us getting a warrant without something more. And don't forget that, as far as the public's concerned, he'll be the bereaved father. If we harass him and find nothing, it won't look good.'

'So what then?'

'I don't think we can do much more than keep a close eye on him. See what we can do to track down this ex-wife. Get something more that means we can bring him in again.'

They both sat in glum silence for a moment. Finally McKay said: 'We've got to find the connection. What is it that links these three women?'

'They're local. Looks like they were all abused. All left home at the first chance, two at least to Manchester.'

'So did they meet? Did they know each other? Did they have some common connection? How did the killer know all of them?'

'Maybe it's not that personal,' Horton said.

'But the candles and roses suggest something personal. Something more than a set of random killings. Some sort of tribute, commemoration?'

'OK. So that suggests some connection. But we're a long way from finding out what it might be. There's no sign it's anything to do with what they were doing at the time of their deaths. We're still working through the list of names that Danny Reynolds gave us for Katy Scott, but not getting much joy. The few we've contacted barely remember her. Same with the other two. They barely seem to have made a dent during their time on earth.'

'Very poetic,' McKay observed, dourly. 'Christ, it's a depressing thought, isn't it? You're here and then you're gone, and no bugger even notices.'

'Maybe that's what our killer thought, too,' Horton said. 'At least these three were provided with candles and flowers. Someone wanted them remembered.'

***

When she heard on the news that they'd found a third body—in the old retirement home up beyond Rosemarkie of all places—she'd almost been tempted to jack in the job. That was what Greg would have preferred, even if he couldn't bring himself to say it. It was what her parents would have preferred, too, but she'd made a point of not discussing it with them.

Kelly wasn't sure how seriously to take any of this. From the little that the police had said, it wasn't even clear the killings had taken place locally. The victims were all from the area originally, but the first two at least had been living in England. It didn't necessarily mean the so-called Black Isle killer was really lurking behind the next corner.

In any case, something brought her back to the Caledonian Bar the next day and the day after. She told herself she was simply being responsible. You didn't walk out on a job without good reason, even if your boss was Denny Gorman. And the money was always useful. Anything she could scrape together before uni was bound to be a help.

But, on top of all that, there was her own curiosity. She couldn't seriously see Gorman as any kind of killer. He seemed far too ineffectual for that. But there was something in the way he'd talked about Lizzie Hamilton. Something that left her uneasy and intrigued.

So the next lunchtime found her back in the Caley Bar, serving well-spaced pints to the usual crowd of elderly men, fending off the unserious advances of the building boys. They were a sweet bunch, most of them. Scarcely out of school, keen to impress each other. About as suave and sophisticated as their bricks, but good natured and lively. Every day they hit the bar like a whirlwind at around twelve-thirty, and forty-five minutes later they were gone, leaving only a haze of beer fumes and sweat.

Gorman himself continued to be well-behaved, perched in his usual spot at the bar, dressed in one of his limited array of heavy-metal tee-shirts, his sparse greasy hair flopping over his badly-shaven face. He was drinking more than ever, increasingly alternating his chain of pints with shots of whisky. The drinking seemed only to make him more morose but he showed no obvious signs of drunkenness. Occasionally he'd offer some comment about the practical running of the bar, but mostly he sat in silence, flicking through his newspaper. She didn't even have the sense that he was watching her the way he had before. It was as if he had something else on his mind.

The first hour or so went pretty much as usual. At around one forty-five, Gorman looked up from his newspaper. 'You in a rush today, Kelly?'

The truth was she was in no hurry at all. Greg was working up with his dad carrying out some running repairs on the holiday chalets and wouldn't be free till after six. She'd no plans for the afternoon other than reading some Anne Brontë. On the other hand, she'd no idea what lay behind Gorman's query.

'Not desperately. Why?'

'Been doing a stocktake. Just wondered if you could help me finish it off.' He waved his glass of whisky vaguely in her direction. 'You can probably count better than I can. I'm likely to see double.' It was the kind of joke he often made, as if by acknowledging his alcoholism he could somehow negate it.

'What do you need doing?'

'I've done all the stock in here and the storeroom. Just need to do a check on what's in the cellar. Shouldn't take you more than half an hour. I'll pay you for the whole extra hour, obviously.'

Obviously, she thought. No-one could accuse Gorman of being tight with money, though that was possibly because he had no conception of its value. She still couldn't see how this business wasn't going to go down the tubes sooner rather than later.

There was no obvious way of extracting herself from this without seeming rude. 'I suppose,' she said. 'Though I need to be away by three at the latest. I've arranged to meet Greg. My boyfriend.' It wasn't true, but she thought it best to leave Gorman in no doubt where things stood.

He regarded her for a moment, as if unsure what to make of her last comment. 'That's grand. Like I say, half an hour max.'

The task was as easy as he'd suggested. Most of the bar's stock was kept in the small storeroom by the bar. Apart from the casks and kegs, the stock in the cellar was mostly boxes of the more obscure spirits that only needed replacing occasionally, plus various oddities Gorman had presumably bought for experimental purposes. He'd given her a flashlight and notebook and asked her to jot down whatever she could find down there. She'd been tempted to include sections headed 'Junk' and 'Spiders'.

Twenty minutes later, she was pretty much done. She took one last look around the darker corners of the cellar to check she hadn't missed anything and turned to leave.

Gorman was standing in the doorway, his bulky frame blocking the light from the stair.

'Just finished,' she said, brightly. 'Here's the list.'

Gorman remained motionless, saying nothing. She held out the notebook. 'Wasn't a lot, but I think I've got everything down.'

'She just left,' Gorman said, quietly. 'You need to understand that.'

She hesitated, conscious that Gorman was showing no signs of moving out of her way. 'You said. It's none of my business anyway.'

'She just left,' Gorman repeated. 'I don't know why.'

'Why does anyone do anything?' Kelly was aware how inane her words sounded. She looked pointedly at her watch. 'I should be off.'

'I just want you to know that. I don't know why she left. It was nothing to do with me.'

'Like I say—' She risked another few steps. Gorman had still not moved. She could smell the beer and whisky on the breath.

'You're all the same, aren't you?' Gorman said.

'I don't know what—'

'All the same. You come here. Dressed like *that*.' He gestured in her direction as if to illustrate his point. Kelly had been dressing in the same shapeless jumpers and jeans since her second day. 'Pretending you're interested. Then you fuck off to your fucking *boyfriends*.' He spat out the last word like an obscenity.

'Look, I think I'd better get upstairs.' She was determined not to be intimidated. Gorman was nothing more than a fat, useless, drunken lump. She walked forward assertively, intending if necessary to push past.

'You're all the fucking same,' he repeated, more morosely now. The moment of anger, whatever might have occasioned it, seemed to have passed. He was on the point of collapsing back into his usual self-pity. She took another step towards him.

Then, unexpectedly, he grabbed her by the shoulders and forced her back, twisting her body so she was pressed against the bare brick wall behind the doorway. 'I told you,' he spat. 'She just left. She just fucking *left*.' His semi-shaven face was inches from hers, the alcohol stench filling her nose and mouth. She swallowed, feeling the nausea rising in her throat, the hard pressure of his fingers through her jumper. His body was touching hers and she could sense, if not feel, his arousal.

156

She had stopped thinking rationally, her mind overwhelmed by a cocktail of fear and anger. Almost without realising what she was doing, she raised her right knee and rammed it as hard as she could into his groin. At the same moment, she thrust him hard in the chest, driving him away from her.

His expression, a mix of surprise and agony, was almost cartoon-like. He staggered back and she gave him another push for good measure, sending him sprawling against the row of casks. He was stronger than she was but he was also very drunk. She realised now that he concealed his inebriation simply by not moving or speaking more than necessary. Having lost his equilibrium, he tottered and fell backwards, ending up awkwardly between two metal barrels.

She didn't wait to see what happened after that, but ran as fast as she could up the stone stairs and out into the bar. A couple of the elderly men were still sitting at one of the tables, half-drunk pints in front of them. Both looked up without curiosity as she passed. Pausing only momentarily to grab her coat and handbag from behind the door, she exited into the street without looking back.

Outside, she was faintly surprised, as she often was after leaving the Caledonian Bar, to realise it was still light. The rain had lessened but there was still a chill drizzle in the air. She'd been dreading the prospect of waiting at the bus stop, knowing that Gorman might emerge at any moment, but a bus was already approaching. She signalled frantically to the driver and threw herself on board. She allowed herself to breathe only when the bus had finally pulled away, leaving the bar safely behind.

Shit. *Shit.*

Part of her—an unreasonable part which she'd disown once she was back in a more rational frame of mind—was blaming herself. She shouldn't have gone back after her previous encounters with Gorman. She certainly shouldn't have gone down into the cellar again. She should have listened to Greg.

But another more sensible part of her was sticking the blame squarely where it belonged—on Gorman. The man had fucking assaulted her. If she hadn't fought back, Christ knew what might have happened. He was a drunken fucking maniac.

Another related thought struck her. If she hadn't fought back, what really might have been the outcome? Physical assault? Sexual assault? Rape? Anything was possible. And if he could potentially do that to her, he could do it to any woman.

Including Lizzie Hamilton.

She just left. It was nothing to do with me.

She just left.

Still shaking, Kelly fumbled in her handbag for the small purse she used to store her bank cards. After she and Greg had found the body at the Clootie Well, that policeman, the detective, had given them one of his business cards. 'Just in case you think of something else,' he'd said. 'If anything occurs to you, even something trivial, don't hesitate to call. You never know what might be important.'

She found the card and held it between her fingers. DI Alec McKay. Major Crimes Division. A PO Box address in Inverness. A direct line number. A mobile.

She'd speak to Greg when she got back. He'd want her to report the assault in any case, though she couldn't really see that going anywhere beyond an informal warning to Gorman.

But this was something else.

She just left.

It was nothing to do with me.

CHAPTER TWENTY-FIVE

This guy had already kept them waiting twenty minutes and McKay wasn't in the best of tempers. Chrissie kept glancing at him, knowing fine well how he was feeling, and no doubt hoping he was still going to play ball.

Well, yes, he'd do that. He'd promised Chrissie he was going to, and, whatever else he might be, McKay was a man of his word. And smart enough to recognise that Chrissie might just be right. This might be what they needed. It might be the answer, or at least part of the answer.

But that didn't mean he had to be pleased that this arrogant bugger couldn't even be bothered to keep to his appointment schedule. Typical of bloody medical types. Always thought their time was invaluable, and the rest of us should just put up with being buggered about.

Chrissie had picked him up at five forty-five as agreed. She'd been waiting in reception, chatting to one of the receptionists who, it turned out, had been at school with her. That was another thing about this neck of the woods. It was such a small world that everyone knew everyone else's business. Even if Chrissie had said nothing— and he knew her well enough to accept she hadn't—it wouldn't take long for word to get around. Well, just let anyone try to take the piss.

The office was part of a medical centre, just outside the main drag. McKay had a vague memory of being here before to deal with some attempted break-in. Some half-addled junkies after the drugs, almost immediately defeated by the centre's security.

'What's his name again?' McKay asked, as they sat in the otherwise empty waiting room watching the clock edge its way towards six twenty.

'Jack Robinson,' she said. 'Doctor Jack Robinson, I think.'

'What sort of name's that?' McKay asked. 'Sounds like a sodding stage name. How quickly can I cure your neuroses? Before you can say Jack Robinson. For Christ's sake.'

'It's probably just his name,' Chrissie said. 'He can't help that.'

'He can help calling himself Jack,' McKay pointed out. 'John would do just fine.'

She'd been tempted to chastise him for being so negative, but she knew this was just McKay's way of coping with his own anxieties. This wouldn't be easy for either of them, but Alec was the last one to talk about his own feelings. He was much happier when he was the one asking the questions.

The receptionist leaned forward to take an internal call, and then looked up at the two of them. 'Mr and Mrs McKay. Mr Robinson will see you now.'

McKay turned to Chrissie as he rose from his seat and mouthed the word 'Mister'. She shook her head and followed him to the door indicated by the receptionist.

Robinson's office was an anonymous workspace that gave little clue to his role or profession, except for an array of framed certificates that presumably denoted specialist qualifications of one sort or another. Robinson himself was a bearded man in an expensive-looking suit, who watched their entrance over a pair of half-moon spectacles. He gestured for the McKays to sit in two low chairs at the end of the room, and sat himself down facing them.

'I'm sorry I can't offer you coffee,' he said. 'I used to have a machine in here but it got banned. Some health and safety thing.' He gave the impression that this was part of a standard chatty spiel, intended to relax his clients.

McKay was watching Robinson closely. 'I've a feeling we've met before,' he said. 'But can't place where.'

Robinson shrugged. 'I don't think I've had cause to meet you in a professional capacity before, Mr McKay.' He laughed to indicate that he was making a joke. 'Shall we get down to business?'

It was an interesting choice of word, McKay thought, given that Robinson was charging them £75 for the session. He wasn't sure what to make of Robinson. The man carried a slightly theatrical air. His greying hair and beard were carefully styled to suggest a bohemian style, the pattern of his mauve shirt and matching tie calibrated to be tasteful but noticeable under the bland suit. The cultivated effect was of a mildly eccentric academic, apparently off-the-wall but no doubt brilliant and highly successful in his field. But, to McKay's eyes, he also looked fit—a man who worked out. There were traces of a local accent, although it was almost lost beneath an upmarket lowlands burr he'd acquired somewhere along the way.

'I don't ask for any information about clients in advance, as I like to hear you describe your situation in your own words. My first question is, quite simply, what's brought you along to see me today?'

McKay glanced at Chrissie, resisting the temptation to offer some facetious response along the lines of 'Because my wife told me to.' It was clear she had no intention of breaking the silence so after a moment he said: 'I suppose because we've been struggling at home.' He looked over at Chrissie again and went on: 'I don't know whether Chrissie would describe it in the same terms—'

'We'll find out in a moment,' Robinson said, smoothly. 'How would *you* describe it?'

'That we're both tense all the time. That when we're together we're walking on eggshells. That we both want to blame each other.'

'Blame each other for what?'

McKay hesitated, hoping Chrissie would intervene. She would know how uncomfortable he found this, but he guessed she wanted to hear him articulate his feelings for himself. He couldn't blame her for that.

'For our daughter, Lizzie. For her death.'

Robinson was motionless. "How did she die?'

'The official verdict at the inquest was an accident,' McKay said, tonelessly. 'She slipped and fell on to the line at Tooting Broadway tube station. Rush hour. A crowded platform. She was hit by a train. Died instantly.' McKay intoned the facts with the air of someone reading a shopping list.

Robinson moved his gaze slowly from McKay to Chrissie. 'But you think it wasn't an accident?'

'Who knows?' McKay said. 'She'd always suffered from—well, mental health problems. Depression. Anxiety attacks. She'd seen the GP about them several times, and he'd recommended various specialist help. But we never knew how seriously to take it. It seemed to come and go. I suppose we—well, I—thought it was probably part of adolescence and she'd grow out of it.'

Robinson nodded. 'And what did you think, Mrs McKay?'

Chrissie seemed surprised by the direct question. 'Something similar, I suppose, if I'm honest. I probably took it a bit more seriously than Alec did, but that's because I saw more of her—' She stopped, conscious of what she was saying. 'I don't mean that as a criticism. Alec was working full-time. I wasn't. And you know what mothers are like. We worry about the slightest thing. If Lizzie had a cold, I convinced myself it was meningitis. But we did what we could for her. Alec's right. We took her to the GP. She did some counselling. Some of it seemed to help but it was difficult to be sure.'

'What was she doing in London?' Robinson asked.

'University,' McKay said. 'That was one of the things. We'd tried to persuade her to go somewhere closer to home, but she was adamant she wanted to go to London. As if she wanted to get as far away from us as possible.'

'A lot of children see university as a way of flying the nest,' Robinson said. 'They don't necessarily want a safety net. It's not unusual.'

'I can see that. It's what we told ourselves. But in retrospect we should have been more aware of the dangers to her.'

'In retrospect,' Robinson echoed. 'I do a lot of work with troubled teenagers, adolescents. It's always easy to decide what was right for them in retrospect. It's almost impossible to know in advance. At that age, their brains are going through huge changes. A lot of the difficulties they face—depression, anxieties, intrusive thoughts—have as much to do with those physical, neurological changes as they have to do with environmental or other factors. And for that reason many of them do literally grow out of it. But of course some don't. It's often very difficult, if not impossible, to work out which fall into the latter category.'

'Even so,' McKay said, 'if you're a parent, it's difficult not to blame yourself if you get that judgement wrong.'

'And you think that this is what lies behind your current problems?' Robinson asked. 'That you're blaming yourselves and each other for Lizzie's death.'

McKay found himself feeling irrationally resentful at the way this man had appropriated Lizzie's name. He'd never met her. He didn't know how warm and lively and joyous she'd been on her good days. Or how blank and morose she'd been when the depression had hit. 'That's part of it, anyway.'

'And the other part?' Robinson prompted.

McKay hadn't really known what he meant. 'I don't know,' he said. 'I guess—well, we've been together a long time. I devote more time to work than I should. We've allowed ourselves to drift apart.' He stopped, his brain pursuing its own thoughts. 'Maybe we've treated Lizzie—Lizzie's death—as an excuse. A reason not to engage with each other.'

'What's your view, Mrs McKay?' Robinson asked.

'Maybe Alec's right. I don't know. I don't know what to think about Lizzie's death. The inquest said it was an accident. It was a crowded platform. Easy to lose your footing. I think in those circumstances they go for the most neutral verdict to spare everyone's feelings. So we'll never know. But it's easy to wake up in the night torturing yourself. If only we hadn't let her go to London. If only we'd made more effort to get serious treatment for her. And it's easier to blame each other than to blame ourselves.' She stopped. 'But, aye, maybe Alec's right and we're just using that as an excuse. It's something more tangible, more specific, than just admitting that we've fallen out of love—' This time she stopped more suddenly, as if she'd said something unexpected. Something she hadn't realised she was thinking.

'Do you think that might be the case?' Robinson asked. 'That you've fallen out of love?'

There was a long silence. Chrissie was staring at the ground. McKay had stretched back in his seat and was staring, with apparent fascination, at one of the framed certificates on the wall. Finally,

Chrissie said: 'I don't know. Sometimes it feels as if we've nothing in common except that we happen to live in the same house. As for love—well, it feels like a distant memory. Something that happened to someone else.'

'How do you feel, Mr McKay?'

McKay tore his gaze away from the certificate. 'Similar, I suppose. But I don't know whether that's because we've let Lizzie— what happened to Lizzie—come between us. Or whether, really, it's because there's nothing for it to come between.'

Robinson jotted something down on the pad he'd kept balanced on the chair arm. As far as McKay could recall, it was the first note the man had made. 'Well, then,' Robinson said. 'There's plenty for us to work on there.'

'Really?' McKay asked sceptically. He supposed that, at £75 per session, Robinson wasn't going to give up on them easily.

'Yes, really.' Robinson leaned forward in his seat. 'I can't tell you whether you're still in love. In the end, only you can decide that. But I can help you get some perspective. See what really matters. Gain some understanding of the factors that are influencing the way you see things. At the end of that, you might look at each other and think: well, that's fine, now I see how things are and I still don't want us to be together. Or you may think—and this is much more common—actually, now the fog's cleared, we're the same people we always were and we're right for each other. But whatever decisions you make will be rational ones, made for the right reasons. That's all I can offer. The question is whether you both want to continue.'

It sounded like a prepared spiel, and, at least to McKay's ears, even Robinson didn't seem to deliver it with much conviction. But what else did they have? At least it would be a chance, finally, to get things properly out in the open.

'I'm up for it,' Chrissie said.

McKay had risen from his chair while Robinson had been talking and had begun to walk around the room, in the same way he prowled around Helena Grant's office when he was feeling uncomfortable or impatient. He stopped in front of another of the framed certificates, half-expecting that Robinson would tell him to sit down.

Finally, he turned around. 'Why not?' he said. 'Let's give it a go.'

***

'Jesus Christ. You're kidding. That slimy bastard—'

Greg's response had been as she'd expected. If he'd been a different sort of person, he'd already be on his way to Fortrose to avenge her honour. As it was, they were sitting on the waterfront in Cromarty, the hoods of their waterproofs raised against the persistent drizzle, staring at the rows of oil platforms out in the Firth. In the gloomy evening, the first lights were coming on across the water, the far shore partly lost in mist. The oily colours on the water were drifting with the incoming tide.

'He's just a drunk,' she said. 'He wouldn't have done anything.' She was feeling more charitable now the terror of the moment was behind her.

'He already did something,' Greg pointed out. 'He assaulted you.'

'Well, it was hardly—'

'It was assault. He grabbed you by the shoulders. He forced you against the wall. Assault.'

'I suppose. But he came off worst.'

Greg laughed. 'Aye, I'd like to have seen that bit. But even so it's a serious business. We need to report it.'

'We?'

'Well, you. You can't let the bastard get away with something like this.'

'That's my decision, isn't it?'

'Yes, but—'

'But that's not the point. That's not what concerns me about this. I mean, I got out OK and I've no intention of going back.'

'Well, I'm not one to say I told you so— '

'So don't. I'm not going back, even if Gorman might be inclined to continue employing someone who'd just kneed him forcibly in the balls. I'm more concerned with what this might mean.'

'What might it mean?'

'If he was capable of attacking me like that, I might not be the first. Or the last. Maybe he's more dangerous than I thought.' She stared blankly into the rain-washed night.

'This is Lizzie whatshername again, isn't it?'

'Hamilton. Yes, in part. He was really weird about that. All this stuff about her having just left. How it was nothing to do with him. He kept repeating it. Like he was trying to persuade himself it was true.'

'You really think he might have had something to do with her disappearance?'

'I don't know. But there was something odd about the whole business. The way he kept coming back to it. And, like I say, if he's capable of assaulting me like that, then who knows?'

'OK. So what do you want to do? Call the police?'

'I think I should do that anyway, don't you? I didn't want to do anything till I'd spoken to you, but I think I need to tell the police what he did. Whatever might have happened before, if he did that to someone else—well, I wouldn't forgive myself.'

'I can't imagine the police are likely to be able to do very much,' Greg said. 'It'll be your word against his.'

'And who would you believe? Me or some creepy drunk?'

'You, obviously, but that's not the point. There just wouldn't be enough to make any prosecution stick. And even if they did it wouldn't be anything more than assault. You were the one committing GBH.'

'In self-defence.'

'Well, yes. But it wouldn't stand up in court.' He giggled. 'Especially after you kicked him in the bollocks.'

'Very funny,' she said. 'So you don't think I should tell the police?'

'No, I think you should. But don't expect them to do much more than give him a warning. Which might be enough to stop him trying it on with someone else.'

'What about Lizzie Hamilton? Do you think I should mention her?'

'I don't know. I imagine they know she worked for Gorman, so it might interest them to know he's capable of something like this.' He paused. 'And, yes, maybe you should tell them what he said about her. I don't know how the case was left, but it might give them a reason to have another look at it. But don't start throwing around accusations. Just give them the facts and let them decide what to do with them.'

'Thank you, Judge Judy,' she said. 'I was wondering about contacting McKay.'

'Who?'

'DI McKay. The guy we saw at the Clootie Well. You remember. He gave us his card. Told us to contact him if anything else occurred to us.'

'I think he was talking about what we saw there. Not something different like this.'

'Who says it is different? I mean, they're hunting this Black Isle killer. What if it does turn out that Lizzie Hamilton was another victim? Then it's relevant, isn't it?'

'It's a big if. But I suppose so. Anyway, from what I saw of that guy McKay, if he's not interested, he'll soon tell you so.'

'That what I thought. And even if he passes me on to someone else, it'll probably have a bit more clout than if I just phone the enquiry number. I'll give him a call in the morning.'

'Thank Christ for that,' Greg said. 'Knowing you, I thought you were going to call him tonight.'

She laughed, then leaned against him, allowing him to put his arm around her. 'Even I'm not that pushy,' she said. 'Now give me a cuddle. It's bloody cold out here.'

***

Only lightweights confined their running to the warm dry days, especially in this part of the world. If you weren't prepared to run whatever the weather, then up here you might as well not bother.

Horton made a point of running every free evening, come rain, hail, snow or blizzards, all of which she'd encountered since living here. By those standards, tonight was relatively mild. The worst of the rain had passed, at least for the moment, and there was just a slow persistent drizzle, little more than proverbial Scotch mist. She hadn't even bothered to don any protective clothing, content to be soaked to the skin as long as there was a hot deep bath waiting on her return. Isla was cooking tonight and, by the time Horton returned, would have cracked open a bottle of red for them to share while the food was being prepared. Life could be worse.

In truth, she liked running in the rain. It kept her alert and refreshed, and she enjoyed the contrast between the heat of her body and the chill damp of the surrounding air. She'd completed her usual circuit tonight, out past Fort George, and then returning back along the waterside towards Ardersier. The lights across the Firth were a hazy orange in the gloomy twilight, and the village itself looked warm and welcoming ahead of her.

As always when she ran, she'd allowed her mind to drift into neutral, her thoughts ranging aimlessly across the day's business. It felt like they were wading through porridge with the murder cases, picking up a fact here and a fact there, slowly building a picture of the victims and the surrounding personnel, but never finding anything to provide the breakthrough they needed.

As McKay had said, the answer was likely to lie in whatever linked the three victims. And that would itself lie somewhere in their respective pasts. All they could do was keep digging away and hope that eventually something would emerge.

The other question, she thought, as her mind ranged aimlessly around the few facts they had established, was whether there was any significance in where the bodies had been found. The Clootie Well. Caird's Cave. The old care home. Those locations had not been selected accidentally. In the latter two cases in particular the killer had gone to some lengths to place the bodies there. The question was why.

As she pounded along the shoreline, she replayed in her head the various interviews they'd conducted with the Scotts, with Cameron, with Reynolds in Inverness, and with Brewster in Cromarty. Something, some point, was nagging away at her, but she couldn't pin down what it was.

She was almost home before she realised. It was only a tiny point, but it had intrigued her. The McNeils had mentioned their elder daughter, Emma, who had died of leukaemia. Horton hadn't quite put two and two together previously, but she'd registered from the transcript of McKay's interview with Scott that, at some point in Katy Scott's childhood her relationship with her father had changed. Scott had hinted that the change was associated with Emma's death—'a tough time for all of us'—but had then suggested that the real cause had been nothing more than Katy hitting adolescence. Emma, he'd said, had gone the same way at the same age.

It was surely possible, though, that the impact of Emma's death on Katy had been more than simply emotional. Perhaps Emma, in those rebellious teenage years, had offered her sister some kind of protection from her father. Perhaps Emma herself had been the primary focus of her father's interest, deflecting his attentions from her younger sister. At the very least, if Emma and Katy had been close, they would have offered each other some mutual company and support in the face of whatever Scott might have inflicted on them. Horton could imagine that Emma's death had ripped away what little comfort Katy might have had in that household.

She wondered now whether, in those last despairing months of Emma's life, Katy had ever made a trip, perhaps with Emma or her mother or both, to the Clootie Well. Whether they had tied one of those sad votive offerings of clothing to the branches around the stream, or left some childhood toy of Emma's to rot slowly in the damp Highland air. A last desperate throw of the dice, hoping for some miracle that would never happen.

It was all too possible. It would have been a clandestine visit—God-bothering Scott would never have tolerated that kind of pagan ritual—but Horton could envisage it happening. And she could imagine that that final visit, perhaps accompanied by her mother and sister, would have gained a special significance for Katy. The last chance she'd had to preserve the only thing that made her life tolerable. A chance that, in her heart, she must have known was non-existent.

Horton paused on the edge of the village, allowing her thoughts to run on. It was nothing but aimless speculation, but she knew that sometimes this kind of random musing, coupled with the pounding energy of her running, led her to insights she could never achieve through more rational deduction.

Had the killer selected the Clootie Well because it had some particular significance in Katy's life? If so, how did that tie into the other victims, the other locations? Joanne Cameron's body had been found in Caird's Cave along the beach from Rosemarkie. Found, as it happened, by a father and son who'd gone there to play pirates. Another passing comment snagging in Horton's mind.

Cameron had said that Joanne and his ex-wife had been 'two of a kind'. He'd talked about them having fantasy tea-parties at the beach, implying that his ex-wife had brought the teddy-bears. The Camerons had been living in Fortrose. If you were visiting the beach from there, where would you go but Rosemarkie? If you were a young child, what would be more exciting than a cave? Had Caird's Cave been selected because it had some particular significance for Joanne? One of the last places she remembered being happy and secure before her mother had left her in the hands of an abusive father?

If that was the case, what was the significance of the former residential care home for their third victim, Rhona Young?

Horton was motionless now, oblivious to the chill evening air, feeling the rain dripping from her dark hair, soaking through her tee-shirt and track suit leggings. Her brain, barely consciously, was ferreting for the nugget of fact that she knew was there. Something on Archie Young's scanty file.

There had been a father. Living in a retirement home in Inverness. Was it possible that at some point he had been in the home near Rosemarkie? It was a long shot. But perhaps Rhona Young's grandfather had played similar role in her life as that played by Emma Scott for her sister. Perhaps the grandfather had been the one source of comfort, perhaps even of protection, after Young's wife had left. Perhaps she recalled visiting him in the care home, knowing that he was being moved further from her. Perhaps Archie Young had deliberately moved his father so it was less easy for the granddaughter to visit. Perhaps he had been afraid of what the girl might say.

Horton shook her head, suddenly aware of how cold and damp she had become. None of this was anything more than the most tentative, unevidenced speculation, just her mind taking an idea for a walk. But that was the way her mind sometimes worked, and she knew better than to disregard the outcomes.

No doubt she had many of the details wrong. But the killer had chosen those locations for a reason. They had some significance to the killer and, most likely, to the victims also. She had identified points in the victims' lives that might explain that significance. A reason why the killer might have chosen to take the victims back to those places. Back to a point in their lives before the worst had happened.

The detail, she thought, wasn't the point. The point was that, even if she was only half-right, the killer must have had access to those details about the victims' past lives. Not just the broad truths about their abusive upbringings. But those specific moments in their lives. The knowledge of what had really mattered to them.

The killer was someone who, in some way and at some point, had been inside the victims' heads. Deep inside.

CHAPTER TWENTY-SIX

McKay was back in the office by seven-thirty the next morning. His mind was still churning through the events of the previous evening, just as it had been for most of the night. The session with Robinson had continued along the same lines. Robinson had continued to ask short but piercing questions, and McKay and Chrissie had continued to open up, finding themselves expressing views they hadn't known they held or referring to events that they hadn't realised had been significant. At least that was McKay's own feeling. Afterwards, they'd both seemed reluctant to discuss what had happened, as if they were each still coming to terms with what had been revealed.

And what was that exactly?

In the cold light of morning, it was difficult for McKay to be sure. At the time, he felt as if he'd opened himself up completely, revealed aspects of his personality or thoughts that were unknown even to him, let alone to Chrissie. But thinking back now it was difficult to identify anything of substance he had said. Similarly, although he'd had the impression Chrissie was speaking with accustomed openness and honesty, he couldn't actually recall any real detail of what she'd talked about.

Perhaps the whole thing was just a sophisticated conjuring trick. He had no doubt that Robinson was very skilled at what he did. It was just that now he was no longer sure quite what that might be. Maybe no more than smoke and mirrors.

And where had it left the two of them? McKay wasn't sure. By the end of the session it had felt as if they'd stripped everything bare, removed whatever illusions had been constraining or sustaining them. As if they'd demolished a stage set and were now ready to start creating a new reality.

That feeling hadn't lasted any longer than it took them to walk back to the car, heads bowed against the ceaseless drizzle. By the time they'd arrived home, McKay had been sure only that there were no longer any certainties. That he couldn't take for granted that his marriage would continue, that Chrissie would always be part of his life. He no longer knew if that was what she wanted. But then he no longer knew if it was what he wanted, either. Equally, he didn't feel that anything was finished. If they were going to make it work— to make anything work—they would have to start from scratch. The question was whether they had the will and energy to do that.

Chrissie had given him no clues to her own feelings, but he suspected she was feeling much the same. Neither of them showed any inclination to discuss the session afterwards. They'd collected a carry-out curry on the way home and eaten it in silence while some implausible crime drama played out on TV. Then they'd gone to bed, exchanging nothing but the most functional of conversation. This morning McKay had left the house before Chrissie had been awake, telling himself he had work to do.

That much at least was undeniable. Progress on the case remained slow and painstaking, and—despite Helena Grant's best efforts to fend them off—the powers-that-be were getting restless. The latest was apparently a barrage of unanswerable questions from one of the local MSPs. There would be more to come. McKay booted up his PC and began to work through his list of e-mails from the previous afternoon, trying to identify those that needed an immediate answer.

Just before eight Horton arrived, and they spent fifteen minutes catching up on what the team had fed back at the end of the previous day. In truth, there was precious little content. More telephone interviews with people who'd known or might have known Katy Scott or Joanne Cameron, most of them going nowhere. From the contacts made to date, neither seemed to have had any close friends, and their workmates and other acquaintances were able to offer few insights beyond what was already known. So far, the contacts mentioned in Katy Scott's texts to her mother had proved either elusive or uninformative.

They were beginning to discuss Horton's thoughts from the previous evening when McKay's mobile buzzed on his desk. He glanced at the screen. A number he didn't recognise.

'DI McKay? This is Kelly Armstrong. From the Clootie Well.'

'You're the wee lass who found the body?'

'That's me,' she said. 'Well, Greg found the body.'

'Aye, well. You both coped very well. Must have been a shock. What can I do for you?'

'You said to call if we had anything else to tell you.'

McKay looked up at Horton, who was clearly following the dialogue. 'Aye, and do you?'

There was a pause. 'Well, not as such. And I'm not sure if you're the right person to contact. But, well, something's happened and I'm not sure if it's significant.'

'Go on.'

Kelly recounted her experience in the Caledonian Bar the previous day. 'You see, I thought I'd better tell you because—'

'Because Lizzie Hamilton worked there,' McKay said.

'Well, yes, but I didn't think you'd—'

'Make the connection. Aye, well, that case is still lingering like a bad smell around here. Tell me again what Gorman said to you.'

'It wasn't just yesterday. He's come back to this two or three times while I was working there. He kept saying things like: "She just left" and "It was nothing to do with me".'

'You think he might be protesting too much?'

'That's the way it felt. It just seemed odd the way he kept coming back to it. Then yesterday when he tried—'

'Aye, I understand, lass. We can follow that up anyway, assuming you want us to.'

'What will it involve?'

'We'll take a statement from you. We'll interview Gorman. We'll consider whether to recommend further action.'

'What's likely to happen?'

'To be honest, it's going to be difficult to make anything stick. At the end of the day, it'll be your word against his. I'm assuming there are no signs of any assault—no bruising or anything of that kind?'

'I don't think so,' she said. 'Like I say, he just grabbed my shoulders.'

'Sounds like he's the one who came off worst,' McKay said. 'So well done you. But he'll probably just claim it was all a misunderstanding. That he hadn't meant to harm or scare you. Blah, blah, blah.'

'So what should I do?'

'Up to you. If you make it formal, we can probably give him a caution which will at least sit on his record. At the very least, we can go up there and read him the riot act. It all reduces the chances he'll do it again to some other woman.'

'In that case, I'll do it.'

'Not for me to offer a view,' McKay said, 'but that's the right answer. Anything we can do to discourage people like him the better. The question, though, is whether he's anything more than a slimy sex pest. It sounds as if there might have been some history to his relationship with Hamilton we didn't uncover at the time. I'd assumed he had the hots for her, but there was no evidence of anything beyond that. From what you're saying, we need to have another word with him on that front as well.'

'You don't think I'm wasting your time, then?'

'Christ, no,' McKay said, with feeling. 'There may be nothing in it. But if there is—well, we'd want to know. If you can come in and give us a statement, we'll get things moving.'

They made the necessary arrangements, Kelly saying she'd come into town with Greg later than morning. McKay ended the call and looked at Horton, who'd been following the gist of the conversation.

'What do you reckon?' he said.

'Well, it'll be good to tell that slimy bastard to keep his hands off the bar staff,' she said. 'He gave me the creeps when I met him last year. As for the rest—I don't know. He's a lech, all right, but I'd have said he wasn't anything more than that. Apart from anything else, he'd be too pissed to do much about it most of the time.' She paused. 'But if I overheard correctly, it does sound like there's something there. That he knows something about Hamilton, maybe, which he didn't bother to share with us.'

'Aye, that's the way it felt to me,' McKay says. 'Well, if he does know something, he'll share it this time, right enough.'

She was watching him carefully, knowing the way McKay tended to think. 'You think this has anything to do with our killings? Lizzie Hamilton, I mean.'

'Christ knows. I can't see how it would.' He stopped, staring into space, as if his subconscious was making connections his brain hadn't yet recognised. 'But, then, like we've said before, it might be that she fits the pattern.'

***

Kelly had been to Divisional HQ, with Greg hanging protectively by her side, and given a characteristically clear and succinct statement. McKay felt as if for days he'd been hearing nothing but accounts of abuse, dysfunctional families, rootless drifters, loveless lives. It was refreshing to see two young people who so obviously cared for each other. Cynically, he wondered how long that was likely to last.

'Time for us to go and have a word with Gorman,' he said. He was conscious that interviewing Gorman wouldn't necessarily be high on Helena Grant's priority list. A couple of uniforms could have gone up there to deal with the accusation of assault. The Lizzie Hamilton case was, in theory, still open and on McKay's books, but Grant would take some persuading that they should be paying much attention to it just at the moment. The solution, as ever, would be to seek her forgiveness afterwards rather than her permission in advance.

The weather hadn't much improved, and McKay had the sense that the dreich downpour was set in for the rest of the summer. He didn't envy those with holiday homes to let or hotel rooms to fill. As they drove over the Kessock Bridge, a bleak band of heavier rain swept in from the Firth forcing Horton to turn on her headlights. It was a mid-afternoon in early summer, but it felt as if the nights were already drawing in.

Horton pulled up on the double-yellows outside the Caledonian Bar, and stuck the official 'Police' sign under the windscreen, not that there was much likelihood of a ticket on a day like this.

Inside the bar was as deserted as ever. The lunchtime rush, such as it ever was, was over, and the elderly regulars had disappeared in pursuit of their afternoon naps. Gorman was at his familiar place at the bar, a half-empty pint and a whisky chaser next to him. He glanced up in surprise at their entrance.

McKay held out his warrant card. 'You remember us, Mr Gorman. We met last year. DI McKay and DC Horton.'

Gorman blinked blearily at them. 'Aye, I remember. What of it?'

'We'd just like another word, Mr Gorman. About a couple of issues.' McKay sat himself at one of the pub tables and kicked out a chair, gesturing Gorman to join him. Horton took the third seat and pulled out her notebook.

Gorman gazed at them for a moment and then slid unsteadily off his bar stool. Clutching a drink in each hand he stumbled over and sat down at the table.

'Quiet afternoon?' McKay peered round the empty room as if expecting to spot a hidden customer.

'Aye, well. It's the weather, isn't it?'

'I imagine so. Do you have a Kelly Armstrong working here?'

'Not anymore.'

'Why's that?'

'She left.'

McKay exchanged a glance with Horton. *She just left.* 'Any particular reason?'

'You'd have to ask her. She didn't turn in today.'

'Is that right, Mr Gorman? The thing is, as it happens, we have asked her. And she tells us the reason she hasn't turned in today is because you assaulted her yesterday.'

Gorman half rose from his seat. 'What's that bloody bitch been—?'

McKay waved Gorman back into his seat. 'Calm down, Mr Gorman. I'm not sure you're safe on your feet. At the moment, we just want to ask you a few questions. What's your version of what happened yesterday?'

The lengthy pause suggested that Gorman hadn't given much thought to his version of events. 'Christ, I don't know. Lass was down in the cellar doing a stock take. I mean, for Christ's sake, I'd offered her some fucking overtime—'

'And what happened?'

'It was just one of those things. A misunderstanding, I suppose.'

'A misunderstanding?'

'I was just going to talk to her. You know, discuss a few things—'

'Advice on the finer points of stocktaking technique?'

'No, I mean, it was just to have a chat. You know.'

'Not really, Mr Gorman,' McKay said, wearily. 'Kelly Armstrong strikes me as a fairly clued-up young woman. I'm not sure how she'd mistake "having a chat" for an assault.'

'It was just one of those things.'

'What sort of things, Mr Gorman? What did you actually do?'

Gorman took a large swallow of his whisky. 'I suppose I sort of grabbed her. You know, to get her attention.'

'You don't think a simple "excuse me" might have been sufficient?'

Gorman seemed drunkenly impervious to McKay's irony. 'Well, she was working. I wasn't sure she'd heard—'

'So you grabbed her? How did you grab her, Mr Gorman?'

'Well, just by the shoulders. It was nothing—'

'And then what did you do, Mr Gorman? To get her attention, I mean.'

'I was a bit—you know.' He gestured towards his whisky glass. 'I probably wasn't thinking straight. I held her against the wall, I suppose.' He trailed off.

'So you grabbed her, and you pushed her against the wall. In the cellar. Because you wanted to have a chat. Is this your standard conversational technique, Mr Gorman? You must be a wow at parties.'

'Look, I didn't mean—'

'What was this chat about, Mr Gorman? What did you want to talk to Kelly Armstrong about exactly?'

Gorman looked as if he wanted, more than anything else in the world, to go over to the bar and top up his glass. McKay had the sense that, deprived of any more alcohol, the man might confess to literally anything. 'Just—you know—stuff.'

'Stuff?' McKay spat out the word. 'What sort of stuff would you want to talk to a young woman about, Mr Gorman? What sort of stuff might you have in common?'

Gorman swallowed the last of his whisky and said: 'She'd been asking about the woman who used to work here. The one who went missing.'

'Lizzie Hamilton?'

'Aye. Lizzie Hamilton.'

'Why was Kelly Armstrong interested in Lizzie Hamilton?'

'You'd have to ask her that.' Gorman stopped and laughed, mirthlessly. 'Oh, don't tell me. You already have. She'd reckoned she knew Lizzie. There was nothing I could tell her. Lizzie Hamilton just left.'

'That right?' McKay said. 'The same way you reckoned Kelly Armstrong had just left when we first asked you? Did Lizzie Hamilton leave for the same reason?'

'She just left,' Gorman repeated. 'I don't know why.'

'Are you sure about that?' McKay said. 'Kelly Armstrong left because you subjected her to a drunken assault in your cellar. Armstrong was feisty enough to fight back. Maybe Hamilton wasn't.'

Gorman looked up sharply, his bloodshot eyes coming into focus. 'What do you mean?'

'What I mean, Mr Gorman, is that Lizzie Hamilton is still missing. No-one's seen any sign of her since she supposedly walked out of your establishment nearly a year ago. She left food rotting in her fridge. She left bills unpaid. She's not used her bank account since that day. And I wonder now if maybe you know something about that.'

The silence was much longer this time. Gorman sat staring into his empty whisky glass as if hoping it might magically refill. McKay was content to let the silence build, sensing there was something Gorman wanted to tell them.

Finally, Gorman said: 'I don't know. Maybe something.'

McKay made no immediate response, but pushed himself slowly to his feet, picked up Gorman's glass, and took it behind the bar to top it up. He slid the filled glass across the table to Gorman. 'Go on.'

Gorman took a grateful swallow of the spirit. 'It was four or five days before she left. She sometimes used to stay behind a bit after hours and have a final drink or two with me and maybe a couple of the lads, depending who was in. Just company, you know. She liked a drink or two, did Lizzie.' He took another mouthful. 'Anyway, that night, she seemed to have one or two too many. Not like her—'

'Who was in the bar that night? After hours, I mean. Who was drinking with you?'

'A couple of the old guys at first. I can give you their names. But they peeled off about half-eleven. So me and Lizzie knocked back a few more.'

'And she got drunk?'

'Seemed to hit her suddenly. We'd moved on to the whisky, but she usually handled that OK. This time, she could barely sit up. Looked as if she was about to collapse at any moment. I said I'd walk her home but she didn't even seem capable of that.'

'And she could normally hold her drink?' McKay exchanged a glance with Horton. The account didn't ring true to him. He had the sense that Gorman was offering them half the story, enough to suggest he was dealing with them in good faith. But not the part that really mattered.

'Aye, I was surprised. But we had been knocking it back. Maybe she hadn't eaten or something, I don't know.'

'So what did you do?'

'I took her upstairs,' Gorman said, adding hurriedly: 'Not like that. Well, not really.'

'Not really?'

'There's a spare room upstairs,' Gorman said. 'I use it mainly to store stuff, but there's a bed. It wasn't made up, but I thought I could put Lizzie in my bed and I could sleep in the spare room.'

McKay didn't want to think about the possible state of McKay's own bed. 'Not really?' he repeated for a second time.

'Aye, well. She was an attractive woman, Lizzie Hamilton. You can't blame me for thinking—'

'We've not made that a crime yet,' McKay said, 'though I believe Holyrood are considering it. So you took her upstairs?'

'More or less carried her, aye. Dumped her on my bed.'

'And?'

Gorman was rubbing his hands repeatedly across his face, as though trying to erase his own features. 'I helped her undress a bit. To make sure she was OK, you know?'

'You helped her undress?'

'Not completely. Just so she was comfortable. She could hardly cope herself. '

'Of course,' McKay said. 'Then what happened?'

The rubbing continued. It was as if Gorman were trying to remove some blemish from his blotchy skin. 'I went back down to finish locking up and turn off the equipment and lights. When I got back up there—' He stopped suddenly, as if he'd forgotten the thread of his story. 'I looked in on her to check she was all right. I was surprised, but she seemed to be awake again. When I poked my head round the door, she looked up at me and, well, beckoned me in—'

'She beckoned you in?' McKay tried hard to keep any note of disbelief out of his voice.

'Aye, well. I didn't know what to think. But she seemed— well, she seemed to want me.'

'Is that right, Mr Gorman?'

Gorman had reddened, as if recognising how unlikely his story was sounding. 'Well, you know, she was drunk. But so was I. You know what it's like.'

'You tell me what it's like, Mr Gorman. What happened after that?'

'Well, I went in. And it was clear what she wanted. So we—you know—'

'You had sexual intercourse with her.'

'I suppose. Yes. That's what happened.'

'And was she sober enough to consent to this act, Mr Gorman?' This was from Horton, and Gorman looked genuinely startled at the intervention.

'I—' He stopped and took another mouthful of whisky. 'Aye. Yes, of course. I mean, we were both pretty stoshied. But yes.'

'You're sure about that, are you?' McKay said. 'That's what you'd say under oath?'

Gorman had buried his face in his hands again. 'I think so,' he said, finally.

'OK, Mr Gorman. What happened after that? I'm guessing this wasn't the start of a beautiful relationship?'

'I—' He hesitated, as if trying to compose the rest of the story in his addled head. 'She fell asleep again. I thought—well, I thought it best to leave her there. I went off to the spare room and slept in there. When I got up the next morning, she'd gone.'

'But this was before she went missing?'

'Yes, she came back to work that night. But it wasn't the same after that. She never said anything, and I never said anything. I wasn't even sure what she remembered. But she obviously knew something had happened. She'd always been a bit of a mate, but after that she just became frosty. Distant, you know?'

McKay could easily imagine. Whatever the circumstances, the fact that you'd slept with Gorman would hardly be something to boast about. 'You think this was why she left?'

Gorman emptied the whisky glass. 'I don't know. But I think she was embarrassed. Maybe she started looking for another job. She was always the restless type. Perhaps it was enough to spark her to move on again.'

McKay stared at him for a moment, this time allowing his scepticism to show. 'That's what you think, is it?'

'Look, I swear to you. I don't know where she is or what happened to her. Aye, it was probably partly my fault she moved on. But I didn't do anything to her.' He shook his head, and McKay was surprised to see tears in the man's eyes. 'Ach, I liked the wee lass. She was good company. I should have left it at that.'

McKay pushed himself slowly to his feet. 'OK, Mr Gorman. We'll stop there for the moment. We'll let you know whether Kelly Armstrong wishes to press charges about what happened yesterday.'

'I didn't mean to—'

'It seems you never do mean to, do you, Mr Gorman? Just a series of unfortunate misunderstandings.' He gestured towards the empty whisky glass. 'Maybe take more water with it if you don't want people to misunderstand you quite so often? And whatever Kelly Armstrong decides to do, you make sure no-one else has any grounds to complain, eh? You're in the last chance saloon, pal.' McKay looked around him at the gloomy interior of the bar. 'In every fucking sense.'

Outside, the rain was falling as steadily as ever. McKay said nothing until he and Horton were heading back towards the A9. 'What do you reckon?'

'I think he's lying through his teeth about what happened with Hamilton,' Horton said. 'But I don't think he's our killer.'

McKay stretched out his feet, his eyes fixed on the rain-soaked road ahead of them. 'Go on.'

'Hamilton sounds to me like a pretty seasoned drinker. Do you reckon she'd have allowed herself to get unexpectedly pissed and end up in Gorman's bed?'

'Stranger things have happened,' McKay said. 'Or so I'm told.'

'Not many. I reckon Gorman spiked her drink. I reckon what happened there was rape. Not that we're ever likely to be able to prove it.'

'That was pretty much my thinking,' McKay conceded. 'I wondered about searching the bloody place, but even Gorman's not dumb enough to have hung on to anything incriminating. Why do you think he was prepared to tell us the story?'

'Because he wanted to get as close as he could to the truth. Convince us that whatever kind of creepy bastard he might be, he's still not a killer.'

'And you're convinced?'

'Oddly, yes. I mean, I suppose I could imagine him killing Lizzie Hamilton accidentally. If she'd fought back when he assaulted her, maybe. But I can't see him having the gumption or the ability to cover it up—you know, find a way of disposing of the body, keep up the pretence for months on end. He's not that smart or that resilient.'

'But what he told us does potentially put him in the frame,' McKay said. 'If Hamilton really is dead. Like you say, he could have just been more violent than he intended. If she was drugged, it might not have taken much.'

'Maybe not. But my instinct is what he told us today was something close to the truth. Edited, maybe, to leave out the most incriminating part, but I think he wanted to get it off his chest. He blames himself for her leaving. I reckon if we pushed him on it we might get him to admit to spiking the drink. But I don't think he killed her. He's not smart enough for that kind of double-bluff.'

'Aye, I suspect you're right. And I definitely can't see him being responsible for the other killings. Can you imagine him manhandling a body down to Caird's Cave or up to the Clootie Well?'

'I don't think he'd be capable of manhandling his own body to those places,' Horton said. 'From what Kelly Armstrong said, today's intake of alcohol was pretty typical. So where does this leave us?'

'I'm not sure. There's just something about the Lizzie Hamilton case that keeps nagging at me—'

'You don't think you maybe took it a bit too personally?' It wasn't a subject that Horton had felt able to raise previously, but she knew more than most about McKay's background.

McKay looked across at her. For a moment she thought she might have said too much, but then he allowed himself a rueful smile. 'That the word on the street?'

She was approaching the busy junction with the A9 and made no response while she manoeuvred the car back on to the main road, slipping neatly between two articulated lorries, pulling over into the outside lane before the spray from their wheels could obscure the windscreen. 'I wouldn't go that far,' she said, finally. 'But, yeah, I've heard one or two people say that. It wouldn't have been surprising.'

'Ach, no, you're right. It struck a chord, right enough. Young woman. Away from home. There was something—you know, poignant about that bungalow of hers. It was so fucking impersonal.' He paused, staring blankly out of the car window. 'I wanted to bring her home, you know? But there wasn't even a home to bring her to—' He stopped, his eyes fixed on nothing. Then he blinked, with the air of someone returning to consciousness, and turned back towards Horton. 'Fuck, I've just realised.'

'What?' She glanced back at him, baffled by his sudden change in mood.

'It's been nagging at me all day. Something my eyes had spotted but my brain hadn't processed. Jack fucking Robinson.'

'Is this some kind of nervous breakdown you're having? Who the hell's Jack Robinson?'

They were heading back over the Kessock Bridge, the Moray Firth a haze of mist and scattered lights, the industrial landscape of the city stretched out in front of them. It looked like a winter's afternoon.

'Jack Robinson,' McKay said, 'is Lizzie Hamilton's father.'

CHAPTER TWENTY-SEVEN

'I met him last year. Went to talk to him as part of the Hamilton investigation.'

'You've lost me, Alec. I'm not sure why this is important.'

They were back in the office. Helena Grant had joined them for a catch-up, and McKay was still berating himself for not recognising Jack Robinson. 'Probably it isn't,' he acknowledged. 'But I've had this feeling right from the start.'

Grant looked over at Horton, who was assiduously tapping away at her keyboard, her bobbed hair concealing her face. 'Go on, Alec. We'll indulge you.'

'Ach, I don't know. Something. Something about Lizzie Hamilton and these killings. Something about the pattern.' He was chewing hard on a piece of gum, as if the answer might lie there.

'So what about her father?'

'He's a counsellor. Psychotherapist. Look, don't tell any other bugger, but Chrissie and I went to see him. Couples therapy.' He shrugged, his face reddening. 'We thought it might help.'

'Jesus, Alec,' Grant said. 'That's the first time I've seen you embarrassed. It's nothing to be ashamed of.'

'Aye, well,' he said, 'you're not a middle-aged Dundonian male, are you?'

'Not exactly, no. OK, you went to see this guy for your session. But you didn't recognise him as Hamilton's father?'

'You know how it is. I was sure I'd met him before, but I couldn't place him. It's because he was in a completely different context. Glasses, beard, smart suit, academic, all that. My fault, too. First time I met him, I had him pigeon-holed as one of those wheeler-dealer types. Some sort of dodgy businessman. Never imagined him with a couch and a stethoscope.' He shook his head. 'Never put me in front of an identity parade.'

'Actually,' Horton said from behind her computer, 'you weren't far wrong.'

'What about?'

'The wheeler-dealer stuff. Just found his website. Counselling, psychotherapy, all that malarkey. But he also seems to have a thriving publishing and events business. Self-help books, personal development courses.' She looked up, her expression suddenly changed. 'Offices here and in Manchester.'

McKay let out a low whistle. 'Well, there's a coincidence.'

'And that may be all it is,' Grant pointed out. 'Manchester's a big city.'

'Aye, there is that. But we have a few coincidences now. We've a man whose own daughter has gone missing. Who works with disturbed young people. Who's in a position to dig into their innermost thoughts. The sort of man who, as Ginny says, would be aware of the important places in their young lives. A man who does a lot of travelling between here and Manchester.'

'You reckon this guy would be up to disposing of the bodies in that way?' Grant said.

'He's fit enough,' McKay said. 'When I first met him, I had him down for a gym bunny.'

'It's all circumstantial,' Grant said. 'Completely circumstantial.'

'But he's the first candidate we've found who appears to fit the bill,' McKay said.

'I do not doubt that, Alec. But that's all the more reason not to jump in with both feet. We've nothing of substance here. Nothing more than your gut feel.'

'Could we find out whether our three victims were clients of his?' Horton asked. 'That would be one coincidence too many.'

'I don't know how feasible that is,' McKay said. 'All his work is private practice stuff, as far as I'm aware. Chrissie got his name as a suggestion from our GP, but it wasn't a referral as such. I don't necessarily think the GP would have a record, and if Robinson is our man, I don't imagine he'll hand us a helpfully incriminating database.'

'Worth a shot, though,' Grant said. 'He may do NHS work, and it's possible that one of our victims was referred there by her GP.'

'Assuming we can track down who their GPs were at the time,' McKay added. 'I suppose the Scotts and Camerons might have had family GPs, but the daughters could well have chosen to go elsewhere once they left home. But, aye, definitely worth a shot.'

Horton was still flicking through the website. 'What's with the name stuff, anyway?' she said. 'Hamilton's father wasn't called Robinson, was he?'

McKay shook his head. 'No, that's another thing that threw me. The man I went to see was called John Robbins. I'm assuming that Jack Robinson's a—what do you call it?—a nom de plume.'

'More like a stage name, I reckon,' Horton said. 'Judging from this website, he's not short of ego. Lots of well-posed images of a moody-looking Jack Robinson staring pensively into the camera. Numerous accolades from supposedly delighted clients. The sort of biog that drops all kinds of academic names without actually telling you what qualifications he's got or where he got them.'

'His office was plastered with certificates from the University of Whatever and the National Association of Please Yourself,' McKay said. 'I was quite intimidated. I was peering at one or two. As far as I can recall, they were all in the name of Jack Robinson. But most of them probably weren't worth the paper they were printed on.'

'But we've still got nothing on him,' Grant emphasised.

'You don't reckon we've enough for a warrant?'

'Christ, Alec, what do you think? This guy's bound to be an upstanding pillar of the community. No-one's going to grant us a search warrant on the grounds that he sometimes visits Manchester.'

'Aye, I know. And even if they did, he'd be too smart to leave anything incriminating about,' McKay agreed. 'I suppose we might find traces of DNA in whatever vehicle was used to move the bodies.'

'Assuming we can track down the vehicle that was used. We can check what vehicles are registered to him, and we can use the ANPR network to track the movement of those vehicles around the relevant times. But at best that'll only provide more circumstantial evidence.' Grant shook her head. 'I've every faith in your gut, Alec, but I can't justify any more direct investigation till we've something more.'

'If you say so,' McKay gloomily. 'All we can do is keep chipping away at the detail. Try to find out if the victims did have any contact with Robinson or Robbins or whatever the hell he calls himself. Do some more digging into Robbins himself. I suppose we can get access to his mobile phone records?'

'As long as you follow RIPA like a good boy,' Grant said. 'And assuming you can get his number.'

'Jesus,' McKay said. 'And in the meantime, if he is our man, he could be off and doing it again.'

'We can try to keep an eye on him,' Grant offered. 'The ANPR network could help us there, particularly if he heads south. But it's still going to be difficult to justify too much resource without stronger grounds.'

'Catch fucking 22,' McKay said, succinctly.

Grant pushed herself to her feet. 'That's the way it is, Alec. You know that as well as I do. And, Alec—'

'Aye?' he said, wearily.

'Don't get too hung up on Robbins, will you? Like I say, I'm happy to trust your instincts. Up to a point. But I know—and you know—how easy it is to fixate on a suspect because they're the only one you've got in the frame. Keep an open mind, eh?'

'Aye, and you also think I'm fixating on Robbins because of my supposed obsession with the Lizzie Hamilton case.'

'I didn't say that.'

'It's what you think. And you probably also think I'm fixating on Robbins because I'm uncomfortable with some semi-qualified shrink sticking his nose into my innermost thoughts.'

'That's not—'

'Well, you'd be right about that one,' McKay said. 'I'll tell you this much. Whatever Robbins might or might not have done, there's no fucking way I'm letting him anywhere near my fucking head again.'

***

McKay called it a day around six, early by his standards. Normally, when he was engaged on a major investigation, he found that the adrenaline was enough to keep him going even when they seemed to be getting nowhere. Tonight, he just felt weary of the whole thing.

He'd been depressed by the meeting with Gorman, that creepy fucking slimeball. Like Horton, he didn't have much doubt that Gorman had drugged and raped Lizzie Hamilton, but it was hard to see how they'd ever have enough evidence to mount a prosecution, even supposing Hamilton ever reappeared, alive or dead. There wasn't really even much point in pursuing Kelly Armstrong's complaint. They might be able to give Gorman a caution, which at least would sit on his record, but otherwise it would go nowhere. On top of that, there were all those poor lasses, who'd spent their young lives being abused, drifting from place to place, rootless and abandoned. Mourned in the end, it seemed, by no-one except their killer.

It was at times like this that McKay felt most impotent. People joined the force for numerous reasons, not all of them wholly honourable. McKay couldn't even remember what had prompted him to apply in the first place. Probably not much more than the lack of other opportunities in the early 1990s recession. Most people he'd known at uni had ended up in boring if lucrative office jobs in insurance or banking. A few more socially committed types had ended up in local or national government, one or two even contributing to the seemingly inexhaustible supply of Scottish politicians. The odd loudmouth had ended up in the media. None of that had appealed to McKay even if that type of employer would have given him houseroom. So he'd ended up here, chasing the bad guys, though these days the chase was largely one of paperwork and bureaucracy. He'd never seen it as a moral calling, but there was some satisfaction when it went right—when you managed to do your bit to make the world a safer or cleaner place.

But all too often the whole thing felt like a waste of time. You lifted up the stone, but could do bugger all about the lowlifes squirming away beneath. What you did, too often, was walk away, shrug your shoulders, and put it behind you until the next time. You couldn't let it get to you. That way lay madness or, worse still, noble corruption. Doing the wrong thing for the right reasons.

As for the killings themselves, Christ knew what to think. McKay's instincts told him Lizzie Hamilton had some part in the story, but there were no real grounds for believing that, except her life had echoed those of the other victims. They had nothing on Robbins except that he loosely fitted the likely profile of their killer. No doubt the same could be said of dozens of men across the city.

The only thing McKay was sure of, as he'd told Helena Grant, was that he wanted no more dealings with Robbins as a therapist. A more cynical part of his mind had suggested he should continue with the sessions, observe Robbins at close quarters, gain some insights into the way the man thought or behaved. But that idea left McKay feeling queasy for countless reasons. Apart from anything else, it would be unfair on Chrissie. If he was going to do this counselling thing, he needed to do it properly. Not play a game because of half-baked suspicions he harboured against Robbins.

It didn't really matter, in this respect, whether he was right or wrong about Robbins. If he was right—well, Christ, that didn't bear thinking about. But even if he was wrong, he'd never be able to look at Robbins dispassionately. He'd wonder about Robbins's relationship with his daughter. He'd wonder to what extent Lizzie Hamilton really did fit the pattern of the other victims.

And, of course, he'd wonder about his own motives. He knew his colleagues—some of them at any rate—thought he'd allowed himself to become too obsessed by the Hamilton case. Maybe they were right. He'd never denied that he'd been affected by the physical and other similarities between Hamilton and his own daughter. McKay was smart enough to recognise that he might be wanting to accuse Robbins of his daughter's death as an alternative to blaming himself for allowing his own Lizzie to die. It was cheap psychology—probably exactly the kind of psychology that Robbins traded in—but that didn't necessarily make it wrong.

The hallway felt colder than usual when he entered the house, and for a moment he wondered whether Chrissie might not be there. But she was in her usual place in the sitting room, slumped in front of the TV, a half-empty glass of wine on the floor. The TV was showing some afternoon game show, but the sound was off, brightly coloured figures swirling across the screen like virtual goldfish.

'You're early,' she observed.

'I suppose,' he said. 'A bit.'

'But then you went out early.'

'Aye. We've a lot on. You know—'

'Aye,' she said. 'I know.'

He sat himself down opposite her. 'We should have a talk about last night. The session.'

'Is there any point?'

'I thought—'

'What did you think? You were barely there. Wandering round the room. Looking at anything but me. Never answering a straight question.'

Was that how it had been? It wasn't the way McKay had remembered it. He remembered being painfully honest. Much more honest than he'd wanted to be. But maybe, it seemed, not honest enough. 'That's not fair.'

'Isn't it? That's the way it felt to me. That it was all just a fucking game to you. Something to placate the little woman. I could see that was what Dr Robinson thought.'

'He's not a fucking doctor,' McKay snapped. 'He's a fucking quack, playing with our heads.' He'd spoken without thinking, but as he said it the words felt more accurate than he'd realised. He'd felt bamboozled by the session with Robbins, as if the man had been systematically unpicking what he thought and knew. At the end of the session he'd felt momentarily exhilarated, as if he'd been granted a new freedom. But within minutes he'd felt—what? As if whatever had sustained him and Chrissie all these years had been stripped away, leaving nothing for them to cling on to.

'That's just bloody typical of you,' Chrissie said now. 'As soon as someone gets too close, as soon as they delve too deeply into that thick head of yours, you want nothing to do with them. He's a professional, for Christ's sake. This is what he does.'

'What he does is destroy people,' McKay said. 'Creates a dependency. He's like a bloody dealer.' Was this right, he wondered. Was that what Robbins had done with those young women? Played on their vulnerability. Taken advantage of them. Taken young people who were already at the bottom and dragged them lower still.

'God, you're always a fucking cop, aren't you?' Chrissie said. 'Always assuming the worst. You can't believe that anyone just wants to help, can you?'

Of course I can, he wanted to say. Lots of people want to help. Lots of people are good, decent, kind. But not Robbins. Robbins is a manipulative evil bastard. Robbins may even be a killer.

He didn't even know whether any of that was true. Maybe Chrissie was right. Perhaps this was just about his own insecurities, his own anxieties. Perhaps this was just him transferring his own fucked-up reality on to an innocent man. Who knew? Who the fuck knew anything?

'Look, I want to do this,' he said, finally. 'I want to make this work. I'll do whatever it takes. But not with Robinson.'

She shook her head. 'That's how it always is with you, isn't it? You'll do whatever it takes, except the thing in front of you. There's always some excuse. Some reason to put it off until the next time.'

'That's not how it is.' He was conscious of how feeble he sounded.

'Then how is it?'

'It's—' He stopped, feeling there was nothing useful he could say. 'I've got concerns about Robinson,' he said, finally. 'Professional concerns.'

'Oh, for fuck's sake,' Chrissie said. 'It always comes back down to that. You're a cop. Different rules apply. There are things you couldn't possibly share with me.'

'That's not how it is,' he repeated, knowing that the argument—and perhaps much more than the argument—was already lost.

'Oh just fuck off, Alec. Just fuck right out of my life.'

He stared at her for a moment, and then turned and left the room, making a point of not slamming the door behind him. After another second's hesitation, he opened the front door and stepped back out into the chilly damp evening.

He hadn't really intended to leave. Not then, at any rate, and not like that. He'd needed a breath of air, a chance to settle his thoughts. They'd reached this point before, or something close to this point. He didn't know whether this time was different. And he didn't know, if so, whether any of this really was Robbins's fault.

Now he was out here, though, he realised he didn't want to go back. There was no point. There was nothing else for them to say. Maybe that would change. But at the moment it didn't feel likely.

He had nowhere else to go, so he climbed into the car and sat there, watching the drops of rain drifting slowly down the windscreen. Still feeling at a loss, he turned on the ignition and backed the car slowly out into the road.

CHAPTER TWENTY-EIGHT

Robbins's house looked no different from the last time McKay had been here, a year before. It was a solid respectable semi, probably built around the turn of the last century when the city had still been a thriving port. Not an inexpensive property, McKay guessed, by local standards.

The rain was still falling, not heavy but persistent, though McKay felt oblivious to the damp on his hands and face. He pressed the bell.

A moment passed before the door was opened. It occurred to McKay now that he had no idea of Robbins's domestic circumstances, whether there was likely to be anyone else in the house. It didn't matter, he reminded himself. He was here on official business.

In the event, it was Robbins himself who answered the door. McKay caught the momentary look of surprise in the man's eyes before his face rearranged itself into the familiar professional mask. 'Mr McKay? I'm sorry, but I don't do consultations without an appointment. And when I'm dealing with couples, I make a point of not seeing either partner alone except at my instigation.' Taking control of the situation, McKay thought. They must teach you that at therapy school.

McKay held out his warrant card. 'Actually, I'm here on official business, Mr Robinson.'

Robbins looked at the card then back up at McKay's face. 'Ah. I was right then.'

'Were you?'

'Yesterday, when you said you thought we'd met before. I thought so too, but I couldn't place you. Then it came to me. You were here last year. About Elizabeth.'

'Well remembered.' McKay wondered when it was that Robbins had made the connection. Had it been during the session itself? Had he been aware of McKay's identity and occupation while leading the two of them through that process of self-questioning? 'Are you able to spare me a few minutes, Mr—?' He stopped. 'Should I call you Robbins or Robinson?'

Robbins laughed, seemingly untroubled by the question. 'You can call me Jack, if that doesn't feel too informal. The Robinson stuff is just a professional thing. More of a brand than a surname.' He gestured for McKay to enter the hallway. 'You'd better come in. Miserable night. Do you always conduct your business at this time of day?'

'If we want to catch people at home,' McKay said, 'then, yes, sometimes.'

'I can see what you meant about the strain on your marriage.' Robbins turned to lead the way into the living room.

'It goes with the territory.'

The living room was neat and well-furnished, but had an unmistakably masculine air. The only pictures on the walls were more professional certificates and some photographs of Robbins himself with local celebrities—a former MSP, a couple of past members of the Caley team, various others whom McKay couldn't place. There were some neatly ordered shelves of CDs and DVDs, but no sign of any books. Robbins gestured for McKay to take a seat. 'Can I get you a coffee? You look like you could do with warming up.'

'I won't keep you any longer than I need to, Mr Robbins. It's about your daughter.'

'Don't tell me you've found her. I'm not sure my bank account could stand it.' The tone suggested a joke, but Robbins's face indicated otherwise.

'I'm afraid not. In fact the news may not be good.'

Robbins lowered himself on to the sofa opposite McKay. 'Go on.'

'You'll no doubt be aware we're currently investigating a series of apparent murders. The bodies found on the Black Isle.'

'You're not saying—'

McKay held up a hand. 'No, no, Mr Robbins. I'm sorry, I didn't mean to imply— We've identified the three bodies. Your daughter is definitely not among them.'

Robbins was staring at him, his expression impossible to interpret. 'Well, I suppose that's something.' He sounded scarcely grateful.

McKay knew he shouldn't be doing this. Helena Grant might sympathise—though McKay was conscious he'd stretched her sympathies to the limit on too many occasions—but she'd want this case done by the book. It would be her arse on the line if things went wrong.

He didn't really even know what it was he was doing. Hoping to stir up the waters a little? Hoping to provoke Robbins into saying or doing something that might give them a lead or at least an excuse to investigate him more directly? Robbins didn't strike him as easily provoked. In truth, McKay's decision to visit Robbins had been simply a spur of the moment impulse, driven by the impetus of his departure after the argument with Chrissie. He didn't want to think too deeply about his possible motives for coming here, of all places.

It was as if Robbins could read his growing discomfort. 'So what does this have to do with my daughter?'

McKay took a breath, already feeling on the back foot. 'In the light of the recent deaths, we've taken the opportunity to revisit and review some of our other outstanding cases. We have a concern that your daughter might also be a victim.'

'Do you have any reason for that concern? Other than that she's missing, I mean.'

None of this was sounding remotely convincing, even to McKay. 'Only that she fits a pattern.'

'A pattern?' The scepticism was unconcealed.

'All the victims to date were young women of approximately your daughter's age. All were living alone, apparently with few if any close friends or acquaintances. All were—well, estranged from their parents or immediate families. All were local.'

There was a lengthy silence. 'With respect,' Robbins said, finally, 'that doesn't sound much. I imagine those circumstances made the victims convenient targets for the killer. It doesn't mean that was why they were killed.'

'But it does mean we have a reason to consider your daughter's case again,' McKay pointed out. 'Along with any other relatively recent disappearances.'

'And I wish you well with that,' Robbins said. 'My own view, for what it's worth, is that she's most likely alive and well and sponging off some other poor sod, God knows where.'

'You sound bitter, Mr Robbins.'

'Do I?' Robbins's face was as expressionless as ever. 'You know how it is with daughters, Mr McKay. Well, yes, of course, you know better than anyone. When Elizabeth was young, I thought she was perfect.' He stopped and, for the first time since McKay had arrived, he smiled. 'The apple of my eye.'

McKay felt a faint chill finger run down his spine. The apple of my eye. The same phrase that Scott had used to describe his daughter. *You know what it's like between fathers and daughters.*

He had a strong suspicion of what it had been like between Scott and his daughter. Had it been the same with Robbins?

'We were as close as could be,' Robbins went on, and for the first time there was a note of genuine emotion in his voice. 'Especially in those years after her mother died.'

'I'm sorry,' McKay said, though unsure what he should be sorry about.

'It was a long time ago. Cancer. Elizabeth was very small— not even at school. I did my best to make everything all right for us. To keep her close. Then she grew up.'

It happens, McKay wanted to say. It's what supposed to happen. You have to let them go. And you can't control what happens when they do.

'She became a different person. Thought only of herself. Took advantage of me every way she could until I put a stop to it. Then she left and went to find someone else to take advantage of. And I imagine that's what she's still doing.' His voice was flat now, toneless. 'I wish I could bring her back. The girl she was, I mean, not the person she is now. I wish I could bring that girl back home.' He looked up at McKay. 'You know what I mean, I'm sure.'

McKay gazed back at him. 'Maybe,' he said. 'Partly. I'd have mine back any way I could.' He pushed himself to his feet, conscious that, whatever his original reasons for coming here, he was getting nowhere. 'I won't take up any more of your time, Mr Robbins.'

Robbins rose with him. 'To be frank, I'm still not entirely clear why you came in the first place.' There was a different, more threatening edge to his voice now.

McKay had a sudden sense that he was being played with. That the last few minutes had been simply a charade, a pretence of emotion. 'I just thought you should know we'll be taking another look at your daughter's case, Mr Robbins. In the light of our current investigation. We'll probably need to talk to you again, perhaps a little more formally.'

'More formally?'

'We may need more detailed background from you. We're trying to identify any links between the victims and—well, any other potential victims. Any information you might be able to provide could be useful.'

'You're barking up the wrong tree. Wherever Elizabeth might be, I'm sure she's not one of your victims.'

McKay said nothing as he followed Robbins to the front door. Outside, the rain was still falling.

'Thank you for your time, Mr Robbins. I'm sorry to have disturbed you. We'll be in touch in due course.' McKay spoke the words automatically, then turned to look at Robbins, making one last effort to read his expression. 'I think in the circumstances, it would be better if we discontinued the therapy sessions. I'm sure you agree.'

'Your choice, Mr McKay,' Robbins said. His smile was bland and unrevealing. 'Have you consulted with your wife about this?'

McKay gazed back at him, matching smile for smile. 'In a manner of speaking,' he said.

***

'You did what?' Grant said.

'Ach, it was stupid, I know. Spur of the moment. Don't know what came over me.' McKay was sitting behind his desk, feeling like death scarcely warmed up. He'd had an awful night. In the end, after a lengthy, rain-soaked walk by the river, he'd been able to come up with no alternative other than returning home. It seemed the right thing to do, practically and emotionally. He didn't really feel he and Chrissie were at the end of the road. Not yet, not quite. He wanted to give it one more shot, and he'd find a way to do that. McKay was certain now that, even if his own more extreme suspicions were unfounded, Robbins was the last person they needed to help them.

In the end, wet and chilled, he'd driven home and let himself into the dark house. He'd waited as long as he could, sitting in the car for another hour or so, to ensure Chrissie would have retired to bed. For all his good intentions, he'd concluded it would be a bad idea to face her again tonight. They'd just rehearse the same old tensions, the familiar grievances, and they'd end up in the same place. Tomorrow, at some point, would be another day.

He'd found an old duvet and slept, fully clothed, on the sofa. He knew he'd managed to get some sleep because he'd woken, after what had seemed like only minutes, to see the first steely light of day around the sitting-room curtains. Feeling barely rested, he'd thrown himself into a hot shower, found a sufficient change of clothes in the clean laundry, and left the house before Chrissie had stirred. It seemed finally to have stopped raining, but the early morning skies remained leaden and louring.

Now he was sitting here being harangued by Helena Grant, the experience not improved by the clear knowledge that she was right and he was very much in the wrong.

'You don't know what came over you?' she echoed. 'The usual red fucking mist, that's what came over you, Alec. Act first and think later, if you bother to think at all.'

'Look, I've said I'm sorry. It was stupid, I know. I shouldn't have gone.'

'Of course you shouldn't have gone. I don't know what you even thought you were likely to achieve.'

'No, well, neither do I now. It just seemed like a good idea at the time. Stir up the waters a bit.'

'Christ, Alec. I told you yesterday. There are no substantive reasons to treat Robbins as a suspect. Just a few coincidences and your gut. It's not enough for us to start harassing him.'

'I didn't harass him. I was very discreet.'

'Aye, I can see that. Alec "soul of discretion" McKay. You should put it on your business cards.'

'Ach, all I did was tell him we were taking another look at his daughter's case, in the light of our current investigation. See if there was a connection.'

'Very discreet, then. We've reason to think your daughter might be the victim of a serial killer. Aye, Mr Tactful.' She paused. 'Apart from anything else, if there is anything in your suspicions, all you've done is tip him off that we're interested in him.'

McKay shrugged. 'On the other hand, if that were to make him think twice about finding another victim, I'd call that a result. At least for the moment.'

'Christ, McKay, you're incorrigible. Aye, I suppose you're right. Seriously, you still reckon he could be our man?'

'It feels even more likely to me after yesterday,' McKay said. 'He's a manipulative bastard. Whether he's manipulative enough to do this—well, Christ knows. He was enjoying playing with my head. And there was something in the way he talked about his daughter. It was like Scott. How she'd been the apple of his fucking eye until she went off the rails.' He paused, thinking. 'He said he wished he could bring home his old daughter. The daughter he'd lost.'

'That's what our killer's done,' Grant pointed out. 'Brought these girls home.'

'And interred them in places they loved when they were small, if Ginny's guess is right.'

'Before they went off the rails?'

'Before they lost their innocence.' He stopped, again. 'Or before they realised how much innocence they'd already lost. Jesus Christ.'

'The question is, Alec: do you think that Robbins is worth investing our time and resource in? Seriously?'

'I think so. You're right—it's no more than gut feel. But there's something there, I'm sure of it. Aye, I think it's worth giving him a good hard look.'

'OK. We'll start with the ANPR Network and whatever we can get on his phones, like we agreed. If that throws up anything that looks remotely suspicious, I'm willing to give it a more serious shot. But we carry on with everything else for the minute.' She leaned forward and stared into McKay's eyes, not allowing him to look away. 'But you better be bloody certain this isn't just about pursuing your own personal obsessions or vendettas, Alec.'

'Trust me, Helena. It's not that. I'm not saying I'm right. I could easily be wrong. But we need to look at him.'

'OK. And one other condition, Alec?'

'Aye, boss?'

'You don't do any fucking thing on this, and not one fucking word to Robbins, without checking with me first. Right?'

CHAPTER TWENTY-NINE

Shit.

He stumbled on the small step leading down into the rear yard, and for a moment lost balance, the world swirling uncontrollably about him. He almost fell, but reached out and grasped the door-frame, clutching tight to its reassuring solidity. Jesus. He ought to be able to do this stuff in his sleep, and here he was, barely able to stand up.

He had to get a grip. Things were getting worse, in almost every imaginable way. Most of it, he knew, was due to the drinking. He'd always knocked it back. That ran in the family, and his father had been worse than he was. Much worse, or so it had felt back then. He could remember his father getting in after a heavy session in one of his blind rages, beating the living shite out of the whole family, wife and kids. Eventually, Denny Gorman had learned how to cope with that. When to make himself scarce. How to avoid provoking the old man. And, in due course, getting to the point where the old man didn't dare to raise a finger against him. If his father had made old bones, if he'd ever reached the point where he'd been dependent on his children, Gorman would have made him suffer. He'd have made the old man's life a fucking misery. But of course it never reached that point. The old man had just caved in one day. A massive coronary, the doctor had said. Only a matter of time till that or something else did for him, given his lifestyle. They'd found him lying stone-dead on the kitchen floor. Halle-fucking-luja. And now Denny was heading the same way. Like his da, only a matter of fucking time.

He had to knock it on the head. He knew he'd never stop drinking entirely—Christ, look at that aeronautical pig—but he ought to be able to cut back. He'd allowed it to creep up, day by day, over the past year or so. He knew fine well why, and who could fucking blame him? But he had to do something about it. Things were getting out of control.

That Armstrong lassie, for example. He'd not intended to harm her. Of course, she was an attractive wee girl, and he'd always had a weakness for a youngster like that. But he knew how to control those urges by now, or he thought he did. He'd just wanted her to know he was all right, that he wasn't the kind of man she might think. That he'd not harmed Lizzie Hamilton either. Or, at least, not in the way the wee lass might believe.

But he'd fucked that up, too. He'd been too rough, too out of control, and he'd freaked the girl out. She hadn't needed to call the fucking police, but he couldn't really blame her for that. Now he was on their radar too, and they'd be thinking that worst of him as well. He'd be lucky not to end up with something on his record.

It was Hamilton he really blamed for all this. Aye, he'd always been a drinker, but not like he was now. She'd egged him on to it—kept up with him glass for glass when she wanted—as well as giving him plenty of reasons to drown his sorrows. She liked him best when he'd had a few, she reckoned. But that was just because then he became even more reckless with his money. She always knew the end of the night was the best time to screw a few more quid out of him.

Things were already well and truly tits up. He was desperate for money and the debts were mounting. Some of his suppliers were already refusing his business, and a couple were threatening legal action. In the past he'd just about kept his head above water with this place, struggling through the winter months and dragging in enough of the tourist custom in the summer. But it had always been touch and go and he'd been eating into the last of his redundancy money to cover any unexpected expenses.

In the last year or so, business had really fallen off. Partly that was the economic climate. If this was an upturn, Christ knew what another recession would look like. Partly it was the competition. The other local hostelries offered a much more attractive proposition to the passing trade than this place ever would, and there were new cafes and bars opening that gave the tourists more and better places to go.

Mainly, though, it was him. He was neglecting the place. He was a bloody miserable host. The Armstrong girl had attracted a bit of extra custom at lunchtime, but he'd buggered that up. In the evenings, apart from a handful of regulars, the place was largely dead and there wasn't much sign the tourist season would change that, especially if this sodding rain continued.

And Lizzie Hamilton had chipped away at what little savings he had left, that small cushion he'd been intending to stash away. There was always something she wanted or needed, and she always gave him the impression he was on a promise if he just kept paying up. It took him a long while to realise the promise would never be fulfilled.

That was why, in the end, he wasn't sorry about what had happened. The bitch had owed him one, in every sense, and he wasn't going to feel guilty for having finally taken what he'd been owed. It was no more than she'd deserved.

He was standing in the yard at the back of the bar, slightly baffled now that he was out here. That was happening more and more, another product of the drinking. He'd find himself confused, forgetting how to carry out tasks that had once been second nature.

The rain had slowed for the moment to a fine drizzle. The yard was a gloomy place at the best of times, hemmed in by buildings on all sides, cluttered with old casks and other discarded paraphernalia. On an afternoon like this, it was mainly lost in shadow. He'd intended to turn on the external lights before coming out, but of course he'd forgotten.

He was gazing round the debris of the yard, trying to recall what had brought him out here, when his nose caught the odd, acrid scent. It took something for him to discern any kind of smell, accustomed as he was to the fug of his own rarely-washed body. But this was something striking, unpleasant.

He turned, wondering where it was coming from. And then he glimpsed, or thought he had, some brief movement from the corner of his eye. Something in the shadows. 'Who's that?' he said, taking a stumbling half-step forward. The stones were damp underfoot, slimy from years of neglect, and he felt his feet slipping under him. He reached for some purchase, but found nothing and toppled headlong towards the grey slabs.

As he fell, he saw someone or something moving towards him, but he was already disorientated and couldn't make out what he was seeing. Something familiar was his last half-thought, or something unexpected. Then his skull hit the solid stone and he was lying, prone and motionless, as the slow rain continued to fall.

***

'I may have something.' Horton was leaning on the door of the office, watching McKay, who looked lost in his own thoughts. She'd never thought of him as a pensive man, and she could imagine he'd be chafing to take some action, make something happen.

'Anything would be welcome.'

'Well, don't get your hopes too high just yet, but something interesting on Robbins.'

He sat up straighter, all attention. 'Go on.'

'We've been trawling through the ANPR data, hoping for some sighting of Robbins's car between here and Manchester around the relevant dates. Not much luck with that. We picked up a couple of sightings, but only on the A9 up at this end so they don't prove he went further south. From the movements looks like just local trips.'

'When you said you had something, I was maybe expecting some good news, you know?'

'Just setting the scene,' she said. 'So we got nowhere with that. But then we found something slightly more interesting. A sighting of his car on the A9 north of Inverness on the night before his daughter went missing—that is, the night before she first failed to show up at Gorman's place for work.'

'So? He could have been going anywhere.'

'He could, but he wasn't. This is where it gets interesting. The camera on the A9 is one of the permanent ones, but at the time there were also a couple of temporary ones on the A832 across to Avoch and Fortrose. Checking car tax and insurance at the start of the tourist season, presumably. He was picked up by both of those, so must have been heading to Fortrose or beyond.'

McKay had found himself a new piece of gum and was chewing hard. 'So he was in the area the night his daughter went missing?'

'We don't know for certain when she disappeared. But she wasn't seen locally after that night.'

'Christ.'

'And there's more.'

'Think before you speak, Ginny. You really don't want me to have reason to kiss you, do you?'

'Jesus, no,' she said. 'But I'll tell you anyway. I started thinking about him travelling to Manchester. I tracked back over the last year or so, looking for other sightings of his car. There were plenty. Tracked all the way down the A9, M90, across to the M74 and M6, all the way into Manchester. It's a journey he's done fairly frequently, for whatever reasons. But none of the timings tie into when our victims went missing.'

McKay frowned. 'You think there might be other victims?'

'There may be, but that's not my point. The point is he spent a lot of time in Manchester, whether for his business or for more dubious reasons. Maybe tracking down our victims? Who knows? But he was there a lot. I've also checked flights. He also made some day trips down there by air over the same period.'

'Doesn't prove anything, though, does it? We know he's got a business office in Manchester. Could be there for countless reasons.'

'Of course,' she said, slowly. 'But what interested me was why the only times he doesn't seem to have made a trip down there are the times our victims went missing. We know precisely when Joanne Cameron disappeared, but timings for the other two are more approximate. Even so, there're no sightings of his car in any of the relevant periods, even though normally he's up and down there at least every two to three weeks.' She paused. 'So I got Josh Carlisle to do a bit of more checking. We'd missed something.'

'Go on.'

'We'd been focussing on the 4x4. But Carlisle did some digging and realised there was a second vehicle.'

'Which we'd missed?'

'It's not registered to Robbins personally. Josh thought to check the business. Jack Robinson Media or some such. It's obviously a company vehicle, at least notionally, with the business shown as registered owner and keeper. A small Ford van. So we checked on that and guess what. According to the ANPR network it made a trip to Manchester that fits perfectly with the Cameron disappearance.'

'Jesus,' McKay said. 'Anybody ever told you you're a fucking genius, Horton?'

'Many people, but never you,' she said. 'And, in fairness, I think it's Josh you should be thanking.'

'So what about the other dates?'

'Same deal. Return trips to Manchester in both cases in the relevant periods around the disappearances. Even more interesting, we can find no other trace of the van being used outside the city centre except on those three dates.'

McKay was on his feet. 'Which, at the very least, means Robbins has some interesting questions to answer. Let's go and talk to Helena. "Any sign of anything suspicious" was what she said. I think we've got that with knobs on.' He was grinning widely. 'Jesus, Ginny. Seriously, bloody well done. Really bloody well done.'

'Like I say, Josh did all the hard work,' she protested.

McKay was already heading off down the corridor. 'That's all well and good,' he said over his shoulder. 'But there's no way on God's earth I'm going to kiss *him*.'

CHAPTER THIRTY

'No sign of his car,' McKay said. 'Bugger.'

Slightly to his surprise, he'd had no difficulty persuading Helena Grant to take this seriously. He'd realised, as he outlined the ANPR evidence to her, that he really had begun to lose perspective on the case. He'd somehow half-expected Grant to dismiss his arguments, tell him yet again he was obsessing over Robbins. He knew—had known for a long time—he was letting his feelings interfere with his more rational judgement, and he hadn't the energy to disentangle what those feelings were or why they mattered.

He was slightly startled when Grant exclaimed: 'Jesus, Alec. You were right.'

'You think so?'

'Well, it looks that way, doesn't it? I mean, it's still circumstantial till we've checked everything out. But there's only so much you can put down to coincidence. The only times that van's been driven to Manchester tie in with the three murders? Be interesting to hear what story he comes up with.'

McKay nodded. 'Though we've done a bit more checking. It was driven to Manchester one previous time, about nine months ago. Other than that, just a handful of sightings round Inverness.'

'That might just mean there's another victim we don't know about.'

'It might. We've only been back twelve months so far, but that's all we've found.'

'Sounds like we've more than enough to bring Robbins in for a chat, anyway.'

'A chat under caution?'

'I'd have thought so,' Grant said. 'A pretty bloody formal chat.'

So here they were, standing outside Robbins's house, with a couple of uniforms in a squad car for back up, about to issue the invitation. Grant had decided she ought to be in on this, and they'd left Horton back at the office still chasing down whatever evidence she could find. McKay might have resented any other senior officer muscling in, but he knew Grant well enough to recognise she was more concerned with being there if anything went wrong than with snatching a piece of any glory.

For the moment, all of that looked academic. The gravelled drive was empty and the house looked unoccupied. As they approached the front door, heads bowed against the incessant rain, McKay looked up at the blank windows. It was late afternoon, but the rain-soaked sky made it feel like evening. If Robbins had been here, some lights would be showing. He pressed the bell with no expectation of a response.

'We can leave our two uniformed colleagues to alert us when he gets back,' Grant said from behind him. 'It's only a matter of time.'

'Aye, I know. I just want that bugger sitting on the other side of an interview table.'

Grant had unfurled a pocket umbrella. Ducking under it, she strode along the front of the house, peering in at the windows. McKay pressed the bell again, holding it down firmly.

'Alec,' Grant said.

'Aye?'

'Come and look at this.' Her face was pressed against the sitting-room window, a hand cupped round her eyes.

'What is it?'

'Have a look.'

McKay reluctantly released the bell and stepped over to join her. 'Christ. See what you mean.'

It was difficult to make out the interior, but it was clear the place had been left in a mess. A table had been overturned, and papers and books were scattered across the carpet. Beyond them, a flat-screen computer monitor lay face down on the floor.

'Some sort of struggle?' Grant said.

'You're the senior officer,' McKay said, 'but I reckon this justifies us entering the house, don't you?'

'I'm happy to take responsibility for that, Alec,' she said, 'as long as you take responsibility for actually getting us in there.'

'I'll see what I can do.' The window in front of them was double-glazed and looked like it might pose a challenge. McKay trudged back to the side of the house, where a passageway led to the rear garden. Its entrance was blocked by a heavy wrought-iron gate sealed with an equally substantial padlock.

McKay gazed at it for a moment, then said: 'Ach, bugger it.' He grasped the wet metal with both hands, raised a foot to the horizontal iron bar in the centre of the gate, and hoisted his wiry frame over it.

'Jesus, Alec,' Grant said from behind him, 'you'll do yourself a mischief.'

He was halfway over, legs straddling the top of the gate. 'If I slip now, I'll do myself more than a fucking mischief.' He lifted his remaining leg over and dropped on to the path inside the gate, slipping only slightly as he landed. 'Piece of cake,' he said, 'and I even managed not to end up on my arse.'

At the rear, there was a large garden, laid mainly to lawn. As McKay stepped forward, a security light clicked on, startling him momentarily. To his immediate left, there was a rear door to the house and, further along, a pair of solid-looking French windows. With no expectation of success, he tried the door. To his surprise, the handle turned and the door opened.

He stepped inside and found himself in the kitchen, a showpiece of granite work-surfaces and stainless steel appliances, none of them looking much used. He clicked on the lights. 'Mr Robbins?'

The pervading silence suggested the house was empty. He made his way through to the front door, half-expecting it to be deadlocked. But again the door opened. If he was out, Robbins hadn't made much effort to secure the place.

'That was quick,' Grant said, as he admitted her into the hallway. 'You've obviously missed your vocation as a housebreaker.'

'I'd like to claim it was down to my locksmith skills,' McKay said. 'Actually, the back door was unlocked.'

She followed him to the entrance to the living room, where he'd paused. 'I think,' he said, 'we might want to treat this as a crime scene. Look.'

The room was illuminated only by the gloomy daylight from the front window, but the scene was clear enough. The disturbance to the room was more severe than it had appeared from outside. The computer had been dragged from the desk, along with a stack of files and papers. A vase lay smashed in the corner by the door, among a scattering of smaller ornaments. Not wanting to touch the light-switch, McKay pulled out a small flashlight and shone it across the carpet. 'There.'

It was a dark stain, perhaps twenty or so centimetres across. As the beam from the torch reached it, it became clear that the stain was a deep red, darkening at the edges.

'Not much question,' Grant agreed.

'There's something else,' McKay said. 'Can you smell anything?' He gestured towards the living room. 'Stick your head in the door.'

Frowning, she did as instructed. The frown tightened into a grimace. 'Christ, what's that?'

'I'm no expert,' McKay said. 'But I reckon it might well be chloroform.'

'We better check out the rest of this place.'

It took them only a couple of minutes to search the rest of the house. Upstairs there were three bedrooms—one clearly used by Robbins himself, one set up as a guest room, and the third apparently used as an office and consulting room for Robbins's counselling work—and a bathroom. All were empty and undisturbed.

'We need to get a bulletin out on Robbins,' Grant said. 'You know his car reg?'

'Not off the top of my head,' McKay said. 'But Ginny's got all the gen.' He pulled out his phone and dialled. Grant was already heading back out to the car to call into the FCR.

The phone was answered almost immediately. It sounded as if Horton was on the hands-free in the car. 'Ginny?'

'Alec? Was just about to call you.'

'Where are you?'

'Heading up to the Black Isle. With Mary Graham. There's been a development, though no idea what it means.'

'We've got what you might call a development here too. Before you tell me your troubles, have you got Robbins's car reg? We need to track him down urgently.'

'It's in my notebook. Hang on. Mary—'

He heard some background noise, presumably Mary Graham finding the notebook in Horton's cavernous handbag. Good luck with that one, he thought, but a moment later Horton was back on the line. McKay scribbled the registration down and hurried into the rain. 'Hang on a sec, Ginny.' Grant was sitting in the car with the passenger door open talking urgently into the radio. She gave him the thumbs up as he handed over the details.

The rain, which had seemed to be lessening while they'd been standing outside the house, had redoubled its force. McKay hurried back to the house, sheltering his phone inside the hood of his rainproof jacket. 'Sorry about that,' he said to Horton, and told her what they'd found in Robbins's living room.

She gave a low whistle. 'Well, that's interesting,' she said. There was silence for a second, as if she were thinking through what McKay had just told her.

'So where are you heading?'

'The Caledonian Bar.'

'I'm guessing you're not popping in for a quick pint?'

'My standards aren't high,' she said, 'but they're higher than that. No, we had a call-out. One of the regulars. Went in for his usual lunchtime pint, but no sign of Gorman. Didn't think much of it at first. Gorman's not the most reliable of hosts. But then a couple of others turned up, and still no sign of Gorman. Reckon they were all getting thirsty. So one of them decides to have a look for Gorman out back. Assumed he was asleep or something. Checks out Gorman's bedroom, but no sign. Gorman's not the type to go out for a day-trip, so they check in case he's had an accident in the cellar or something. But they don't find anything till they go into the yard out back—' She paused and he heard her swear. 'Bloody lorries. I've a good mind to take his bloody number. Sorry—nearly sideswiped off the Kessock Bridge.'

'Gorman?' he reminded her.

'Yeah, there's apparently a yard at the back of the pub with access to the road, where Gorman takes deliveries. No sign of Gorman there either. But what they do find is one of Gorman's shoes.'

'What?'

'Lying there in the middle of the bloody yard, like it's fallen off his foot. So one of them talks the others into calling the police. And of course we don't take it seriously but eventually a couple of uniforms pop in on their way past. And find a pool of blood out back.'

'Which the regulars hadn't spotted?'

'In fairness it's pretty gloomy out there apparently, especially on a day like today. They'd just thought it was a puddle. But our colleagues were a bit sharper. Enough blood that even this bloody rain couldn't wash it away.'

'What do they reckon?'

'It's still a mystery. They did a thorough search of the place, but no other sign of him. Checked the neighbouring properties but still nothing. They were reporting him as a misper when someone was alert enough to spot we'd interviewed him so I got a call.' She paused. 'Don't know if I did the right thing, but something about it set the alarm bells ringing. I persuaded them to treat the place as a crime scene, at least provisionally, so that no-one tramples over it until we've had chance to have a look. Like I say, I was about to call you.'

McKay laughed. 'You're learning, Ginny. Forgiveness not permission. But, aye, I think you were right. I don't know how any of this fits together, but it's another bloody odd coincidence. Two pools of blood and two more missing people. Too many bloody coincidences. It makes me nervous.'

He turned, still talking, to see Helena Grant standing inside the front door, signalling to him. 'Hang on.'

'Got the bulletin out on Robbins,' she said. 'But I also got them to check the ANPR network while we were on. Sighting of Robbins's car on the A9 north of Inverness, late this morning. Then another sighting on a temporary camera on the A832 west of Munlochy, heading east, a few minutes later. No sign of it returning according to the latest data.'

McKay nodded. 'Back on the Black Isle, then.' He spoke back into the phone: 'I don't know what's going on up there, Ginny. But I want you to be bloody careful. It looks like we have another coincidence on our hands.'

CHAPTER THIRTY-ONE

Mary Graham pulled up outside the Caledonian bar, not worrying about the double-yellows or being halfway up the pavement. It was barely 6pm but the rain was coming harder than ever and it felt like night had already fallen. The street ahead was deserted, except for one man under a flapping umbrella scurrying over to the fish and chip shop. The start of the bloody tourist season. Horton could imagine the families clustered miserably in their holiday lets and B&Bs, peering into the grey evening and wondering when the hell this was ever going to let up.

She'd been afraid the uniforms would have made a big deal of securing the crime scene, envisaging the bar draped in police tape and surrounded by flashing blues. The last thing they wanted, though she didn't fool herself word wouldn't already be getting round in a small town like this.

In fact, they'd handled it discreetly enough. The marked car was tucked around the corner and they'd obviously done nothing more than lock the main bar doors and shut the wooden gates to the delivery yard.

After a moment, the bar door opened a crack and a face peered out. 'Aye?'

She was about to brandish her warrant card when the door opened further. 'I know you. Alec McKay's gopher.'

'DS Horton to you,' she said. 'Or Ginny to my friends. You were at the Clootie Well.' Murray something, she recalled.

'Aye, come in,' he said. 'Make yourselves at home.'

The two uniforms—Murray and another she didn't recognise—had been sitting by the doorway waiting for someone to turn up. It looked as if they'd been smart enough to minimise their impact on the crime scene, if that was what it turned out to be. The bar looked even more dreary and lifeless than when she'd visited with McKay, as if its last spark of hospitality had finally been snuffed out.

'We OK to bugger off now?' Murray was already gathering up his possessions. 'Shift finished the best part of an hour ago.'

'Anything else useful you can tell us?'

'Not really. You'll have seen what we reported. The pool of blood's in the yard out back. I didn't know what to do about that or the shoe. Didn't want to disturb it if it was evidence, but didn't want this bloody downpour to remove anything that might be helpful. In the end, we found a sheet of plastic in the back and laid that over them to keep the rain off. That's the only thing we touched. Even kept our hands off the beer. Not that it was much of a temptation in this place.'

'You did right,' she agreed. 'Though the examiners will whinge whatever we do.'

'Aye, tell me about it,' Murray said.

'OK, push off then,' Horton said. 'But make sure you're both contactable if there's anything we need to check with you.'

She and Graham settled themselves in the corner vacated by Murray and his colleague to await the arrival of the crime scene examiner. He was, they'd been assured, on his way. No doubt at his own speed, Horton thought. In the meantime, there wasn't a lot they could do. Murray and his colleague had already checked the adjacent properties and learned that all but one—an elderly woman who'd seen and heard nothing of interest—were unoccupied during the day, their owners at work. There was little point setting any more hares running until they'd a better idea of what had happened here.

'Can't even help ourselves to a bag of crisps,' Graham said, morosely. 'I'm starving.'

'More than your job's worth,' Horton agreed.

'Aye, and they're probably stale in this place anyway.'

She was about to respond when her mobile buzzed on the table. McKay. 'Alec?'

'Aye, I'm heading in your direction. Another bit of news.' She could hear he was on the hands-free now, voice raised against the white noise of the car engine, the repetitive brush of the screen-wipers. 'I told you we put out a bulletin on Robbins's car. No response to that yet, but it was tracked by the ANPR heading up to the Isle this morning. Then one of the FCR operators spotted the same reg in a call she took earlier. Some old bugger from Rosemarkie. One of those houses on the seafront. Phoning up to complain that some inconsiderate bastard had left a bloody great 4x4 parked outside his house all afternoon. Operator pointed out it wasn't actually illegal to park on an unmarked public street, but the old bugger kept blethering on about how they'd taken his parking spot so he'd had to get wet on his way back from the supermarket. And they'd just left it there blocking his view of the sea. Like there's anything to look at on a day like this—'

Horton reflected, not for the first time, that it was fortunate that McKay wasn't expected to take 111 calls from the general public. 'You're saying this was Robbins?'

'Aye. The old bugger had taken the number. When the bulletin came in, it rang a bell with the operator, so she checked back and—bingo.'

'Do we know if it's still there?'

'No idea. The operator fobbed the old bugger off with a promise we'd check it out, and then promptly stuck it at the bottom of the priority list. There were no further calls, so maybe it's moved on. Old bugger reckoned there was no sign of the driver and he couldn't see into the back as the thing's got tinted windows.'

'Want me to go and check it out? I can leave Mary here to hold the fort.'

There was a pause, filled only by the incessant background noise on the line. 'Aye, I suppose you can go and have a look. But I'm only fifteen-twenty minutes away. Don't take any risks, Ginny. If there's any sign of Robbins, get the hell out and call for back-up.'

'I'm not an idiot, Alec.'

'Aye, but you're a police officer, Ginny. We're all daft bastards when it comes to that sort of stuff. OK. Call me and let me know what you find, if anything.'

***

She left Graham to watch the bar and stepped back outside. There was no sign of the rain lessening, and its force was increased by the chill wind blowing off the sea. The street was deserted, except for the occasional passing car, and the lights of the bars and restaurants along the road looked welcoming but forlorn. On nights like this Horton sometimes wondered why she'd ever left the Home Counties. But then she knew the answer to that well enough.

She took the road through the town out towards Rosemarkie. In the short open stretch between the two adjoining villages, you could normally make out the open firth but tonight there was nothing but a haze of cloud and rain. She came down the hill into Rosemarkie and took the right turn down to the seafront. McKay had given her details of where the vehicle had been parked, down at the far end, just before the parking for the beach.

As she'd expected, there was no sign of it now. The few cars parked along that end of the front were standard saloons, with nothing resembling the large 4x4 she was seeking.

She parked up in one of the parallel spaces intended for visitors to the beach and dialled McKay's number. He was either on the phone himself or in a dead spot, and the call went immediately to voicemail. She left a brief message saying she'd found nothing, and then prepared to turn back.

She hesitated for a moment, her attention caught by something in her peripheral vision. She had parked facing the sea and whatever she'd seen, or thought she'd seen, was off to her left, further along the shore, somewhere in the area by the beach cafe.

Probably just her imagination. Curious, though, she leaned over into the passenger seat and lowered the side window, peering into the rainy gloom.

At first, she could see nothing but the sheets of endlessly falling rain. Beyond the short row of houses to her left, the path to the beach cafe disappeared into the grey mist. The cafe itself would have closed hours ago and was visible only as a darker silhouette. The other smaller shapes would be the wooden benches that dotted the grassed area above the beach.

Then, as her eyes adjusted to the mist-shrouded twilight, she spotted it again. A flickering movement of light. The play of a torch beam on the empty beach.

Horton pulled her hood back over her head and climbed out into the rain. The wind buffeted her coldly, drumming the water into her face. Who would be out there on an evening like this? She peered over the railing. The tide was rapidly coming in, the beach disappearing under the relentless encroachment of the wind-whipped waves. Even the most ardent dog-walkers would have left the beach.

She'd taken McKay's warning to heart and had no intention of advancing further if she saw any signs of Robbins. She glanced back along the empty seafront, confident that she could outrun him if he should appear ahead of her. She took another few steps forward and stopped.

A figure had appeared along the shore, rising white and ghost-like above the beach. It took Horton a breathless moment to realise that the figure was making its way up the steps from the sand to the grassy bank in front of the cafe. The flashlight flickered in the figure's hand, scattering a diffused glow through the rain.

Her first thought was that it must be Robbins. Almost immediately, she realised the figure was too slight. McKay had described him as well-built and muscular, someone who looked as if he worked out. This figure was shorter and slimmer than McKay himself.

As Horton watched, the figure walked slowly and steadily across the grass, coming to a halt at one of the heavy carved benches in front of the cafe. In the teeming rain, the figure remained motionless, staring out to sea, the flashlight beam pointing vainly into the gloom.

There was no other sign of life or movement. Horton walked cautiously forward, half-expecting some other figure to step out of the shadows ahead. But there was nothing except the slim, pale figure on the bench.

As Horton drew closer, she saw the figure was a young woman, blonde hair plastered across her gaunt white face. Horton had expected the pale clothing to be some kind of waterproof, but the woman was wearing nothing more than a sodden white blouse and a pair of pale-coloured jeans. She was soaked to the bone, but her posture suggested an indifference to the rain and cold.

Horton had assumed she was still out of the woman's sight, lost in the copse of trees that lined the path. But the woman suddenly called: 'Hello.'

Horton froze, unsure whether the woman was addressing her or someone else. Then she realised the woman was staring directly at her.

'Hello,' the woman said again. Her voice was clear and loud enough to carry above the roaring of the wind and the incoming tide. 'I didn't know there was anyone else here.'

Horton glanced back, fearful that someone was behind her. The pathway and the street beyond were deserted, stained orange by the glow of the streetlights on the rain-washed surface. 'Are you all right?'

The woman nodded thoughtfully. 'I'm fine now,' she said.

'Aren't you cold?'

'Not really.'

Horton walked cautiously towards the woman. 'Do you want to borrow my coat?'

'I'm fine now,' the woman said again.

'I've an umbrella back in the car. Help keep you dry?' It sounded absurd.

'No, I'm really fine.' The tone was a little sharper.

'Can I take you anywhere?'

'No, I really am fine.' The woman gestured behind her. 'Anyway, I can drive myself.'

Horton's gaze followed the gesture. She hadn't noticed it before, but there was a vehicle parked in the shadow of the cafe building, twenty or so metres from where they were standing. A large vehicle.

She turned and looked more closely. It was what she had thought. A substantial 4x4. A Mitsubishi Shogun.

Robbins's car.

***

McKay banged heavily on the bar door, irritated at being left standing in the rain. After a moment, he heard the sound of the lock being unfastened inside and the door was pulled open.

'Oh,' Mary Graham said. 'It's you. Sir.'

'You sound disappointed. What were you expecting, a visit from the chief constable?'

'We're still waiting for the examiners to arrive.'

'Ah. Even more exalted company. If it's Jock Henderson, he won't be hurrying on a night like this.' He followed Graham into the bar. 'Where's Ginny?'

'She's still out.' Graham's expression suggested that even facing the weather outside was preferable to being stuck in the Caledonian Bar.

'Out?'

'After your call. She went to check out this car up in Rosemarkie.'

McKay looked at his watch. It had taken him longer than he'd expected to get here, his passage slowed by wet roads and low visibility after he'd left the A9. He'd picked up Horton's message confirming that there was no sign of Robbins's car, and had assumed she'd have returned by now.

He thumbed her number. The number rang for a minute or so and then cut to voicemail. 'How long's she been gone?'

'She left straight after you called,' Graham said.

'Best part of half an hour then?'

'Something like that.'

It was maybe five minutes to Rosemarkie, even in weather like this. McKay called Horton's number again, but the call again rang out to voicemail.

'Shit,' McKay said. 'OK, Mary. You hold the fort here. I'm going looking for her.'

'If you say so, sir,' Graham said, but only once the door had closed behind McKay's disappearing back. 'If you fucking say so.'

CHAPTER THIRTY-TWO

'Is that yours then?' Horton said, gesturing towards the Shogun parked in the shadows. 'Your car?'

She had sat herself on the heavy wooden bench next to the woman. The edges of the bench were carved with a Biblical quotation and the name and dates of a local boy who'd died before reaching adulthood. In the dim light, it resembled nothing so much as a wooden tomb.

'Sort of,' the woman said. 'It was my father's.'

Horton's eyes were fixed on the young woman's face. 'Your father's?'

'Yes, it was his.'

'John Robbins?'

The woman turned towards Horton, surprise in her eyes. 'You know him? Aye, I suppose you would. He always liked your type.' A small smile played round her lips. 'My type.'

'What's our type?' Horton asked.

'You're troubled, aren't you?'

'Troubled?'

'You don't need to pretend, you know? We're all in the same position. We're all victims.'

Horton felt as if her blood had frozen in her veins. She had told no-one of her own troubles, her own past. Not even Isla. Not properly. She'd shared some of it on one or two half-drunken nights when they'd downed too much wine. But not the whole story. Isla didn't need that. She had plenty enough troubles in her own past. That was why they'd come up here. To put all that—or as much of it as they could—behind them.

'Are you a victim too, Elizabeth?'

'You know my name?' Elizabeth Hamilton said. 'Did he tell it you?'

'No, Elizabeth. It's a long story.'

'It always is,' Hamilton said. 'You can call me Lizzie if you like. We can be friends. I want friends.'

'We all do. Why are you sitting here, Lizzie?'

'I'm just waiting.'

'What are you waiting for?'

'I've been waiting all day. For the tide. I was too late this morning.'

'Why are you waiting for the tide?'

'I like watching the tide. Waiting for it to come in and go out.'

Horton followed Lizzie Hamilton's gaze. It was scarcely possible to see anything through the thick twilight and heavily falling rain.

'Why are you here, Lizzie?'

'Watching the tide, that's all.'

There was something in the way she spoke that Horton found unnerving. Something inexplicable even in this absurd situation. 'Why are you here?' she asked again.

'I needed to stop him. I should have done it before. Long ago. It was my fault. It was always my fault.'

'What was your fault, Lizzie?'

'Everything was my fault. It was my fault that my mother died. It was my fault we were alone. It was my fault he couldn't help himself.'

'You don't believe that, do you, Lizzie? You don't believe it was your fault?'

She shook her head, not entirely a gesture of denial. 'I don't know. Some of it was my fault. I could have stopped him before.' The rain was dripping from the angles of her cheeks. 'I should have stopped him before.'

'He's responsible for what he does, Lizzie. Not you.'

'I don't know. I'm like him. I'm too like him.' She was staring out across the beach, eyes fixed on the almost invisible sea. The roar of the waves was drawing closer, crashing below them.

'Why don't you come with me, Lizzie? I can take you somewhere warm and dry, where you'll be safe. Then we can talk properly.' Horton looked over her shoulder, conscious how vulnerable they were in this semi-dark. There was no movement other than the constant pounding of the wind and rain.

'I have to wait,' Hamilton said.

'What are you waiting for?'

'I'm waiting for the tide.'

Horton felt the same chill she'd experienced moments earlier. Nothing to do with the cold, wet night. 'Where's your father, Lizzie?'

Hamilton turned to face her. 'I'm safe now,' she said. 'We're all safe now. You. Me. All the victims.'

'Where is he, Lizzie?' Horton had half-risen, peering over the grassy bank towards the beach and the encroaching sea. It was impossible to make out anything from here.

'He was right,' Hamilton said. 'He was always right. After the first one, it becomes easier. It becomes part of who you are.' Her gaze had shifted. She was no longer looking out to sea, but staring down across the beach. Horton walked cautiously over to where a short flight of steps led down to the path at the top of the beach. The tide was nearly in now, only a short strip of beach left exposed.

Then she saw it, twenty yards away along the shore, where the rising sea hit what remained of the beach. Something long and dark, and another shape beyond it.

Not stopping to think, Horton ran along the beach path and, reaching its end, jumped over the low wall on to the wet sand and shingle. She sprinted the last few metres, the ground sinking beneath her weight, the lash of the spray on her face.

It was a human body, as she'd expected, face down on the wet sand, the waves already beating against its torso and legs. The arms and legs were tied and the ropes weighted with piles of stone. Horton looked further along the beach. Another similar body, again face down, already half-sunk in the rising tide.

She ran to the far body first, suspecting she was already too late. She grabbed the nearest arm and leg and hauled the body as best she could back up the beach. It was a dead sodden weight, dragged down by its wet clothes, constantly being sucked back by the pull of the waves.

After what felt like far too many minutes, she managed to drag it on to the stones above the debris that marked the high point of the tide. Not stopping to check the body, she turned back to where the first body still lay. The tide had risen another few centimetres. Elizabeth Hamilton was standing a few yards away, her frail body whipped by the wind. Horton wanted to call for her help, but knew there would be no point. Instead, she turned to the first body and began to drag its resistant bulk from the clutch of the sea. The body was weighted more heavily by the stones and its own heavy clothing, and the effort was almost too much. But slowly, inch by inch, she pulled the body away from the sea, up towards the tide-line.

She'd almost dragged the body to safety when she finally looked up. Hamilton was standing behind her. She was holding the flashlight at her side, its beam glittering on the wet sand and pebbles.

'No,' Hamilton said. 'Don't listen to him. Don't believe him. We were safe. We were almost safe.'

And she raised the flashlight and brought it down hard against the side of Horton's head.

CHAPTER THIRTY-THREE

Where the bloody hell was she?

McKay pulled into the space by Horton's abandoned car and climbed out into the wet night. He'd kept calling during the short drive over, but the calls had simply rung to voicemail. Why the hell hadn't she called before buggering off on whatever fool's errand she was pursuing? Visibility was down to a few metres, and he could see nothing beyond the narrow inlet where the burn ran into the sea.

'Ginny!' His voice was almost immediately whipped away by the sharp wind.

With nowhere else to go, he took the path to the beach cafe, peering into the gloom for any sign of movement. There was nothing but the roar of the tide, the clatter of the wind in the trees.

Then, suddenly, he saw an unexpected flash of light by the water's edge. Something moving in the near dark.

With no rational thought, he began to run towards the sea, slipping and stumbling down the wet grassy bank until he reached the firmness of the beach path. It was only as he reached the end of the path that he realised what he was seeing.

Out on the narrow strip of beach, two figures were struggling, the waters already around their ankles. McKay jumped on to the sand, trying to work out exactly what was happening. One slender ghost-like figure, pale against the roaring sea. The other larger, bulkier, stumbling backwards as if about to topple into the water.

He dragged his own powerful flashlight from his waterproof. 'Police!' Again, he was conscious his voice was almost inaudible, but the shout was sufficient to cause the pale figure to turn. Almost immediately, the other figure jumped, pushing the pale figure further back up the sand.

'Police! Stop!' McKay screamed again. The bulkier figure, he realised now, was buried in a heavy dark waterproof. Horton.

'Hold her,' Horton yelled. 'Just fucking hold her!'

McKay grabbed the pale figure, a slender young woman dressed only in flimsy everyday clothes. She wriggled and almost managed to extract her slippery body from his grip, but he threw his arms around her and dragged her back up the beach on to solid ground.

Horton was wrestling with something large and heavy further down the beach, dragging it away from the waves. It took McKay a moment to realise it was a body. Still gripping the struggling woman, he watched as Horton pulled the body above the tide-line. She was crouching, feeling for a pulse, and then she began pounding on the chest, trying to extract the water from its lungs. Trying, it seemed, to bring the dead back to life.

She hammered at the body for what seemed an eternity, long after McKay knew there was no chance of success. Finally she stopped and looked up at McKay. 'I was too late,' she said. 'Too bloody late.'

Almost immediately, the young woman in McKay's arms relaxed, the fight suddenly gone from her body.

'Safe, then,' she said. 'Finally. We're all safe.'

***

McKay wrapped Elizabeth Hamilton in his own waterproof and led her back to his car, Horton following behind. Hamilton was a passive figure now, meekly accepting McKay's direction.

McKay looked back at Horton. 'We need to get you to hospital. And this one. How are you feeling?'

Horton fingered the bruise already appearing on her temple. 'I'll survive,'

'We need to get you checked.'

'I've always said I need my head examined, working for you.'

'Sounds like you're making a good recovery already.'

They helped Hamilton into the back seat of the car, and Horton climbed in beside her. 'Turn on the heater. I'm bloody frozen, never mind her.'

McKay had called for back-up, including an ambulance, and there was nothing they could do until that arrived. They'd left the bodies at the top of the beach. Strictly speaking, McKay supposed, one of them should have stayed out there, but Horton was neither in a condition to do that nor to look after Hamilton by herself. In any case, he reasoned, he was buggered if either of them was going to get any wetter than they already were.

'I take it that's John Robbins?' McKay said, gesturing back to where the bodies lay.

'And Denny Gorman,' Horton said. 'No question.'

'Not the best night for a swim,' McKay said. 'What's the story, Lizzie?'

Hamilton looked at him, as though surprised by the question. 'We're safe now. Me. Her.' She waved her hand towards Horton. 'All the victims.'

'You did it to make yourself safe?'

'All the victims.'

'Were there many victims, Lizzie?' Horton said.

She frowned, thinking. 'Lots. I don't know how many. Girls he damaged, like me. He wanted to control them, like he controlled me.'

'How did he control them?'

She shrugged. 'He had ways. Power. Money. Violence.' She stopped. 'He wanted them to be little girls. Like I used to be. They came to him—they were sent to him—because they were damaged. He said he'd make them better but he wanted to take them back to what they used to be. Make them small again.' Her eyes were fixed on nothing, as if remembering something from long ago. 'When he couldn't control them anymore, when they went away, he went to bring them back. Bring them home. Make them his forever.'

There was a smile playing round her lips. 'When I was small, he'd bring me here. He'd make me sit here with him, on the beach. Not playing. Just sitting. Telling me I wasn't allowed to play because I'd been naughty. Even though I hadn't. Then later he'd punish me. But first I had to do what he said. Just sit and wait.' She paused, the smile wider now, as if she were recalling some private joke. 'Watching the tide come in.'

CHAPTER THIRTY-FOUR

It was nearly midnight before McKay arrived home. The rain had lessened slightly, but as he'd driven through the city the sky was still fogged with drizzle. The house was in darkness. He pulled into the drive and turned off the engine, sitting for a moment to drink in the silence.

The aftermath of a major case always took much longer than the investigation itself. Whatever the exact outcome here, there'd be weeks of gathering and collating evidence, preparing documentation, making sure that everyone's backsides were covered when it eventually came to court. Even the thought exhausted him, but now wasn't the best time to worry about what the next few weeks would hold.

He hadn't realised till afterwards how shaken he'd been. Or quite how worried about Ginny Horton. She was more than capable of looking after herself, he knew. But that had no doubt been true of most of the officers listed on the memorial plaque in HQ. You could never afford to think the worst. When it came to it, you could only assume that, this time, it would somehow work out all right. That would take you safely through until the time when it didn't.

Horton herself had seemed unaffected by her experience. Well, of course she did. She was running on adrenaline. Maybe it would hit her tomorrow. Or sometime in the future. Or not at all. Who knew?

They'd kept her in overnight at Raigmore for observation, though she'd repeatedly insisted she was fine to leave. The doctors were fairly certain there was no concussion, but no-one was taking any chances. As McKay had been leaving, he'd met Horton's partner, Isla, who'd turned up to spend the night sitting by the bedside. They'd met briefly at a couple of office social dos, but he couldn't claim to know her. A lawyer, Horton had said. She was a tall woman with swept back blonde hair, more patrician in manner than Horton. Someone who wouldn't take any nonsense, McKay thought.

'How is she?'

'She insists she's fine. And I'm pretty sure she is. Docs just want to keep an eye.' He was wondering whether the woman was inwardly blaming him for allowing this to happen.

'She's very resilient. A bit too resilient, sometimes. She won't let anyone in, you know what I mean?'

'Aye,' McKay had said. 'I know exactly what you mean.' He left the sentence hanging, then said: 'Take care of her, won't you?'

'We take care of each other.'

'Aye.' He'd had nothing else to say, so he'd turned and headed out towards the car park.

Elizabeth Hamilton was in the same hospital, in a private ward being watched by a couple of uniforms. She'd been sedated so they had no expectation much would happen before morning, but McKay had wanted to take no chances. He didn't know what mental state the young woman was in. The docs had said she appeared to be in shock and had been on the verge of hypothermia when they brought her in.

In the morning, assuming she was well enough, she'd be charged with the murders of John Robbins and Denny Gorman. Then, perhaps, they might get a clearer idea of the story.

Perhaps.

McKay climbed out of the car with some reluctance. After everything, its womblike warmth felt more enticing than entering that unlit, unloved house. He fumbled for his keys and opened the front door.

He'd assumed that Chrissie would be in bed. But, even as he opened the door, something about the quality of the silence told him that wasn't the case. He turned on the hall and landing lights and, without bothering to check the ground floor, made his way up the stairs.

The door of the main bedroom was open and the bed was empty and undisturbed. He checked the two spares—one of them still decorated in the teenage style Lizzie had chosen before she'd left home. How many years ago? They'd packed away what few possessions she left behind, but never changed the wallpaper or furnishings.

The downstairs rooms were equally empty, equally tidy. There was a folded sheet of paper in the middle of the kitchen table. He picked it up but dropped it back on to the table without opening it.

Time enough for that tomorrow, he thought.

Time enough for everything.

***

'So before we organise the press conference,' Helena Grant said, 'we are sure he's our man?'

'As certain as we can be,' McKay said, already wishing that he could be more so. 'In the circumstances.'

'It's not going to come back to bite us?'

'No,' McKay said, more confidently this time. 'I'm sure of that.'

They were in Grant's office and for once McKay was sitting peaceably in his chair. He looked, she thought, utterly knackered, but that was understandable enough. 'OK,' she said, finally. 'Tell me about it.'

As it had turned out, Hamilton had been kept under sedation for most of the next day. She'd been running a temperature and the medics had been worried about some kind of infection. Her condition had improved by the following evening, but the police had been dissuaded from taking any further action until she'd had another night's sleep.

It had only been that morning, therefore, that McKay had finally been able to charge her with the murders. She looked frail lying in the hospital bed, but seemed calm and unsurprised, a much more coherent figure than the shivering wee thing curled up in the back of his car two nights earlier. The doctors had allowed her to be interviewed, with a warning that the interview should be adjourned if Hamilton showed any significant signs of fatigue. McKay had offered her the option of delaying the interview, but she'd seemed keen to get it over with.

Horton had been released from hospital after her overnight stay and, despite McKay's protests, had insisted on returning to work the next day. He'd known there was no point in arguing. She wanted to be there when Hamilton was interviewed and, in the circumstances, McKay felt she'd earned that right.

'Tell us about Denny Gorman first,' McKay said. He and Horton were seated by Hamilton's hospital bed. They'd set up the recording equipment close to the bed and arranged for a solicitor to be present, but Hamilton seemed uninterested in those details. The solicitor, a local lad well accustomed to being patronised by McKay, sat making copious notes but saying almost nothing.

Hamilton took a moment before replying. As she lay there, washed and rested, McKay was struck even more by the resemblance to his own Lizzie. The similarities were only superficial, of course—the pale hair, the slender, vulnerable-looking face and clear blue eyes—but they were sufficient that McKay knew he'd have to control his inclination to protect her. This woman was responsible for two men's deaths.

'He scared me,' she said, finally, her voice small.

'Scared you how?'

'He was—you know, he was only interested in one thing. He was like that with all the women who worked in the bar. Hands everywhere. Most came and went pretty quickly. I stayed longer than most.' She shook her head. 'It was my fault. I shouldn't have put up with it.'

It would be a constant refrain in the interview. *My fault. Always my fault.* Later, he discovered she'd said the same to Horton when the two women had been alone together in that rain-soaked night. It was, he imagined, what had been drilled into her head by her father. *Your fault, Lizzie, always your fault.*

'Put up with what?'

'I could see what he was doing. He started off friendly enough. Tried to buy his way into my affections. You know, presents, topping up my pay. But he thought he was owed something for it.

Just the usual groping and pawing at first. Then once he tried to force himself on me, but I fought him off and he pretended he'd been joking. He kept trying to get me drunk—' She stopped, those pale blue eyes staring at McKay. 'I thought I could look after myself,' she said. 'I thought I was big enough and strong enough.'

'What happened?'

'We were drinking one night after hours. I knew I could hold my drink. Better than he could. And then, suddenly, a couple of drinks in—bang. It hit me like a sledgehammer.'

McKay exchanged a glance with Horton. 'Go on.'

'There must have been something in the drink. One of those date-rape drugs, I suppose. I could barely keep upright, could barely think. Next thing he was taking me upstairs, undressing me, putting me in his bed—'

'Can you remember what happened after that?' Horton said.

Hamilton shook her hand. 'Not clearly. But I'm fairly sure he assaulted me. Probably raped me.' She shivered. 'I shouldn't have been so stupid.'

'It wasn't your fault,' Horton said, firmly. 'Whatever happened, he did it. Not you.'

'I know, but—'

'Did you report this?' McKay said.

'No. I didn't think anyone would believe me. And even if they did—'

They'd think it was your fault, McKay added silently to himself. It was maybe true, if you came up against the wrong officer. And there were still too many of those.

'We understand,' Horton said. 'So what happened after that? I mean, with you and Gorman.'

'It was—well, awkward.' Hamilton smiled at the inappropriateness of her language. 'Listen to me. Awkward. I left before he was up the next morning. I remember going home and standing under a scalding shower, trying to wash myself clean of him.'

'But you went back to the bar?'

'There was nothing else I could do. Not straight away. I needed the money. But we both knew, even though neither of us would say anything. I started looking for other work. There wasn't much going locally, but I thought I'd find something before long.' There was a long pause, as if she was trying to find the right words. 'Then, a couple of weeks later, I started to think I might be pregnant. I was—well, late, you know. And if I was pregnant there could only be one candidate.'

'Gorman?'

'There was no-one else. I got into an almighty panic. I mean, I couldn't afford to have a child anyway, but Gorman—' It was as if she was reliving that panic now, McKay thought. The look of horror in those blue eyes. 'I didn't know what the hell to do. In the end, I could think of only one thing.'

'Go on.'

'I called my father.'

CHAPTER THIRTY-FIVE

McKay had called a short break at that point, conscious of the emotions he could read in Hamilton's eyes. He and Horton left Hamilton with the solicitor, while they retreated to a nearby coffee vending machine to compare notes.

'What do you think?'

'It ties in with what Gorman told us.' Horton took a sip of her coffee and grimaced. 'Christ, must be kill or cure in this place. But, yes, it all rings true. Whether it justifies what she did—'

'That's for the jury and judge to decide,' McKay said. 'All we can do is make sure we've got the facts.'

'Unpleasant as they are.'

'Aye, no question of that.'

They reconvened five minutes later. Hamilton looked slightly more settled, the expression in her eyes less haunted. At least for the moment.

'Tell us about your father.'

'You know about my father, don't you?' she said. 'You know all about him?'

'We think we know something,' McKay said. 'Tell us what you know.'

Another lengthy pause. 'When I was small—when my mum was alive—I idolised him. I thought he was the perfect father. He used to take me down to the beach, play with me there.'

'Rosemarkie beach?'

'Aye, among others. It was one of my favourites.'

'So what happened?' McKay asked. 'Was it when your mother died?'

'He changed. He thought we should have looked after her better. He blamed himself. And he blamed me. I was too young to see it, but he must have gone through a bad time. I think he was drinking too much. He was made redundant—he'd been working in a managerial job for some US company who pulled out of Scotland. He didn't know what to do with himself.'

'This was before he started the counselling work?'

'He eventually did the training for it. Used his redundancy money. It must have given him some direction.'

McKay couldn't imagine she would have been aware of these issues at the time. He could imagine Robbins telling her this, justifying himself, what he did. 'How was he with you?'

She shook her head. 'Awful. I mean, looking back, he was abusing me. Not, you know, sexually. Not then.'

'Not then?' From Horton.

'That came later. When I was older, a teenager.'

McKay said: 'At this point?'

'Psychological abuse, I guess you'd call it. Leaving me on my own. Scaring me. Piling all his own guilt on to me. And physical, too. He used to spank me. He used to say I'd been bad when I hadn't. He used to make me sit silently for hours, doing nothing.'

'Watching the tide?'

Involuntarily, her gaze moved away from his. 'That, too. And then later there was the sexual abuse. Me and others.'

'Who were the others?'

'His—patients, clients, whatever you want to call them. He built up this practice. Specialising in troubled teenagers and young people. People already damaged by their backgrounds, by what had happened to them. He took them on. Sometimes referred by their doctors. Sometimes just private cases. If they were deserving, as he put it, he didn't charge them. You can guess which ones were deserving.' The last sentence, for the first time, had a real edge of bitterness.

'He had a technique,' she went on. 'I watched him do it. I realised it was what he'd done to me, over the years. He took you back into the past. Back to the last place, the last time, you'd been really happy. And then it was as if he unpicked your whole life, everything that had happened from that point on. Slowly demolished it until there was nothing left. He said it was to free you, to enable you to rebuild your life. But what it did was put you in his control, make you dependent on him. It was like he was playing with you.'

McKay swallowed. It was all too recognisable. It was what Robbins had done in the session with Chrissie. He'd unpicked them, taken everything away. Begun to create that dependency. 'No-one complained?'

'Not as far as I know,' Hamilton said. 'When he'd had enough of them, or when they stopped playing his games or whatever, he got rid of them.'

It was as if the air had grown suddenly colder. 'Got rid of them?'

'Sometimes he'd just cut them off and that would be it. But sometimes they were more persistent. He had contacts in Manchester—he was building up a subsidiary practice with some associates down there—and he'd arrange for them to move. Told them it was for the best that they got away, that he'd continue to look after them. Helped sort out their accommodation, sometimes helped find them work.' She paused. 'They were troubled souls. Most of them would do whatever he said.'

'Lizzie,' McKay said slowly. 'You're aware we're investigating three recent murders?'

'Aye, I know,' she said. 'That's why I'm here.'

McKay raised an eyebrow in surprise. 'Why you're here?'

'Why I came back, I mean. As soon as I saw the first one reported on the news, I knew it was him. I don't think it was the first—'

'Go on.'

'It was when I called him up. After, you know—'

'Why did you call him? You hadn't seen him for, what, the best part of ten years?'

'Something like that. I'd walked out. I'd made a couple of friends. They helped me to see what he was doing, what he'd done. And they helped me leave. I went to Glasgow. It didn't work out, not for long. But it got me away from him.'

'But now you phoned him?'

'I was desperate. I thought I was pregnant. I didn't want the child. I wanted to get away from Gorman. I had a bit of savings, but nothing worth talking about. He was the only person I could think of.'

'What happened?'

'We met up. He drove up to Fortrose. I didn't want him in my house so I let him take me down to Chanonry Point. You know, where the dolphins are. It was a beautiful afternoon. I picked a place where there were plenty of people around. So there was no danger of him—well, you know.' She took a breath. 'I told him what had happened. I asked for help.'

'How did he react?'

'He was the same as ever. Just laughed. Began playing his usual mind-games. Began trying it on again.'

'And that was it?'

'No. I'd thought about this. I knew how he'd react. So, in the end, I did the only thing I could think of. I threatened to expose him. I told him I'd report him to the authorities, to his professional body. Tell them what he'd been up to with his clients. I'd done some checking up on him on the internet. He'd become quite a star in his field. He wasn't short of ego, and he'd got himself on various committees. Speaking conferences, all that stuff. There'd been one or two allegations about his behaviour over the years, but he'd been able to shrug them off. His specialism was dealing with troubled young people, after all. You couldn't trust what they said. But I thought it would be different coming from his own daughter. And over the years I'd gathered the names of a few other women who'd be able to support what I was saying. Other victims.'

'At first he laughed. Told me I wasn't the first to try. Told me no-one would believe me. So I started telling him the names of some of the other women who'd support what I had to say. He carried on mocking me, but I could see he was beginning to take it more seriously.'

'The names you mentioned,' McKay said, gently. 'Did they include any of our victims?'

Another pause. 'I shouldn't have told him their names,' Hamilton said. 'That was my stupid fault. That was why I felt responsible.'

'How did you know them?' Horton asked.

'I'd met them when he was treating them. I knew Katy Scott fairly well, the others less so, but I'd talked to them then. I knew a bit about them. They were women I knew had moved to Manchester. Women I knew he'd been involved with.' She shook her head.

'What did he say?'

'I could tell he was rattled. He told me I was talking rubbish. He said he'd pay me off, just once, just to stop me bothering him. Offered me five thousand. It was a lot more than I'd expected, to be honest.'

'What happened after that? You left Fortrose?'

'His condition was that he wanted rid of me, then and there. Said he'd drive me to Inverness station, buy me a ticket anywhere and stick me on the train. I'd got a friend I knew I could stay with for a bit in Aberdeen, so I agreed. And that's what happened. I didn't much care by then. It was when we were driving down that he got more threatening. Said I should be more careful. That I needed to watch myself. That I should leave it here or I wouldn't be the first he'd had to *silence*.' She stopped, as if surprised by her own words. 'It was that word "silence" that shook me. Then he leaned forward and said that I needed to realise that, after the first time, it became easier. That it became easier every time.'

There was a protracted silence. The solicitor—McKay had almost forgotten his presence—was scribbling furiously. McKay asked quietly: 'What do you think he meant?'

'Killing,' she said bluntly. 'That's what he meant.' She was silent for a moment, those piercing blue eyes fixed on his. 'And you know what? He was right.'

***

There hadn't been much more after that, not then. Hamilton was already looking exhausted, and McKay had been conscious that there was no point in pushing her too hard. They'd have plenty of time to continue.

'It was my fault,' she said yet again, as they were finishing up. 'My fault they ended up dead, those poor girls. And it was all a joke to him, wasn't it?'

'A joke?' McKay had asked.

'Bringing it back to where he'd started. To where they'd started. Doing what he did in those sessions of his. Taking them back to the places where they'd last been happy. Pretending to commemorate them with those bloody candles and roses—'

McKay had stood watching her, thinking. Then he'd nodded to Horton and the solicitor. 'We'll leave it there for now,' he said.

Now, a couple of hours later, sitting in front of Helena Grant, he was still thinking. *Are we sure he's our man?*

'We'd need a lot more if we were in a position to be prosecuting Robbins,' he said. 'But that's academic. We just need enough to be sure we're right.'

'And we have that?'

'We've found traces of the DNA for two of the victims in the old van,' he said. 'The van was parked in a garage round the back of the house, accessible from the street behind but on Robbins's property. We know the van made trips from Inverness to Manchester on or around the key dates. We've got Hamilton's evidence that he knew these three women, and we've been able to trace that one of them—Joanne Cameron—was referred to him by her GP.'

'Any DNA in the Shogun?'

'Can't find any. Maybe he was more careful with that, or maybe it wasn't the vehicle he used to take the body up to Caird's Cave. Who knows? You could probably do it with a standard vehicle if you were prepared to drag the body a bit further.'

'You think it's enough?'

'Like I say, we'd need more if we needed to make it stand up in court, but in the circumstances—' He shrugged.

'It sounds pretty cut and dried,' she said.

McKay nodded. Cut and dried.

Except, he thought, for that strange moment at the end of the interview when Hamilton had mentioned the candles and roses. It had taken him a moment to realise that it was a detail they'd never released to the media. He supposed she could have picked up the information from some insider source. And, if he were to ask her, he had no doubt she'd be able to conjure some story to explain how she knew. He could tell she'd registered his hesitation and had known what he was thinking.

Then there was the van. It had been found in Robbins's garage, but neither of the immediate neighbours could recall seeing it being driven in recent months. He'd apparently bought it cheaply to transport equipment for the various conferences and exhibitions he'd attended. It was registered to his company, and they'd been able to trace a few sightings of it on the ANPR Network in and around Inverness but—other than the trips to Manchester—there were no records of it further afield.

They had only Hamilton's word about the trip to Inverness station. She'd claimed her father had paid cash for the ticket, so there was no way of checking whether it had really happened. What they did know—because Hamilton had told them—was that she'd stayed in Aberdeen only for a couple of weeks until she'd received the money transfer from Robbins into an account she'd set up for the purpose. Then, having discovered she wasn't pregnant after all, she'd returned to Inverness and found herself some lodgings and a couple of cash in hand jobs. And, McKay thought cynically, perhaps found the opportunity to screw some more cash from some other lecherous male.

He knew he wasn't thinking rationally about this. It was the resemblance to his own Lizzie. No doubt, as he'd done with Chrissie, he was transferring his own guilt. Wanting Hamilton to be something other than another victim.

But there was something about Hamilton that reminded him of Robbins. Like father, like daughter. Another manipulator. Who knew if Robbins had agreed to lend her the van as a way of getting her out of his hair, or even if she'd just taken it, knowing he wouldn't have the bottle to risk reporting her?

And if Hamilton had possession of the van, their only real evidence against Robbins was no evidence at all. They'd found nothing in his house other than traces of the chloroform used to overcome Gorman and Robbins himself, with the remaining bottle left in the rear of the Shogun. But that didn't mean that the chloroform had belonged to Robbins.

So who knew?

Someone had brought those young women back. Brought them back to the places where they'd last been happy. Had commemorated their lives and deaths with shop-bought roses and plastic candlesticks.

Maybe to silence them. Maybe to frame someone else. Maybe simply to bring them home.

But someone had done it.

'You OK, Alec? You've been unprecedentedly quiet for at least two minutes? Not even an expletive.'

'Ach, I was just thinking.'

'Don't let it become a habit, will you?'

'Lot on my mind, you know?'

'Aye. How are things at home?'

'Not so good, you know?' The truth was he didn't know. He hadn't been able to bring himself to open Chrissie's note before he'd left that morning.

'Sorry to hear that, Alec. I mean, really sorry.' She shuffled embarrassedly with her papers, wishing he'd begin his usual prowling instead of just sitting there. 'Look, you in a hurry to get home tonight?'

He looked up, not even sure what his answer ought to be. 'Not so's you'd notice.'

'When I've got this bloody press conference out of the way, let's go and grab a pint. And maybe a bite to eat. You've deserved it, and I'll bloody well need it.'

He stared at her for a moment, surprised, and then allowed himself a grin. 'Aye. Why not?'

The truth was that he could think of a dozen reasons why not, not least the question of whether he should keep this investigation open. But no-one, least of all Helena Grant, would thank him for suggesting that, so just at the moment none of them seemed worth mentioning. After all, he thought, when this was all out of the way, he'd be back with those bloody burglaries.

Not to mention the whole of the rest of his life.

'Aye,' he said again. 'Why not?'

THE END

Acknowledgements

Thanks as ever to all the people who helped make this book possible. Above all, I'm forever grateful to Helen not just for her unfailing support in everything but also, in this case, for her invaluable comments on the earlier drafts. And thanks to James, Adam and Jonny for their help and encouragement.

I should also acknowledge all the necessarily anonymous folk who contributed insights and advice in respect of policing practice. As always, the credit for the detail should go to them, but any errors or artistic licence are mine alone.

Special thanks to all the people of the Black Isle for their unfailing friendliness and hospitality over the years. It's a magical place, whatever Alec McKay might try to tell you, and I hope to become a full part of it one day. Particular thanks to Jim and Anne Anderson of The Anderson in Fortrose for the beer, food and friendliness, and to Jim for not objecting to his cameo appearance in the book.

And, finally, thanks to Betsy and Fred of Bloodhound Books for being the best and most helpful publishers I've worked with.

CPSIA information can be obtained
at www.ICGtesting.com
Printed in the USA
LVHW042240221020
669596LV00005B/283